A FINE SCOTTISH SPELL

A SCOTTISH ROMANTASY

THE MAGICAL MATCHMAKERS OF SEVEN CAIRNS
CAIRNS
BOOK TWO

MAEVE GREYSON

Contact Information: maeve@maevegreyson.com

Author Maeve Greyson LLC

55 W. 14th Street

Suite 101

Helena, MT 59601

https://maevegreyson.com/

Published in the United States of America

PROLOGUE

The cool smoothness of the tarot cards, worn to a comforting, familiar softness, brought Mairwen, Master over all the Divine Weavers, little solace today. The faded blues and reds of the symbolic images, all the colors, in fact, were tired, and she understood that feeling completely. Struggling to earn her husband's freedom from mighty Danu's prison seemed futile of late, especially with the loss of their son, imprisoned along with his father and supposedly protected—but that had turned out to be a promise too fragile to survive the evil of the witch Carman's sons.

Even though the goddesses Danu, Bride, and Cerridwen had recovered the shards of her son Valan's essence crystal and intertwined them with Jessa and Grant MacAlester's firstborn son's soul, her beloved Valan was still gone. Mairwen pulled in a deep breath and released it with a heavy sigh. How did a mother come to terms with the loss of their precious child? How was life supposed to go on even though she occasionally glimpsed her dear Valan in wee Lucian's laughing eyes?

"Mairwen?" Keeva, more like a daughter than an apprentice, gently knocked on the open door. "I have tea for ye."

1

"Any word from Bedelia?" Mairwen didn't bother to look up from the tarot spread that refused to speak to her. The cards had taunted more than guided ever since her cruel sister Morrigan had shared the news of the attack on their sons. Mairwen had done a rare thing that now muddied her second sight. She had aimed her mournful fury at the goddesses. She gathered up the cards and dealt them again. "Bedelia and the Love Weavers must make haste. The only true reason Emily remains in Seven Cairns is to maintain contact with Jessa, and that hold is waning. If we do not find Emily's fated mate soon, she will leave us and return to her family across the waters."

"How could New Jersey possibly tempt our Emily away from the magic of Scotland and Seven Cairns?" Keeva set the steaming cup of tea on the table and gently nudged it closer. "Drink yer tea, Mairwen. I brought yer favorite biscuits too."

"A family who loves and cradles Emily in caring and familiarity begs her to come home. I hear them calling to her. Their love pulls at her heart and soul. Ye can see it in her face too. Her loneliness unites with theirs. We are not enough, Keeva, even with our temptation to teach Emily how to connect with her ancestor's magic."

"But she enjoys her lessons with Ishbel and loves Jessa like a sister. Surely, she would never leave to return to New Jersey. Especially not with her being the godmother to the babies. Lucian, Kiran, and Meira need their Auntie Emily. They would be lost without her."

"Emily was never meant to live her life on the sidelines watching others fulfill their destiny." Mairwen swept the tarot cards off the table with an irritated flick of her hand. "Fetch Bedelia. I want answers as to why the Love Weavers have yet to locate Emily's mate."

Keeva bowed her head and backed toward the door. "Yes, Mairwen. Right away."

Mairwen closed her eyes and covered her face with shaking hands while sagging forward to prop her elbows on the table. Never in the history of the Highland Veil or the Divine Weavers had they ever experienced this much trouble finding a chosen mortal's fated mate. Perhaps it was because of the trace of Spell Weaver blood running through Emily's veins, or a sign of the times, this world's age of disbelief in magic. Mairwen didn't know what it was; all she knew for certain was that the Highland Veil cried out for the strengthening it would receive when Emily bonded with her one fated love. The Veil had to remain strong at all costs. The many worlds, planes of time, and realities it separated could not be allowed to merge into apocalyptic chaos.

"Mairwen?" Bedelia stood in the doorway, waiting.

Mairwen lifted her head. Her heart fell at the somber weariness slumping the Master Love Weaver's shoulders. "Why can you not find him for her? Help me understand why, Bedelia."

Bedelia slowly shook her head. "All my Weavers sense Emily's mate. It's as though his spirit dances just beyond our fingertips, teasing us with his presence while refusing to tell us where he is. But the main thing is—he exists. We know it. We simply must find him and bring them together."

"The tapestry of the Veil needs them. Jessa and Grant's bond strengthened it immensely, but the darkness picks at its threads, threatening to unravel it. We must make haste."

Bedelia offered a resigned nod. "We will find him, Mairwen. I swear it."

"I hope so," Mairwen whispered. "I truly hope so. This time feels more crucial than any of the others."

CHAPTER 1

Modern Day - Autumn
Scottish Highlands
Village of Seven Cairns

"Mama...Mama..." Emily Mithers gave up. She snapped her mouth shut and nodded in all the right places of her mother's long diatribe about missing her, missing Jessa, and wanting to hold Jessa and Grant's babies rather than coo at them over video calls. What her mother didn't realize was that it had taken a battle of epic proportions to convince the goddesses and the Weavers to back down off their stance of erasing the memories of family and friends to protect the secrecy of fated mates brought together through time travel and magic so their loving bonds could strengthen the weave of the Highland Veil—a mystical shield of sorts that separated all the worlds, realities, and timelines in existence.

Emily and Jessa were the first outsiders able to convince the goddesses that they should be allowed to maintain contact with their loved ones as long as they handled it delicately and protected the secrets of the Highland Veil, its Order of Defenders, and the Divine Weavers who cared for it.

"If you are not going to listen, we might as well end this call—even though it is long overdue." Her mother sniffed and assumed the aloofness of a parent more than willing to hand out a generous helping of guilt. "But I'm not complaining. I am just thankful you spared a few moments out of your busy schedule for a brief chat with your mother."

"Passive aggressiveness is beneath you, Mama. Save it for the fearsome five. It always works on them."

Her mother just jutted her chin even higher. "At least your brothers adore me."

"I adore you, too, and you know it." Emily rested her fingertips on the computer screen, wishing she could reach through it and touch the softness of her mother's cheek. As the youngest of six and the only girl, her parents had lovingly spoiled her rotten, and she missed them with a fury. "You and Papa are still coming to Seven Cairns in the spring. Right?"

"Are you coming home for the holidays?"

"I'll be there for Christmas. You already extracted that promise. Remember?"

"And what about our Jessa? And the babies? We consider her family too. I never want her to forget that."

"Jessa and Grant aren't brave enough to make an almost eleven hour flight with seven-month-old triplets." Emily couldn't add that by the goddesses' order, eighteenth century Grant MacAlester's forays into the twenty-first century were limited to the boundaries of Seven Cairns, the way station sanctioned by the goddesses for the use of fated mates and the Weavers.

"I suppose that would be a bit much. I'll simply ship their gifts to them. I assume I'll have to send them to your cottage there in Seven Cairns, since Royal Mail still hasn't figured out where their castle is?"

"It's a keep, Mama. Remember?" And she couldn't very well tell her mother that the twenty-first century Royal Mail didn't deliver to the eighteenth century. "If you don't want to ship them, I can always bring them back when I return after Christmas." Emily braced herself. That particular subject was still a raw nerve with her mother. Her parents couldn't understand why she had decided to stay in Seven Cairns indefinitely, and she had given up on trying to explain it in vague yet convincing terms.

"That won't work. I doubt the airline's weight limits would allow it." The self-ordained grandmother wasn't the least bit ashamed that she might have overdone it a bit in purchasing gifts for the babies.

Emily couldn't very well tell her mother that, depending on the gifts, they might not be allowed into the eighteenth century. That was another rule from the goddesses, and this one, she understood completely. They had to be cautious about fouling history's timeline with knowledge or items from the future. The results could be disastrous. The babies would have to enjoy their presents in Seven Cairns and leave them there whenever they went home. She gave her mother a stern look she knew would be ignored. "Remember Papa's back. Don't pack the boxes too heavy."

Her mother rolled her eyes. "Don't get me started on your father's aging insecurities and determination to prove he's still as fit as a twenty-year-old."

The video on the laptop froze before Emily could comment. A sure sign that Ishbel, Master of the Spell Weavers, was tired of waiting for Emily to show up for their daily work in spell casting. With a resigned sigh, Emily pulled out her phone and texted: *Sorry! Lost the signal. Love you!*

Her mother responded with a long string of heart emojis and *Love you too!*

Emily tucked her phone back into the thigh pocket of her black, fleece-lined leggings, then pulled on her favorite creamy white cable knit sweater over her sleek black workout tank. She had learned early on that layers were the best defense against the damp chill of Scotland in late November. Thick wool socks. Waterproof hiking boots. Wool gloves. All the accoutrements she never thought she would wear for anything other than climbing a mountain on a cold, windy day had become everyday garments here. She tied back her mane of long black braids into a neat twist that would keep them out of the way and pulled on a chunky knit beanie. A backpack with a change of clothes completed her preparations for her magical work-out. Even though it was a short walk from her cottage to the Weaver's meeting house, and she and Ishbel always practiced inside, past experience with the unpredictability of Seven Cairns had taught her to be as prepared as possible for the unexpected.

"Ye should never call yer mother when ye know ye're due to be somewhere," Ishbel said as Emily entered the practice hall. "It makes ye tardy every time."

Emily gritted her teeth against telling the Master Spell Weaver that it was none of her business. Wasn't it enough that she had put her life on hold and remained in Seven Cairns to get in touch with her Spell Weaver ancestry as the Weavers had requested? Of course, she had also stayed because of Jessa, but the more she saw how happy and settled Jessa was, the more restless she felt. Not that she wasn't happy for Jessa—but...well...it was complicated, and she wasn't in the mood to get into it with Ishbel.

She dropped her backpack onto the bench against the wall and started stretching as if about to lift weights or run a marathon. Sometimes, magic turned physical, and she had the bruises to prove it. "So, what are we working on today? Same old stuff?"

When Ishbel remained silent, she turned to find the Weaver studying her with a worried scowl. Emily tensed, or more aptly, her already tensed muscles ratcheted into even tighter knots. Of late, she stayed so overly wound it was a wonder she wasn't a cramped bundle of misery. "What?"

"We have talked about how yer emotions feed into the magic, ye ken?" Ishbel moved closer, her long, silky robes of purple and red splashes fluttering around her as if she were a colorful butterfly. She had released her gray hair from its usual messy bun, and the silvery curls cascaded down well past her waist. "Yer aura is full of chaos, child. Murky with troubled shades. Perhaps ye best spend yer day elsewhere and leave the energies be. They dinna take kindly to those who poke at them with negativity. Mayhap Mairwen could give ye a massage."

"I am not negative." Emily huffed at her own snappishness. She sounded like a sullen brat even to herself. "Or at least I wasn't until you accused me of it."

"What is wrong, child? What has ye so upset?"

"I am not your child, and I'm not upset."

Ishbel spread her hands and offered an apologetic bow.

The Weaver's placating dramatics and faint smirk made Emily even pricklier. She plopped onto the bench and dropped her head into her hands. She was upset, had felt that way for days, and was sick and tired of it. "I don't know what's wrong with me, and nothing I try helps."

"What about meditation? Seeking the problem and working it out the way I showed ye?"

"No luck." Emily stared at the toes of her boots and noticed some of the stitching had torn free. Great. She had spent a bundle on those and even sang their praises to her bazillion followers on her influencer channel. Looks like she would have to go back online and tell everyone she had been wrong. And that was just it. She had been wrong about so many things. "I am tired of being wrong, Ishbel. Tired of screwing myself over by making the wrong choices." She snorted a sad laugh. "And I have no one to blame for my misery but myself."

Ishbel settled down beside her and wrapped an arm around her shoulders. "I have never seen ye like this, child...er...Emily. Ye worry me when ye are so troubled. Is part of it because we have yet to find yer fated mate?"

Every frustration churning within Emily roared even louder, making her twitch to shake Ishbel away, then immediately feel guilty about even thinking that. "I didn't come here looking for a fated mate and don't expect to find one."

"Why did ye come here, lass?"

"To help Jessa find happiness. She deserved it."

"And ye dinna believe ye deserve that same happiness as well?"

"I didn't say that."

"Ye nay had to." The determined glint in the Spell Weaver's pale green eyes warned she was not yet finished. She shook a finger as if winding up for one hell of a sermon. "Why do ye not believe ye have every right to be as happy as yer friend?"

"Why do you believe I can't be happy without the complication of a relationship?"

"The *complication* of a relationship?" Ishbel nodded. "I see now. Ye have been burnt by that fire before and still feel a bit singed, I reckon. Is that not what ye worked so hard to help yer Jessa overcome? The *complication* of a relationship that had soured?"

"Enough therapy, Ishbel. Shall we get started?" Emily jumped up from the bench, strode to the center of the room, and bounced in place while flexing her fingers. "What spell are we working on today? Same one as yesterday?"

Ishbel's eyes narrowed with a displeased glare. "I doubt verra much ye can manage the serenity spell today any better than ye managed it yesterday. The thatching on Innis's cottage is still smoking."

Emily rolled her shoulders and stretched her tensed neck muscles by tipping her head from side to side. "I apologized for that and even made it rain to put out the fire."

"I was the one who made it rain, lass, and shielded the rest of the village from the lightning ye conjured with yer weather spell."

"I'll do better today." And she would. She would concentrate. Clear her mind and her heart, and swim with the energies as if she were a magical dolphin. She forced a smile she didn't feel. "I promise."

Ishbel did not appear convinced, but she nodded for Emily to proceed.

Pulling in a deep cleansing breath, Emily closed her eyes and struggled to calm her thoughts—never an easy task, even on a good day. She had always considered it a strength, the way her mind jumbled with limitless possibilities, and prided herself on the ability to juggle any number of ideas while handling whatever needed to be handled in the forefront. It was simply a matter of channeling all her lively internal wiring into successfully firing on all cylinders at the same time.

Unfortunately, magic was a greedy energy that demanded her full focus, or at least her version of focus. As a child, her teachers had labeled her with all the usuals: ADHD, hyperactive, dyslexic, neurodiverse, or just plain difficult. Thankfully, her psychiatrist mother and internal medicine physician father had lovingly embraced her unique way of thinking and refused to allow the education system to make her feel ashamed or ostracized. But even though she had thrived and amazed them with her brilliance, as her father had always said, she still struggled when it came time to focus on one finite thought and block out all the others. Magic was hard, and hard frustrated her. How dare that energy not cooperate with her way of thinking!

"Yer aura is flaring red, Emily. Rage will poison yer power. Go to yer vision and rid yerself of it."

"My vision," Emily repeated calmly, even though she wanted to tell Ishbel to be quiet and let her work this out for herself. That would be rude, and Ishbel didn't deserve rude. The Weaver had always been patient and kind. Emily counted her breaths, concentrating on slowing them while bringing forth the memory of a pristine white beach she had enjoyed while visiting the island of Saint John in the U.S. Virgin Islands. She returned to the waters that had been bluer than the bluest crayon in the jumbo crayon box she had always prized as a child. The gentle shush of the waves stroked the shore like a devoted lover. A gentle breeze tickled across her as she basked in the warmth of the tropical sun after a nice, long swim. Her heart rate slowed, and breathing came easier. The impossible to explain feeling she needed, the relaxing fluidity of centering herself, flowed through her.

"*Tranquillitas*," she whispered, envisioning herself as a serene being floating up into the clouds.

"Emily!"

Ishbel's panicked screech exploded through her like an electrical jolt. Emily hit the ground. Hard. The magic turned on her and attacked with a fury. She thrashed to be free of the painful energy searing through her. If she didn't release it, she would surely burst into flames. "Stop it! Leave me!"

"Feckin' hell!"

Clods of dirt and grass showered her as a monstrous horse leapt over her. Instinctively, she curled into a ball and covered her head. Thankfully, the fiery barbs of mystical energy nipping at her bones had eased, but now she was in the middle of a field somewhere. And she had dropped herself into the path of somebody riding a horse. Damn, magic! She tried to push herself to her feet, but agony knifed through her hip and knocked her back down. "Shit!"

Head pillowed on her arms, she pulled in several deep breaths, fighting the horrendous pain and trying not to give in to the nausea it stirred. Then she opened her eyes. Whatever damage she had done to her hip was the least of her worries.

A very large, angry man had alighted from the horse and was headed her way. She didn't know him, and that meant she had spelled herself somewhere away from Seven Cairns. Wasn't that just freaking wonderful? Then she noticed his clothing and clenched her teeth even tighter. From his manner of dress, the twenty-first century was not his time. The *where* of her landing was no longer the larger problem—the *when* was.

"Shit, shit, shit," she hissed under her breath. Now, what was she going to do?

His worn leather boots rose to his knees, and with every forceful step, his kilt molded itself across the muscular powerhouse of his long legs. His impressively broad shoulders were encased in a black wool coat that didn't come close to matching the sooty darkness of his shoulder length hair and the short beard that enhanced the angular lines of his face. The coldness living in his flinty stare made her wonder if he was going to kill her. This man made mountains look small. She might've held her own when it came to tussles with her five older brothers, but she would never stand a chance against this guy.

"I am sorry," she blurted out, instinctively raising an arm as if that would somehow protect her from his wrath. "I didn't mean to land in your way. I didn't mean to land here at all."

Silent and grim as death, he stopped, then crouched in front of her, eyes narrowing as he raked his furious gaze across her.

Maybe he didn't speak English? He looked like a Scot. An eighteenth century Scot, in fact. His clothing reminded her of what Jessa's husband, Grant, always wore. Had she sent herself back in time? If she had, she prayed she had hit Jessa and Grant's 1786 timeline. "Uhm...I'm Emily. And again, I am really sorry. Is your horse okay?"

The man's baleful expression darkened even more. He tipped his head to the side as if struggling to decide what species she was. "My horse is Avric—not *Okay*."

"Sorry." She chewed on her bottom lip. Jessa had told her about the problem of using modern words in a different time and the confusion they caused. She would have to filter herself more carefully. "I'm Emily," she said again, as if he might've missed that, even though he knelt within a foot of her. "Would you mind telling me the date?"

"The date?"

His hard eyes reminded her of onyx, or black quicksilver, if there was such a thing, or maybe some sort of dark molten ore. A sudden shiver stole through her along with an unmistakable certainty that he meant her no harm. In fact, she felt as if she had met him before. That was pure crazy. She didn't know this guy. How could she *know* on the deepest level imaginable that he wouldn't hurt her?

"Today's date," she said, flinching at the quiver in her voice. She cleared her throat and tried to push herself to a sitting position, only to cry out as pain burned through her hip.

"Ye are injured." His deep voice washed across her, making her catch her breath. "Where are ye hurt?"

"The date?" She had to know the date. He couldn't possibly understand how important that was way more important than whatever was wrong with her backside.

"Late November, I think. I dinna ken for certain the day." He leaned closer. "Where are ye hurt?" he repeated with a gentle sternness that clearly said he wanted an answer.

"My pride. I landed on it." She gingerly rested her hand on the joint of her left hip. "And the year is?"

"1786." He tipped his chin higher, as if daring her to lie. "What of it?"

"Thank goodness. 1786. You don't happen to know Grant MacAlester, do you?" The lack of recognition in his eyes disappointed her immensely. Where the devil had she landed? "The village of Seven Cairns? MacAlester Craig?"

Still scowling, but maybe he was one of those who always scowled, he shook his head. "Is Grant MacAlester yer husband, then? Are ye running from him?" The growling ferocity rumbling through his voice surprised her.

"No. He's my friend's husband. I thought you might know him." She shifted on the cold, hard ground, hoping she could convince her rear end to let her sit upright this time. It did not. "Shit!"

The glowering Highlander's expression softened somewhat, but he still didn't smile. "Ye'll not be able to ride with that injury."

"Can you just help me stand? I don't like being lower while I'm trying to have a conversation with someone. It's like I'm a rabbit in a trap or something."

He didn't move. Just studied her, sweeping his gaze from the top of her head to her feet once again.

"Is that a *no,* then?"

14

"I think I should carry ye. Yer arse may be out of joint."

She bit her tongue to keep from firing off a smart remark. Her entire life had been *out of joint* for a while now. "Just help me stand, and we'll go from there, Mr...?"

"MacStrath—Chieftain Gryffe MacStrath of the Midlands. Ye may call me *Gryffe*." He caught her by the shoulders and swept her to her feet as if she weighed no more than a blade of grass.

Her hip raged against the move, punishing her with a dangerous slap of nausea. Dots of blackness swirled through her vision, making her head swim. She fell forward and fisted his shirt in both hands while breathing deep to keep from losing the pot of tea and toast she'd had for breakfast. Eyes closed, forehead braced against his chest, she prayed she wouldn't throw up all over his boots. "I apologize in advance if I puke on you," she whispered, then swallowed hard and willed herself not to vomit. This first impression was not going well at all, and she needed it to. She would need his help to get back to Seven Cairns, since her freaking magic had turned on her.

He held her with a gentleness that helped her catch her breath and reconsider pulling away. This man was a total stranger—and yet, he wasn't. His nearness, his warmth, the reassuring hardness of his muscular chest against her face both calmed and confused her. She should pull away. Stand on her own. But—she couldn't and wasn't all that mad about being mesmerized into breathing him in and resting in the moment. He smelled of an exciting wildness, cold crisp air warmed by a smoky fire that made you want to curl up and enjoy it. Stroking her hair, he softly murmured a string of words she didn't understand, but she *felt* them wash over her. What the devil was happening here?

"What are you saying?" she whispered without opening her eyes.

"Just words, lass. Dinna fash yerself."

Breathing him in yet again, she found the strength to lift her head and look up at him. He was so tall. At just a whisper shy of six feet in height herself, he was a full head and shoulders taller than her. "I am better now. Thank you." Her hip still throbbed, but it wasn't as bad as it had been. She could bear it as long as she didn't put any weight on her left leg, which would be a problem. "I need to get back to Seven Cairns. What part of Scotland is this, so I can get my bearings?"

He studied her for a long moment, looking deep into her eyes as if walking into her soul and wandering through the shelves of her innermost thoughts to learn more about her. "Seven Cairns is several days' ride from here. Due north. It could take ye nigh on a sennight, depending on the weather, and how hard ye push yer mount. This is my land. Edinburgh is a wee bit to the south of us. Not far from here at all."

"Edinburgh?" Her heart fell. Seven Cairns was north of Inverness, about an hour by rental car—not horse, and it was well over a four hour drive from Edinburgh, depending on how many sheep blocked the road in various places. How had she managed to shoot herself so far south and into another century with what was supposed to be a simple serenity spell? Then it hit her that he knew of Seven Cairns when earlier, he had shaken his head that he didn't. "I thought you said you didn't know about Seven Cairns?"

With his arms still around her, he twitched a shrug. "I never said that."

"You shook your head when I asked about Seven Cairns and MacAlester Craig."

"I shook my head because I dinna ken MacAlester Craig nor the name of yer friend's husband." His expression darkened again. "Or was that a lie?"

She tried to shove out of his embrace, hobbling most of her weight onto her right leg and nearly falling. "Shit!"

Baring his teeth, he caught her arm and steadied her. "So it was a lie, then, was it?"

"Grant MacAlester is the husband of my friend, Jessa, who is more like a sister to me than a friend. In fact, my parents even think of her as family, and I consider myself an auntie to their three babies. Their favorite auntie, I might add!" She thumped his chest with both fists, then almost fell before grabbing hold of his arms. Why was she telling him all this? He obviously didn't care. "If you don't want to help me, then don't, but nobody calls me a liar."

"I dinna make it a habit of leaving the injured to fend for themselves until the wolves end their misery."

"Wolves?" Mairwen had told her that Scotland had hunted wolves to extinction by the seventeenth century. "Wolves survive on your land?" She loved wolves, had even gone so far as to sponsor several sanctuaries, and raised donations for them on her influencer channel.

A leeriness settled across him as he slowly pulled one of his arms free of her hold and only allowed her to steady herself with the one. "Wolves roam the vastness of the United Kingdom of Scotland. King Roric IV respects their right to survive alongside the rest of us."

"King Roric IV?" While she had never been a history buff, she'd never heard of a King Roric or known Scotland to ever be called the United Kingdom of Scotland.

"Aye. Roric rules this land."

"He rules Scotland."

"Aye. He rules all Britannia."

All Britannia? "Scotland rules England? They not only won their independence but also overcame England's rule?"

"Aye. The English made a poor attempt at an uprising in 1746, but we convinced them of the error of their ways. Both them and the French."

The leeriness in his eyes seemed to shift to concern. Maybe. She had never really been that good at reading people. "What about England's royals? Their peerage? The dukes and earls and stuff?"

"They all pay fealty to Roric. In return, they are allowed seats in parliament. Some say our king is a wise and fair ruler for doing such, hearing the opinions of those who once opposed him. Some say otherwise." His scowl tightened with a narrowing of his eyes. "Where are ye from, lass? Ye dinna speak like anyone I have ever known, and the questions ye ask are worrisome. I am thinking Seven Cairns is nay the home of yer birth."

"I am from..." She didn't know how to finish that sentence and wished she had paid more attention to her history lessons. Or maybe she was better off because she hadn't paid that much attention to them. This eighteenth century defied what little history she happened to remember. Almost like it was flipped. Scotland over England. An entirely different reality. What had Mairwen said about alternate realities? Emily's throat closed up, making her gasp for air as the dark spots returned to her vision, spinning at a dizzying pace this time until everything went black.

CHAPTER 2

"No. It canna be." The vial of infused oil slipped out of Mairwen's hand and shattered on the slate floor. The Ether, the thread of consciousness shared by all Weavers and wisely hidden from the goddesses and Defenders of the Highland Veil, had to be wrong. According to its whispers, the unthinkable had happened. A mortal, a fated mate, had been lost, disappeared from existence. Mairwen immediately knew it was Emily's soul that was gone. She searched for the child's energy, then closed her eyes and searched again. Emily's signature was gone from every level of awareness.

Stepping over the mess of broken glass and oil, Mairwen fisted her colorful skirts of sienna and dusky blue out of the way and ran to the meeting hall without regard to the cold, sleeting rain stinging her face. In a distracted, subconscious way, she felt the weather was warranted. The skies and all creation should weep for the loss of their precious Emily—not only a mortal but a direct descendant of their beloved Esme and the mortal the Spell Weaver had so fiercely loved.

"How?" she demanded as she burst into the practice room she knew Ishbel and Emily always used. "How could this happen?"

Crumpled in a heap on the floor, Ishbel lifted her gaze and slowly shook her head. "I dinna ken," she said, her voice quaking with despair. "I thought the serenity spell would be one of the safest, especially with her habit of setting things on fire."

Mairwen sank to the floor beside Ishbel and touched the ancient flagstones the goddesses had laid as the foundation of the building an untold age ago. "The warmth of her energy remains. It is strong."

"Aye," Ishbel said, "but for how long? And where did she go? Never in all my centuries have I ever had a student cease to exist as though they had never been. She did not gently fade away as most do when transporting." Ishbel kept shaking her head as if wishing to change the memory. "She simply went away. Was gone. Disappeared as if the goddesses erased her from all creation."

"The goddesses?" An ill feeling of dread wrapped icy fingers around Mairwen's heart and squeezed. She struggled to breathe. "Did you sense them? Do you suspect their hand in this?"

With heartbreaking despondency, Ishbel shrugged. "I sense nothing. There is no hint, no trail of anything anywhere. It is as though our precious Emily was never born. All that remains is her warmth in the stones." She pressed a shaking hand to her cheek as tears spilled over. "What are we to do, Mairwen? I know she could be a tempest at times, but I loved her like a daughter."

"Love, Ishbel," Mairwen corrected. "You *love* her. Not *loved* as if she is gone from us forever. We must find her. Every plane, every reality, every timeline must be searched. We have never lost a mortal, and I intend to keep it that way. We shall send a clearer alarm through the Ether to all our Weavers on every level. Our Emily will be found."

"Shall we seek help from the Defenders of the Veil?"

"No." Mairwen clutched a fist to her aching heart. "They might seek wisdom from the goddesses, and I prefer to be better armed before the mothers demand that I explain. We will find her, and all will be well. I refuse to think otherwise."

Ishbel covered her face and bowed her head. "I am so verra sorry. Please forgive me."

Mairwen hugged her dear friend and whispered, "This is not yer fault. Come. We must make haste while the stones hold a remnant of her energy. Send her image with the alarm through the Ether, then join me in a search."

Tears still flowing, Ishbel nodded, pausing for the slightest moment before she leaned forward and rested her hands on the flagstone where Emily had stood only moments ago. After a few moments, Mairwen joined her, holding Emily's memory in her mind while focusing her mystical senses on the whisper of heat Emily had left behind.

"Show me," she whispered. "Show me where ye are, child."

CHAPTER 3

The lovely being who called herself Emily went limp and started to fall. Gryffe swept her up and cradled her like a babe against his chest. "Daren't ye die on me, woman. Daren't ye do it." He leaned in close to ensure she still breathed. When he discovered she did, he found that more consoling than he should. He shook off the feeling. 'Twas probably more of Nicnevin's infernal meddling. She had more than likely cast a glamour over this tempting lass to make him believe the dark haired beauty was the one. He never should have told his mother about his vision.

"Avric, come. Let us get the lass back to the keep so old Grennove can heal her."

The great black horse obediently ambled closer, then halted. His ears swiveled forward, then flattened back close to his head. He snorted and gave a single hard stomp.

"I shall hold her. I ken well enough that she canna ride because of her injury."

Avric snorted again, stomped harder, then backed away, shaking his head.

"If I use magic to return to the keep, it will flag Nicnevin. Is that yer wish?"

The stubborn beastie turned away, lifted his tail, and dropped a steaming pile of dung.

"Ye are an arse, Avric. A pure evil arse that I shouldha left with the kelpies where ye belong. Do ye wish to return to the loch this evening or be confined to the stable on dry land?"

The ebony beast shot him a warning glare and bared his teeth. As a rare hybrid born from the mating of a legendary shire stallion and a fierce kelpie mare, Avric much preferred a loch or a river rather than the stable when Gryffe no longer needed his services for the day. The horse wheeled about, came in close, and gave the unconscious woman a thorough snuffle. After taking in her scent, he stared at Gryffe for a long moment, then backed away again.

While Gryffe couldn't exactly hear the horse's thoughts, the two had always understood one another and known what the other felt. Perhaps it was because Gryffe had been the one to save Avric and his dam when they had both hovered near death after Avric's birth. Kelpies were never meant to breed with stallions of the land. Unwilling to leave the pair to die, Gryffe had called out to Nicnevin to save them. And she had. By mixing Gryffe's blood with that of the kelpie mare and the rare foal. Gryffe's strength had saved them. After all, even though his father was a mere mortal, the chieftain of Clan MacStrath, his mother was the Queen of the Dark Fae, the powerful Unseelie, none other than Nicnevin herself.

"Ye are a stubborn arse," Gryffe told the horse again as he shifted the lass higher against his chest and took off at a brisk pace. He would feckin' walk, before folding time and space and drawing Nicnevin's attention. She needed to stay at Court and out of his life. After all, he was considered the bastard son. Why did she even bother with him? She had named Roric the prince and heir of the Unseelie, a title his half-brother cherished but rarely spoke of since it tended to make the pureblood mortals a tad nervous. Roric enjoyed ruling the United Kingdom of Scotland and would do nothing to risk that crown.

A steady thumping behind him, Avric's plodding walk, made Gryffe shake his head. "Ye'll not let me ride, but ye will follow along behind me like a dog. Damn ye, Avric. Damn ye straight to hell."

The horse snorted, and something hit Gryffe square between his shoulders. He halted and turned. "Snot on me again, and I'll tell Cook to roast yer arse for supper, ye ken?"

The beast bobbed his head and whinnied, laughing in Gryffe's face. Avric knew Gryffe would never bring harm down upon him.

The lass, Emily, shifted and eked out a strained groan. "Could you put me down, please?" Yet, she clutched the front of his linen shirt as if she would never let it go. "This is killing my leg. Please. Set me down."

He had no doubt the position was hurting her hip, but she couldn't walk. "I shall carry ye this way for a while." He threw her over his shoulder. Her arse in the air would take the tension off her injured joint.

"Are you kidding me? Put me down. I am not a freaking sack of feed."

He almost smiled. Or at least, he thought it might be a smile tickling at his mouth. It had been so long since he'd been pleased about anything, he wasn't rightly sure how it felt anymore. "This takes the pressure off yer arse. We'll not be long. The keep is but a good stretch of the legs from here."

She reared up and propped herself on his shoulder so her head wasn't hanging downward. "Why didn't you just throw me over your horse like some kind of carcass?"

"Avric took a sniff of ye and decided he would nay give ye a ride."

"That is not remotely funny." She squirmed a bit more. "I do not stink."

Unable to resist, Gryffe turned his head and buried his face in her side, treating himself to a deep inhale. Damn. She was right. She smelled of warmth and all things good and comforting. She smelled like a woman he needed in his bed. Permanently. He clenched his teeth and forced himself to set aside that ridiculous thought and pick up the pace. "Ye dinna smell foul. All I know is Avric refused to let ye ride. Probably because of yer injury."

"So you let your horse make all the decisions?"

"Not all. But in this case, he seemed more than a little certain."

"There is something gross on the back of your coat."

"Horse snot. He thinks that great fun when he wishes to get his point across."

"Lovely." She wriggled again, drawing back from the mess the horse had made. "I really would like to try to walk. I can take care of myself, you know."

"Aye, lass." He gently eased her down and helped her steady herself on her good leg. "I have seen how ye take care of yerself. How ye landed yerself in the path of a horse, knocked yer arse out of joint, and have no idea how ye got here."

She glared at him, and he hoped she would never stop. Her eyes were the dark caramel hue of well aged whisky filled with fire.

"Yer name should be *Ember*—not Emily," he said before he could stop himself.

She blinked, almost flinching, then bared her teeth as if about to bite him. "I will be out of your hair as soon as possible, Mr. MacStrath. You can bet on it."

"Gryffe."

"What?"

"Call me Gryffe since ye are nay a servant, a merchant, or a crofter. Although they tend to call me Chieftain or the MacStrath. I dinna recall them ever saying, *mister*." He kept an arm around her, steadying her as she doggedly tried to hop one step at a time. "And ye'll nay be leaving me until ye're not only healed, but I am also damn sure I can no longer stand the sight of ye." Deep down, he knew he would never tire of her. She drew him in like honey tempting a badger. Nicnevin must have cast one hell of a glamour on this one. Feckin' hell, he wished this attraction was real. More than that, he wished the beauty felt the same for him.

"You cannot keep me prisoner," she snapped. She hopped again, then pulled him to a stop. "Wait. I have to rest for a minute. Apparently, I need to add hopping to my daily workout to increase my stamina."

"I canna keep ye prisoner, eh?" He increased the distance between them but kept hold of her arm so she wouldn't fall over. "Now is yer chance, my lovely Ember. Run for yer freedom."

"Oh, just shut up!"

Feckin' hell. She was about to cry. He had meant her no harm, merely intended to make his point. "Come here to me, lass." He pulled her close and tucked her tightly against him. "Hold fast, and close yer eyes." Breathing her in, he envisioned his bedchamber. "*Domus.*"

As soon as the familiar scents of leather, fresh linens, and beeswax candles hit him, he opened his eyes. "Let me help ye into the bed, and then I shall call for Grennove. She is the clan healer."

Emily opened her eyes and went still as a hare that had just spotted a wolf. "Where are we?" she whispered while casting a panicked glance all around the room.

"My keep, but more exactly—my bedchamber. 'Tis the most comfortable of all the rooms. At least, by my thinking, it is." He gently but firmly attempted to turn her. "To the bed with ye, aye? Then I'll summon the healer. Dinna fear. I mean ye no harm."

"I know you would never hurt me," she murmured so softly he almost missed it. She cleared her throat and stiffened, straightening her spine as if embarrassed by what she had just said. "So, you can do magic. Are you a Weaver too?"

"A Weaver, *too*?" he repeated, a chilling leeriness making him swallow hard. "Ye are a Weaver, then?"

Her eyes narrowed. "You do know what a Weaver is? You know I am not talking about making baskets or rugs, right?"

"I am not a Weaver." He would leave it at that for now. If this lass was a Weaver, that complicated things immensely and made his attraction to her even more impossible. Why the devil would Nicnevin choose a Weaver for her ridiculous game of trying to get him to sire an heir? Weavers were not of this world, and while many called his mother the goddess of winter and magic, half his bloodline was still very much mortal. He would never live as long as a Divine Weaver. But if Emily was a Weaver, why hadn't her leg already healed?

He tucked a finger under her chin and tipped her face higher, peering at her closer. "Ye nay answered my question, lass. Are ye a Weaver?"

The bewilderment and sheer panic in her eyes hit his heart as surely as an arrow.

"I am not a Weaver," she said. "My great-great grandmother was." She swayed off balance and tightened her hold on his arm. "You're right. I need to lie down."

He yanked back the bedclothes and helped her ease down among the pillows.

Struggling to lean forward, she grimaced as she yanked on the lace of her boot with one hand. "And, of course, it's knotted."

"Feckin' hell, woman. Lie ye back, and I shall rid ye of yer boots."

She relented with a pained groan, then patted her leg and drew out an odd thin square from a pocket in the seductive black trews that fit her like a second skin. After pecking several times on the gleaming bit of strangeness that was about as large as her hand, she heaved a great sigh and shoved the thing back into her pocket. "Idiot. No cell towers in the eighteenth century."

Gryffe didn't comment, as it didn't seem as though she was speaking to him. As he unlaced her boot, he noted the stitching giving way on one of the seams. "I'll send this out to Mathy. He can repair it."

Lying with her arm over her eyes, Emily flipped her hand as if she didn't care what he did. "Thank you. Who is Mathy? Your cobbler?"

"Nay. Mathy manages my stables. He is the best there is when it comes to working with leather." With her heavy sweater rucked up, he noted her long, lithe form that flowed into the perfect curve of her hips. Aye, perfection was indeed the word to describe her. Legs long enough to wrap around him and squeeze as he sank into her. The sweater hid her breasts, but he felt sure they were exquisite too. And her face. Surely, she was descended from the goddesses themselves. Elegantly arched brows, high cheekbones, a long slender nose, and whisky eyes filled with fire. She mesmerized him.

As he realized Nicnevin's spell was about to consume him, he blinked hard and sucked in a deep breath, drawing upon every strength he possessed to break free and regain his sanity. His mother's glamours were strong, but he had overcome them before and would do so again. When he finally found his *one*, it would not be because of manipulative magic. He set Emily's boots aside on the bench at the end of the bed.

"What time are ye from, lass?" Nicnevin had taken him to several eras through the Dreaming, but he hated it. He nay belonged anywhere but here. But not Emily. She did not belong here. By her clothes and her language, she was not of this time.

She scrubbed her face with both hands as if fighting against tears. "Twenty-first century—and I need to get back as soon as possible. I am not good at fitting in where I don't belong."

"Everything happens for a reason." How many times had he scoffed whenever Nicnevin had told him that very same thing? "Have ye any idea how ye came to be here?"

She let her hands drop and stared up at the ceiling with such a look of despair, he almost climbed into the bed and pulled her into his arms to comfort her.

"I'm not so sure I should say," she said with a heavy sigh. "A lot is at risk if I mess up and say something that might reveal a secret that's supposed to remain unsaid..." She propped herself up and looked at him, making him ache to join her among the pillows. Her eyes narrowed to critical slits. She was sizing him up. He could feel it. "You said you weren't a Weaver," she said, "and yet you used magic to get us from wherever we were to here. And you also seemed to know what a *Weaver* is. How is that?"

"I am the Grand Chieftain of the Defenders of the Veil." He clenched his teeth, immediately filled with second thoughts about sharing that he headed the Order of the Veil, the protectors of the blessed Highland weave.

"The Defenders I know, the ones from my time, aren't able to use magic. Only the Weavers can, and it's usually the Spell Weavers who manage the more complicated doings." Her critical look turned to one of disgust. "I am trying to learn because my great-great grand-mother was a Master Spell Weaver. Unfortunately, I suck at magic."

"Suck at magic?"

She huffed. "I catch everything on fire while trying to learn a spell and have only managed to conquer a few of the most basic ones."

So *Ember* was an apt name for her. He struggled to keep his amusement hidden. "Magic can be verra difficult."

"Then how come you do it so easily?"

"I am half Unseelie." He braced himself. Most mortals familiar with the Dark Fae ran screaming when they heard an Unseelie—or even a half Unseelie—was in their midst.

Emily's sleek, dark brows drew closer together. "What exactly is an Unseelie?"

"My mother is Queen of the Dark Fae, goddess of winter and magic, the magnificent Nicnevin—or so she tells everyone whenever she announces herself at Court." He wouldn't add that his meddling mother had also cast a glamour across Emily to make her so unbear-ably enticing.

"Fae," Emily repeated slowly, still frowning. Her eyes narrowed even more. "You're a fairy? Fairies are real?"

He didn't know whether to be insulted or not. "I am half Fae. My father was a mortal. The previous chieftain of Clan MacStrath." Nicnevin had told him about the mortal stories of the future that described the Fae, or *fairies* as Emily had called them, as winged bugs that sprinkled children with some sort of magical dust that made them fly. He was not now nor ever had been a feckin' bug. "And yes, the *Fae* are quite real."

"Sorry. I didn't mean anything by it. I didn't realize *fairy* was a racial slur." She primly folded her arms across herself and jutted her chin higher. "I'm a mix of Caribbean, Asian Indian, Belgian, and Cuban. And among that smorgasbord of DNA is my Spell Weaver ancestry. Trust me. I understand racial slurs and would never knowingly use one." She flinched as she adjusted her position. "I promise. As soon as I'm able, I'll get back to Seven Cairns. The Weavers there will help me get back to my time and out of yours."

That infuriated him even more, and he didn't understand why. It had to be Nicnevin's feckin' spell. "What did I tell ye about leaving here?"

She stared at him for a long moment, her confusion appearing to deepen the longer she studied him. "Something about I couldn't go until I was well, and until you decided whether or not you were sick of me. From your current tone, I think I have already achieved option number two."

Rather than argue or risk becoming ensnared even tighter in the web of magic that was to trick him into believing she was the one, he stormed across the room and yanked on the bellpull. "Grennove will heal ye, and Mrs. Thistlebran will assign a maid to serve ye." He pointed at her, stabbing the air with his finger. "Stay put until they get here. I'll not have ye injuring yerself further, ye ken?"

Her expression taut and stormy, she slowly nodded. As he yanked open the door, she shouted, "Hey!"

While he wasn't certain why she was bellowing about hay, he stopped and looked back at her.

"Thank you for helping me and for not being some sort of beast and doing unspeakable things," she said. "I know I could've landed myself in a lot worse situation than this, and don't think I don't appreciate your kindness." She drew up and swallowed hard, barely holding back the tears that made her eyes shimmer like rare jewels.

"It's just...complicated, and it really pisses me off when I make a mess that requires more than just me to clean it up."

Damned if he could fight the temptation any longer. He charged back across the room, tenderly cradled her face between his hands, and claimed the exquisite kiss he had hungered for since first setting eyes on her. His entire being shuddered with the wondrous connection, and it frightened him to the very depths of his soul, making him rip away and flee the place before he said more than he should.

Once safely in the hall, he slammed the door shut and fell back against it, breathing as hard as if he had run the length of the kingdom. He must never do that again. To taste her lips once more would surely be the death of his freedom and his oath to the vision he'd once had, his one true love—a woman hidden in shadows. He had to wait for her. His heart had whispered that he would know her when he found her, his one fated mate.

CHAPTER 4

E mily barely brushed her fingertips across her mouth. "I have never...what a...what a kiss." Her lips still tingled like she had just tasted something she'd always longed for but hadn't known what that thing was until she got it. What in the world had just happened? She had kissed and been kissed before, but never like that.

Taking care to keep her weight off her left side, she gingerly pushed herself higher among the pile of pillows against the massive oak headboard at her back. She stared at the bedroom door, half wishing Gryffe would return and half hoping he wouldn't. How had she managed to spell herself into an alternate eighteenth century, into the life of a man claiming to be half fairy, and then been totally gobsmacked by his kiss? Yes. Gobsmacked, one of her favorite new British words. It perfectly defined what that kiss had done to her. She huffed a soft laugh. He had said he was half fairy. Well, that fairy was no lightweight myth that fluttered around with gossamer wings. This breathtaking alpha male was a conqueror. A man, half mythical being aside, who took what he wanted.

"No. Not *fairy*. Fae," she whispered in case he was still on the other side of the door. That hard thump against it after he had slammed it shut sounded as though he had fallen back against it. That consoled her a little bit. The way he'd torn out of the room, he seemed to be as gobsmacked by that powerful kiss as she was.

A frigid breeze gusted in through the partially open window, and rain mixed with sleet pattered against the panes. He had said it was November—the same month as it currently was in her time. Mairwen had said all the worlds and timelines the Highland Veil kept separate ran parallel to one another. It would seem that the same rule applied to alternate realities, too.

Emily wondered if every world, every timeline had an alternate? The sheer enormity of how many levels the Weavers had to work with in their search for fated mates made her head hurt as badly as her rear end. Speaking of which, had she dislocated it as Gryffe suggested, or just badly bruised it?

Teeth clenched against the pain, she brought her sock feet together and compared the length of her legs. "Still the same. Good. It shouldn't be dislocated, then." A heavy sigh left her as she traced the outline of her cell phone in her pocket. "I wish I could text Papa." She drew up her good leg, propped her elbow on her knee, and held her head. Maybe it was better that she couldn't text her parents. They would really freak out about this. But if she could at least text Keeva, Mairwen's assistant, that would get her out of here. But texts were out. She was completely disconnected from all she had ever known, and she had never felt so alone in her life. She stared at the door again. Well...maybe not alone...but she sure was isolated in her confusion.

Gryffe was so...grumpy bearish, but he didn't come across as mean. And his announcement that she wouldn't be allowed to leave until she was healed, *and* he decided he was sick of her, was kind of exciting. He was most definitely an assertive male. That usually rubbed her fur the wrong way and goaded her into challenging any man with that mindset. But Gryffe was different. It might be fun to poke that bear and make him growl, but she wasn't sure she was ready for whatever might happen after that. There was so much in his eyes that both drew her in and pushed her away.

She pressed a hand to her chest and swallowed hard. Her heart was still pounding from their *exchange*. She had to escape this. Get back to Seven Cairns and go home. Home was safe. Home was normal. Maybe it was even time to move back to Jersey. Jessa was well settled and could portal to twenty-first century Seven Cairns and video call whenever they felt like a visit. Jessa had Grant and the babies. Another heavy sigh worked itself free. Yes. It was time. Emily nodded. She needed to forget about the craziness of Seven Cairns, forget about her great-great grandmother, and head back to Jersey and *normal*.

But what about Gryffe MacStrath? She closed her eyes tightly against the inner voice that never failed to get her into trouble whenever she listened to it. "Gryffe MacStrath will get on just fine with his life right here in his own little world." But that conviction sounded like pretty weak tea even to her, especially when her voice quivered whenever she said his name. "Gryffe MacStrath," she repeated louder and firmer, as if demanding he appear out of thin air.

She jumped as the door creaked open, then hissed as fresh agony shot through her behind and down her leg.

"Himself said ye was in a lot of pain," said a plump, white-haired woman who couldn't be more than four feet tall. "Add an extra kettle to the hearth, Breenoa. Moist heat will help our lady. Gather the resin cloths to keep the bed dry."

The much younger Breenoa, tall and gawky, and so thin a strong wind would blow her away, hurried to do the elder's bidding.

"I be Grennove Cobbledust," said the gnome-like matron as she kicked a footstool to the side of the bed with the aim and precision of a professional footballer. With minimal grunting, she climbed up on it and smiled down at Emily. "I be the healer of Clan MacStrath, and that lass over there be my assistant, Breenoa Swiftsong."

"Pleasure to meet you," Emily said, somewhat dazed by the

women's unusual names. Were they Fae or human? "I'm Emily. Emily Mithers."

Breenoa pulled a table closer to the bed and set up a pitcher and bowl along with any number of colored bottles and crocks from a large basket. "We be honored to serve ye, Lady Emily. Himself has been waiting for ye for such a verra long time." The girl beamed with an adoring smile and bowed.

"Breenoa." Grennove shot a stern look over the wire-rimmed spectacles perched on the end of her bulbous nose. "Run see if Mrs. Thistlebran has chosen a maid yet for our lady, and also ensure there is tea heading this way. No matter what be wrong, a cup of tea never goes amiss."

The *our lady* title worried Emily, but she tried to shake it off as a regional thing. After all, several at Seven Cairns referred to her on a regular basis as *our Emily*. "Tea would be lovely," Emily said, hoping to nudge the oddly fan girlish Breenoa out of the room before the girl dropped to her knees and started worshipping her.

As soon as Breenoa left them, Grennove clucked like a restless hen while sprinkling some sort of yellowish powder into the steaming bowl of water on the table. "Pay her no mind, m'lady. She is verra young."

"She is fine. Really." Emily recoiled at the rotten egg odor rising from the basin. "What is that?"

"Dinna fash yerself, m'lady. 'Tis a poultice for bandaging. Not a tonic for drinking."

"I am glad to hear that." Emily gingerly shifted and rubbed her left hip. "I think I just bruised it when I landed. I'm sure it'll be fine by tomorrow."

"Bruised it when ye landed," Grennove repeated while grinding some unknown substance in a mortar. She hugged the chunky stone bowl against her thick middle and grunted as she worked the pestle to crush its contents. "And where did ye fall from, m'lady?"

"I don't remember," Emily lied, instinctively feeling it best to be cautious.

Grennove shoved her spectacles higher up the bridge of her nose and squinted at her. "Hit yer head too, then?"

"Could be. I don't remember that either. I woke up with Gryffe carrying me." There. That was the truth. At least, most of it was. "He thought my hip might be out of joint, but my legs are the same length, and I haven't lost any feeling or gone all tingly, so I think it's just badly bruised."

The old woman's face puckered with a more judicious scowl. "Are ye a healer, then?"

"My father was—is. He is a healer. So is my mother. Sort of."

"Sort of?"

"Mama helps people with their minds." Emily tapped her temple. "When they are upset or having problems they can't seem to overcome."

"Hmm." Grennove studied her, ever so slightly tilting her head. Her wild, silvery brows knotted over her pale green eyes. "I see."

The healer didn't sound as if she *saw*, but Emily couldn't help that. It was best she kept things as vague as possible.

"Shed yer trews and show me yer hip," the matron ordered.

With no small amount of pain, Emily slipped her leggings down as far as she felt necessary for Grennove to examine her hip. Eventually, she would be forced to don the clothes of this century, but she intended to hang onto her twenty-first century garb as long as possible. She lightly ran her fingers high on her thigh, closer to the hip joint. "It hurts the worst right here."

Grennove frowned, then gently laid her pudgy hand on the spot Emily had indicated. "No bruising yet, but with yer rich coloring, 'twill be harder to see. Pale skin like mine tells its secrets quickly. Yer richness is proud and keeps its pain hidden as long as possible." She bowed her head and closed her eyes. "Aye, ye've bruised it badly, m'lady. I feel the heat of the injury. 'Twill take days for it to show and even longer for the pain to leave ye." She opened her eyes and pinned Emily with a hard look. "How far did ye fall? Several centuries?"

Did everyone here know about time travel and accept it as an everyday occurrence? Emily stared back at the healer, determined not to blink. "About three, to be exact."

Grennove smiled as if she had just won a bet. "Ye can trust me, m'lady. Never worry about that, ye ken?" She nodded at Emily's bare behind. "Straighten yer trews, if ye wish. We'll not be using the poultice. 'Twill do no good for what ails ye." She dried her hands on the towel hanging from the thin belt buckled around her middle. "When yer maid arrives, she can help ye don a shift. Ye will be more comfortable then. Moist heat and several days in the bed will cure what ails ye."

Emily nodded and fixed her clothes, still unsure as to just how much she could trust the little old woman with the eyes of an old soul, as her father used to say. "Thank you."

Folding her pudgy hands in front of her, Grennove tipped a nod at the items on the table. "We shall still add a few herbs to yer tea. That will help ye as well." She resettled her stance on the stool and nudged her chin higher. "Himself refuses to believe ye are his one. Fears to believe it, in fact."

"His one what?" Why did everyone here talk as if they belonged in an epic fantasy movie? They were as bad as the Weavers of Seven Cairns.

Grennove frowned and wrinkled her nose to adjust her glasses. "The *one*, m'lady. The missing part of his soul. His fated mate."

Fated mates. Emily refused to say the term aloud, especially when she was more like a thorn in Gryffe's side rather than the other half of his heart. *But what about that phenomenal kiss?* She shook away the thought. "Maybe he refuses to believe it, because he knows it's not true."

"So, ye feel nothing for him, then?"

"We just met."

"Aye, but the bond rekindles quickly as the fire from all yer past lives returns to revive the love ye shared. Ye feel no drawing to him? No faint memory of having met him before?"

"Are you a Weaver?" Emily curled deeper into the pillows and eased away, putting a bit more space between her and Grennove. The old woman asked too many pointed questions that hit entirely too close to the mark.

"No." The healer's expression softened with a look that spoke of a cherished memory filled with sorrow as well as joy. "But I loved one, once." She smoothed the bedcovers, tugging them wrinkle free. "As I said, ye can trust me, m'lady. I never betray a confidence." She turned her head and smoothed a silver curl behind her faintly pointed ear. "I am an excellent listener."

"He kissed me," Emily said without meaning to say it. She clapped a hand over her mouth to keep from blurting out anything else.

"Good." Grennove nodded. "I thought he might have, considering the state he was in when he spoke to us in the hall."

"I am going back to my time. To my world. I'm going back to where I belong." Emily hugged the knee of her uninjured leg to her chest, curling into herself while gathering up the bedclothes and pillows like a shield. "I can't stay here."

Grennove jutted her chin higher still and looked down her nose, wrinkling it again and making her glasses wiggle. "And why not?"

"My family. My friends. Everything I know and love is *not* here."

"Ye are a Weaver and can open the portals of Seven Cairns any time ye wish to visit those ye cherish. Ye should know that. Weavers are blessed with that boon from the goddesses themselves."

"I am not a full blooded Weaver and didn't find my way here by passing through a portal. My great-great grandmother was a Spell Weaver—all I ever do is catch things on fire, and apparently, shoot myself into alternate realities." Emily covered her eyes. She hated to cry worse than anything in the world. Crying helped nothing. All it did was make her nose run, her eyes burn, and her head hurt. "Is that tea ever going to get here?"

The bedroom door swung open as if it had heard her childish whininess that even made her cringe.

Breenoa marched in, smiling broadly as if proud to be the leader of the parade. An older woman dressed all in black followed her, and next came a petite, young girl who didn't look sturdy enough to even lift the large tray she carried. It bore a teapot, a milky white pitcher, cups, and an assortment of plates and bowls covered with white linens. Not only did the enormous round tray look heavy, but unwieldy as well. But the girl carried it with agility and finesse, as if it were light as a cloud.

The lady in black, silvery haired and an old-fashioned grandmotherly sort, drew closer to the bed and offered a graceful nod. "Good day to ye, m'lady. I be Mrs. Thistlebran. Housekeeper. Anything ye be needing, I shall see that ye have it." She tipped a nod at the delicate young woman still holding the tray. "This be Inalfi Shadowfen. Yer personal maid. She will take the verra best care of ye, I assure ye." She motioned Inalfi forward. "Come, Inalfie. Our lady needs her tea."

Inalfi had the lightest blonde hair Emily had ever seen and was so pale she was almost translucent. She stepped forward and managed an impressive curtsy while still holding the tray. "Would it be to yer liking if I rest the tray here on the bed with ye, m'lady, so ye might easier reach what ye need? I also brought a few nibbles and bits I thought ye might enjoy. Healing takes food, and lots of it. Leastways, that's what my grandmam always said."

"That would be fine, thank you." Emily managed a nervous smile, not entirely comfortable with the idea of having a personal maid. But the bed was huge, much larger than any standard, king-sized bed, so Inalfi might as well make use of it.

"And what would ye be having in yer tea, m'lady?" Inalfi poured a cup, then adjusted the chunky knit tea cosy that had shifted slightly. "Silly thing. Not tied properly." Fingers flying, she corrected the oversight.

Emily blinked hard to focus more sharply. No one's fingers moved that fast.

"Milk, sugar, honey?" The wisp of a girl held the cup and saucer aloft in one hand while uncovering everything on the tray.

"A bit of honey, please." Emily stared at the stack of neatly folded linens that had previously covered all the plates and bowls. How had they gotten that way, as if they had folded themselves? She rubbed her eyes, then pressed a shaking hand to her forehead. Maybe she *had* hit her head when she landed. It was starting to hurt, and everything was so—strange. "Uhm...maybe I should just try to sleep. I'm not feeling very well all of a sudden."

"Bring me her tea," Grennove told the maid. "She needs the herbs. 'Twill help her."

Inalfi hurried around the bed and set the tea on the table beside the healer. Grennove scraped some of the greenish substance out of the mortar, added it to the tea, and stirred, then nodded at Inalfi. "Now."

"Here ye are, m'lady." Inalfi ever so gently placed the cup and saucer in Emily's hands. "Steady now. Verra good, there. Now, have ye a wee sip and let me know if ye wish more honey or less."

Less? What would the maid do if she wanted less sweetness? *She would add more tea, silly.* Emily sighed. She hated it when her logic and good sense waited too long to kick in. She took a hesitant sip and closed her eyes. It tasted exactly like the tea Lilias always served her at the pub, so much so, it was about to make her cry. She wished she was back at Seven Cairns.

"Oh no, m'lady. I got it wrong, then."

Inalfi moved to take the cup, but Emily stopped her. "No. No, you got it perfect. It's just like the tea I always had at The Fearless Scottie. It reminded me of home." Another sigh shuddered free of her as she wrestled with her churning emotions. "It's fine. I'm just...I'm just tired."

Grennove gave Mrs. Thistlebran an almost imperceptible nod.

The housekeeper immediately stepped closer. "I shall be leaving ye then, m'lady. Should ye have need of anything, let Inalfi know, and she will fetch me." She shifted in place and looked as though she was trying to decide if she should say more or keep her thoughts to herself. Then she cleared her throat and bowed as if Emily were some sort of royalty. "We are all verra glad to have ye here, m'lady. Please know ye are as welcome as welcome can be."

Something about the housekeeper gave Emily an eerie shiver. Not necessarily a bad shiver, but the kind she got whenever she suspected something about a person. Mrs. Thistlebran was trying to tell her more without actually saying the words. Hugging her tea closer, she tried to smile and failed. "Thank you, Mrs. Thistlebran. Everyone here has been most kind."

"Good, then. Good day to ye, m'lady." After a curt nod, the housekeeper swept out of the room and softly closed the door behind her.

Emily breathed in the steam rising from her tea, then consoled herself with another sip. She had to stay calm and get a grip on her emotions. Everything would be fine. Once she healed enough to walk, she would borrow a horse and head to Seven Cairns as fast as it could carry her. Or maybe she'd try that serenity spell again. Excitement and hope stirred within her. Yes. She could try the spell before she was fully healed. All she had to do was center her thoughts and say the words. She could do that once everyone left her alone. The prospect sent a much needed shot of adrenaline through her, giving her the strength she needed.

"Breenoa, bring the resin cloth, so we might get our lady settled on her warm padding afore the tea makes her sleepy." Grennove pointed at Inalfi. "Steady our lady's tea and tray to keep us from causing a messy topple."

"Aye, Grennove." With a reassuring smile, Inalfi took Emily's tea away, returned it to the tray, then lifted that and held it aloft. "Once they get ye settled again, I shall have ye a fresh cup to enjoy. Daren't ye worry," she told Emily.

With less pain than Emily anticipated, Grennove and Breenoa soon had her settled on a pallet of warm, damp linens that worked as efficiently as a proper heating pad—even though the moisture was seeping through her leggings. She wished they had used one of those resin cloths between her and the linens, but she supposed that would defeat the whole *moist heat* therapy idea. Thank heavens they hadn't pushed the *shift* issue. She needed to be fully dressed when she tried the spell.

Inalfi once again presented a fresh cup of tea to Grennove for more herbs, then offered it to Emily. "Would ye like a biscuit or two? I brought shorties, treacles, and jam prints all. Some of Cook's best."

Emily was afraid to eat, especially with her plan of trying the serenity incantation again as soon as everyone left the room. "Just tea for now, thank you."

Inalfi's tranquil demeanor didn't falter. She simply nodded and stepped back as though waiting to jump at Emily's next command.

"Well, then," Grennove said. "Breenoa and I shall be off. We will return in the morning to see how ye fared through the night. Inalfi can manage changing the cloths and seeing to yer comfort." She bowed before hopping down off the wooden step stool. "Good rest to ye, m'lady. Have Inalfi fetch us should aught cause ye concern."

"Thank you and Breenoa both." Emily sipped her fresh tea, wondering how she could get rid of Inalfi, too, since it sounded as though the maid intended to stay in the room and watch over her.

After the healer and her assistant left, Inalfi flitted about the chamber, tidying anything that might be remotely out of place, even going so far as to return the large, round table that had been pushed over to the bed, back to its place in front of the window.

"Once all the heat leaves those linens," the maid said, "we shall get ye into a nice fresh shift. That will help ye settle in for the night."

Settle in for the night, my Aunt Fannie. Emily smiled and nodded while holding the teacup to her lips, as if she could hide behind it. She really didn't want to change before trying the spell again. She was more comfortable, more self-assured in her twenty-first century clothing. They acted like an anchor, a trail of breadcrumbs back to her time. Ishbel had often advised her to use something besides her beach vision to focus her thoughts. Her clothing and her cell phone would serve that purpose just fine.

She finished her tea, then stretched to place the cup and saucer on the bedside table.

Inalfi jumped to take it from her. "There, now! Dinna hurt yerself. I am here to serve ye, m'lady. Please dinna hesitate to ask me for whatever ye need."

"Thank you, Inalfi. I'm just not used to having someone jump to do everything for me."

"Well, ye have me now." Inalfi threw out her chest and preened like a tiny peacock. "I am proud Mrs. Thistlebran chose me to care for ye."

"I'll try to remember to ask for help." Emily shifted her left leg and smiled. The pain wasn't nearly as bad as before. "My hip already feels better because of everyone's care. I appreciate each of you." She hoped they would remember that when they discovered she had disappeared back to her time. *Think positive.* The spell would shoot her back to her time just like it had shot her here. That would definitely grant her some serenity.

A slight misgiving niggled at the back of her mind. *What about Gryffe?* She would never see him again. She rubbed her knuckles up and down her breastbone, trying to erase the subtle burning ache that had settled deep in her heart at the thought of him. How could she already miss him? She'd only known him a few hours. It had to be heartburn from whatever herbs Grennove had added to the tea. "Uhm...would you mind stepping out of the room for a little bit so I can use the chamberpot?" There had to be a chamberpot. After all, this was the eighteenth century—even if it was an alternate reality.

Inalfi stared at her in befuddlement. "Ye will need my help, m'lady. Yer leg might be feeling better, but Himself and Mrs. Thistlebran both said ye couldna walk." She nodded at the wooden privacy screen partitioning off a corner of the room. "That there is a fair few steps for ye to make all by yerself. I can bring the bourdaloue to the bed for ye. Or do ye need the full sized pot for a hearty shite?"

"I can walk over there." Emily tried to sound calm and firm

without appearing too anxious. She didn't want to arouse any suspicion. "I can do it. Really."

Inalfi folded her arms across her chest, narrowing her eyes and slowly tilting her head. "Himself insisted ye should never be left alone."

"But that's when he thought I couldn't walk. I can now."

"Show me."

Determined to hide any amount of pain or discomfort, Emily slid to the edge of the bed and stood, placing all her weight on her right side, but resting her left foot on the floor to look as though some weight was on it as well. Her hip throbbed and sent off a warning zing of pain down her leg. She gritted her teeth and forced a smile. "See?"

"Ye've nay walked yet." Inalfi was obviously unconvinced.

Clenching her teeth even tighter, Emily forced herself to take a step without flinching, and then she took another, and another. Cold sweat peppered her brow, and she was so glad she hadn't eaten. As it was, the tea was about to slosh back out as her stomach stormed with the pain ripping up and down her leg. She tossed a victorious look back at Inalfi. "See?"

With her delicate features puckered in a displeased scowl, Inalfi shook a finger at the door. "I shall leave ye long enough to fetch fresh linens. Not a moment longer, and when I return, we will be changing ye into yer shift so ye can keep yer bare arse against the warmed linens, ye ken?"

Emily forced an even wider smile and gave the maid a thumb's up. "Perfect. Thank you." She held her breath until Inalfi left, then sagged to the floor, struggling not to vomit from the pain.

"I can do this," she said, forcing the words through clenched teeth. She closed her eyes and hugged her cell phone to her chest, forcing herself to think of nothing other than using her phone in twenty-first century Seven Cairns. Yes. She had it firmly in her mind. This would work. "*Tranquillitas!*"

A ring of fire exploded around her. The flames crackled ever higher as the raging inferno's circle slowly closed in to consume her. Panic shot through her, fueling the blaze even more. "No! Help!"

CHAPTER 5

E
mily's shriek shot through Gryffe at his self-appointed post
in the hallway across from the closed bedroom door.

He barreled into the room, immediately knowing what
she had done. She had tried to leave him by using magic. Why? Had
she not told him that whenever she did spellwork, she caught everything on fire? He clapped his hands. "*Recedo!*"

The ring of fire disappeared, as did any damage it had caused,
revealing Emily slumped in the floor with her head buried in her
arms. Unable to decide whether to shake her, leave her there, or risk
kissing her again, he settled for dropping to his knees in front of her.

"Did ye learn anything?" he asked as calmly as possible when she
refused to lift her head and look him in the eye.

"I still suck at magic," came her muffled reply from the depths of
her arms.

His heart ached for her pain but it hurt even more because she
was in such a hurry to leave him. The kiss had meant nothing to her.
She had not felt a thing. Proof yet again that she was not his *one*.
This unholy burning that consumed him, the insistent urge that she
was meant to be his was most definitely Nicnevin's damned spell.

He would have a few choice words for his mother when next he saw her.

"Come. Let's get ye back to the bed."

Emily lifted her head and fixed him with such a forlorn expression that it tore a groan from him and made him pull her into his arms.

"I have made such a mess of my life," she sobbed, clinging to him like a soul lost at sea, trying not to drown.

He closed his eyes and clenched his teeth, steeling himself against the feelings she stirred. With gentle shushing and stroking her hair as if she were a wee bairn, he carefully cradled her, taking into account her poor injured arse. "Ye've nay made yer life a mess," he told her quietly. "Ye've merely taken a turn ye nay expected. Once ye heal, once ye're strong enough, we'll get ye back to where ye belong, ye ken?"

"I don't belong anywhere." She hugged him tighter, wailing and mumbling incoherently with her face tucked under his chin.

"Ye belong with me." He flinched, closed his eyes, and prayed she hadn't heard him. Nicnevin's glamour must be one that strengthened over time. He silently cursed his conniving, dark-hearted mother to the hottest pits of hell. "Come. Let us get ye into the bed, lass. A bit of sleep will do ye a world of good."

She had gone suddenly quiet, barely snuffling and only hiccuping occasionally with her face still buried in his chest. Ever so slowly, she slid her arms out from around him and tucked into herself—a tight little bundle of misery. "If you could stand me up, I'll try to walk."

His heart sank even lower. Growling against the painful rejection, he swept her up, carried her to the bed, and gently lowered her into the nest of pillows. As the backs of his hand brushed the bedclothes, he recoiled and hoisted her back to his chest. "The feckin' linens are wet. Would no one bring ye anything so ye could piss and keep yerself dry? Inalfi! Get yer arse in here!" He swung about and glared at the door. "I'll have that girl's hide and send her straight back to the kingdom."

"I did not wet the bed, and stop yelling at Inalfi. Grennove was using moist heat to make my butt feel better. Could you please set me down? This position pulls my leg and makes everything hurt worse."

Inalfi flew into the room, came to an abrupt halt, and bowed her head. "Forgive me, my chieftain. I should never have left her. Please forgive me for failing our lady."

"You did not fail me," Emily said before Gryffe could further reprimand the maid. She twisted in his arms. "Please set me on the bed. I am dying here."

"What?" Panic shot through him. "Fetch Grennove immediately!" he said to Inalfi as he eased Emily onto a dry part of the bed but kept his arm under her shoulders, supporting her so he could gaze into her eyes. "Dinna die, my precious ember. I beg ye." Then he noticed *his precious ember* looked far from being at death's door. Instead, she appeared ready to burst into a flaming ball of irritation.

"Inalfi, don't go! That was just a figure of speech," she said, spitting the words as if they tasted bad. "I'm not really dying. At least, I don't think I am. My butt just throbbed a lot worse because of the way you held me."

She had made him look the fool. He stepped away, letting her fall back among the pillows.

"Ow!"

Ignoring the infernal woman sent to torment him, he turned back to the maid. "If I am not in this room, dinna leave her again for any reason, lest she burn down the keep with her spellcasting. Ye were chosen because of yer ability to snuff magic. Am I quite clear this time?"

Head still bowed, Inalfi curtsied. "Yes, my chieftain."

"Get her into some dry clothes and dry that bed as well. I slept on wetness and much worse during the wars, but I'll not be doing it in my own home."

"Yes, my chieftain."

"You're not sleeping in this bed with me," Emily said, pushing herself back against the headboard with her uninjured leg.

"These are my private chambers, and that is my bed. I am chieftain here, and I sleep where I damn well please."

"Then move me to another room." She clutched the front of her heavy knit tunic as if determined it would stay put. Stubbornness flashed like fire in her dark topaz eyes.

"No, my lady." He went to the cabinet in the corner and poured himself a whisky before turning and arching a brow at the maid. "Well?"

"Yes, my chieftain?"

"Do as I told ye. A dry shift for our lady, and a dry bed for us both. Now."

"I am not stripping down in front of you," Emily said with a feralness that made him want her even more. Damn, the woman made him ache for her in every possible way. But he had withstood Nicnevin's spells before. He'd withstand this one as well.

"Ye'll not be stripping down in front of me, my lady." He turned back to the cabinet and refilled his glass. "Ye will be stripping down behind me. Inalfi—proceed." When he heard no movement, he rapped a knuckle on the cabinet. "Shall I turn to inspect the progress the two of ye are making?"

"No—you shall shut the hell up before I hobble over there and throw that drink in your face."

He snorted, the closest he ever came to laughing anymore. "Now, now...we dinna waste good whisky around here, my fiery ember. Would ye care for a glass to warm ye? 'Twill also help numb the pain in yer arse."

"Drink more, then, because *you* are currently the biggest pain in my arse."

And then a hearty laugh did burst free of him, startling him with how good it felt. At that sudden realization, the mirth left him, but didn't fade completely. How long had it been since he had laughed? How long had it been since he'd even smiled? He shook away the foolish ponderings. What the devil did it matter? He selected one of the finer glasses from the tray on the cabinet and filled it with a prudent amount of whisky, then topped off his own. He squared his shoulders and stared straight ahead, ready to turn. "Are ye dressed yet, my lady?"

"Yes."

The sullen fury in her voice threatened to make him smile. *Nicnevin's spell*, he silently chanted to keep himself in check, but as soon as he turned and beheld Emily in his bed, in her thin shift untied at the throat as if she were his eager bride, it nearly undid him. Such a glorious woman. Why could she not be his one?

With forced nonchalance, he sauntered over to the bed and held out her glass. "Yer whisky, my lady."

She glared at him, eyes glowing with even richer heat than the golden liquid in the glass. With a flare of her delicate nostrils, she accepted it from him but didn't drink.

"I'll be fetching our lady more tea with Grennove's herbs, if that be to yer liking, my chieftain?" Inalfi said. "Be it all right for me to leave the room and do so?"

"Yes." Gryffe didn't break from Emily's damning glare. "I shall be here till morning. Bring a tray of fruits, cheese, and meats as well, since we shall miss our supper. Have Cook send up her best and make the lads help ye, ye ken?"

"Yes, my chieftain." Inalfi hurried out of the room.

After a sip of whisky, he pulled his favorite chair from its place beside the hearth and set it close to the bedside table. The leather cushions squeaked and groaned as he settled into the chair's depths. He offered Emily a nod. "Whisky does ye more good if ye drink it rather than just hold it 'twixt yer hands."

She tore her focus from him and stared down at the drink, gently swirling it until the sparkles of light danced through the golden nectar. After the barest sip and while still glaring at the glass, she asked, "What did you mean by what you said?"

Her voice had lost its edge. A hesitancy echoed through it,

making it quite clear which of his statements she meant. The problem was—he had not said those words willingly. Nicnevin's glamour had pulled them from his lips. The only way to keep his oath to his *one* was to confess the truth to Emily. "It was not I who spoke those words. I did not say *ye belong with me*."

An endearing bewilderment came over her, drawing her sleek black brows closer together as she stole a glance at him. "I distinctly heard you say that."

"Aye—I did *speak* the words, but 'twas Nicnevin's spell that pulled them from me. She has placed a glamour upon ye."

Emily eyed him as if he'd sprouted a horn out of the top of his head. "She has done what?"

"A glamour. Placed it upon ye. Have ye not studied glamours yet?"

"I've heard of them—in movies and stuff—but I don't think they are part of a Weaver's arsenal, or Ishbel would've told me. Are you telling me they're real?"

"Aye, quite real. Ye're nay the first that Nicnevin sent to fool me."

She straightened and squared her shoulders as if insulted. "A lot of women have dropped in your horse's path, have they? Are you as charming to all of them as you are to me?"

"I easily sent them back to where they belonged. Their glamours were weak." He shook his head and fortified his courage with another sip of whisky. The slow burn down his gullet gave him strength. "Ye appear to be different, though. The spell she placed upon ye is strong."

After another sip of her drink, Emily seemed even more bewildered as she stared upward. "Wouldn't I know it if Nicnevin had done that to me? Wouldn't the Weavers sense her presence in Seven Cairns? They're pretty secure there. They sense magic whenever it's used."

He hadn't taken that into consideration. Emily's Weaver ancestry might make a difference. But her bloodline had to be weak. After all, if she had been a pureblood Weaver, she would've already healed. Unless—he had heard stories of the goddesses dabbling in the lives of Weavers, all for the greater good and the strength of the Highland Veil. Above all else, it had to be protected, or every world, every timeline, and reality would plunge into unbearable chaos.

"Have ye known of yer Weaver's blood all yer life?" He flinched for her as she shifted positions and appeared to still be in quite a bit of pain. "Drink more whisky, lass. Trust me, it will help."

"I don't want to become too..." She narrowed her eyes at him. "Compliant."

"Compliant?"

She pinned him with a pointed glare. "You said you were sleeping in this bed tonight—remember?"

"I have never forced myself on an injured woman, and most especially, not an unwilling one. No matter how *compliant* she might temporarily think herself because of drink." Mildly insulted, he tossed the rest of his whisky back and rose to get another. "More or no?"

She finished hers off as well and handed him the glass. "More."

"Now, as I asked before, have ye known of yer Weaver's blood all yer life?"

"Not really."

"Ye sound confused, lass. Either ye knew it or ye didn't." He filled their glasses and returned, handing hers over before settling back into his chair.

"I knew who my ancestor was—not *what* she was." She ran a fingertip around the rim of the glass, causing him to take in the gracefulness of her long fingers. She twitched a faint shrug. "All I knew about her was her name. My great-great grandmother Esme." She shifted to more fully face him, studying him as if he were an oddity in a book. "You said you sent the others back where they belonged. Why haven't you done the same for me?"

"Ye are different from the others." He wouldn't add that he hadn't sent her away because he hadn't wanted to—a dangerous weakness he refused to admit. "Nicnevin's spell is stronger this time and gaining strength by the moment."

Emily relaxed deeper into the pillows, staring straight ahead now as she occasionally sipped her drink, then hugged it to her chest. "Ishbel says the reason I have so much trouble with my magic is because my emotions are in an uproar. She thinks it's because they haven't been able to find my fated mate."

He choked on his whisky, thumping his chest as he tried to clear his windpipe of the fiery fluid.

She watched him with concern. "Are you okay?"

"I am Gryffe, remember?" He cleared his throat, thumped his chest one last time, then reached for her glass. "If ye canna remember my name, ye have had enough."

"*Okay* means the same thing as *all right* or *well*. I was checking to see if you were all right or if I needed to help you beat on your chest, so you wouldn't die on me."

"Why do ye care if I die, lass? Ye set the room on fire trying to get away from me."

"I did not." She took a big swig, then blinked from the fumes and wheezed in and out from the overly large sip. "I was trying to get back home, not get away from you."

"If ye return to yer time, ye will be away from me, ye ken? I can travel across the centuries whilst in the Dreaming, but I hate it."

"The Dreaming?" She paused with her glass partway to her mouth. "What is that?"

"Exactly what it sounds like. Traveling wherever ye wish through dreams. The Dreaming is the plane that holds them. That place is an unholy chaos, constantly fluid and ever-changing depending on who is there and who is not. Some have more control over their dreams than others. It's none too pleasant when ye become snagged in someone else's nightmare." He drank the last of his whisky and set it aside. He'd had enough. "Nicnevin loves the place. She thrives on chaos."

"Is she evil?" Emily rubbed her nose, then held out her glass for him to take. "Here. The tip of my nose is going numb. I have had enough." Still gently squeezing her nose, she asked again, "Is Nicnevin evil?"

"She can be, depending on her mood."

"Is she as bad as Morrigan?"

That surprised him. "What do ye know of the Morrigan?"

"She almost killed my best friend while trying to keep her from bonding with her fated mate." Emily shuddered as if suddenly cold.

He rose and tucked the bedclothes up around her shoulders, then sat on the bed beside her. "Nicnevin is not as heartless as the Morrigan, nor as hungry for death or the destruction of the Veil. But she is a vain, selfish beastie, and more often than not, leaves a feckin' mess wherever she goes." Seeing how Emily still appeared worried, he impulsively reached out and cupped her cheek. "Dinna fash yerself, lass. I would never allow her to harm ye."

"There is so much kindness in your eyes," she said as if speaking more to herself than him.

He pulled his hand away as if the touch of her burned him. And it did. Her very existence set him ablaze. He needed quiet to turn within himself and strengthen his resolve, to find a way to undo Nicnevin's spell. "Shall ye sleep some afore ye eat? Inalfi should return soon with yer tea and our supper."

"I'm not sleepy." Her eyelids drooped lower. "I'm lost."

"Ye're nay lost, my precious ember. Merely a bit confused." He eased off the bed and silently shifted away. "I wish ye were mine to claim," he added softly as he moved to stand in front of the hearth fire. "With all my heart, I wish ye were my *one*."

EMILY OPENED her eyes and froze. Didn't breathe. Didn't blink. Didn't twitch so much as a finger. This wasn't her room in her cozy cottage at Seven Cairns. Even in the dim lighting, she could tell this wasn't her bed. Then, she remembered where she was and exhaled, sagging deeper into the pillows.

Steady breathing beside her dared her to turn her head in that direction. Gryffe hadn't lied. Even though he was fully clothed and lying on top of the covers, he was sleeping in his own bed, just as he had said he would. On his back, hands folded on his broad chest as if ready to be lowered into the grave. He slept soundly—and didn't snore. At least, he didn't snore compared to the noise her father and brothers always made whenever they slept. They had made it easy to sneak into the house after curfew. The loud, rumbling snores of the Mithers males drowned out any possible sound she might make while creeping up to her room.

A comforting sense of security and contentment washed across her as she studied the handsome profile of the growly chieftain of Clan MacStrath. Gryffe was a good man. She could've landed in the hands of someone so much worse. But good man or not, he made her heart hurt, made it burn with such a lonely ache that sometimes she had to swallow hard to get past all that he made her feel. If she had been brave enough to answer Grennove's questions about feeling drawn to him, feeling as though she had known him all her life, feeling as though something about him completed the crazy puzzle of her soul, she would have said, *yes to all the above.* But she had evaded the questions. She had to—to protect herself. After all, how could she possibly feel all those things about a man she had just met?

Ishbel had told her she would know when she found her fated mate, but how could she be sure? She had made so many wrong choices when she'd thought she was following a good instinct, a solid gut feeling. But sometimes, her gut lied. And a lie that made her decide to settle down in an alternate reality of eighteenth century Scotland would be an *epic* disaster.

The slow rise and fall of Gryffe's chest mesmerized her, lulling her into almost going back to sleep. But she couldn't. The unrelenting need to pee jabbed at her, warning her she had better pay attention to it soon. Now that her vision had adjusted to the darkened room, she could see quite well, considering only a single candle burned on the mantelpiece. If she went slow and used the furniture between the bed and the wooden privacy screen to keep her balance, surely she could make it. She wasn't about to wake Gryffe and ask for help, and Inalfi was nowhere to be found. A wave of guilt washed across her. Poor Inalfi. Emily hated that she'd gotten the maid into trouble, but she did need to ask the maid about what Gryffe had said about her ability to *snuff* magic. What exactly did he mean by that?

Ever so slowly, Emily pushed herself upright, bracing for the pain that turned out to be a great deal less brutal than it had been. Thank goodness for that. She'd always had a high pain tolerance, but this one had nearly made her vomit several times.

"What is it, lass? Are ye unwell?"

She clenched her teeth to keep from cursing. How had she awakened him so easily? She had barely moved, and the bed hadn't shifted in the least. "Go back to sleep," she whispered. Why was she whispering? He was already awake. "Go back to sleep," she said louder. "I am going to the..." She nodded at the privacy screen in the corner.

He rolled off his side of the bed, hurried around to her side, and started to pick her up.

"No! I can do this." She pushed his hands away and scooted to the edge. "I am not hurting nearly as badly. Let me try it on my own. Besides—there is no way you're going back there with me."

"Everyone pisses and takes a shite. There is no need for embarrassment. If ye fall, ye might hurt yerself worse."

She glared at him, willing him to understand. "I cannot do what I need to do with an audience."

"Once I get ye there and seated on the close stool, I will come away and give ye yer privacy until ye are ready to return to the bed. Will that suit ye?"

"Do I have a choice?"

"Ye do not."

"Fine." If she didn't get to the facilities soon, he'd be calling for Inalfi to dry the bed again.

He swept her up into his arms and strode to the area behind the screen. It was bigger than she'd expected, containing a long cabinet with several pitchers and bowls and what looked like a short, squat nightstand against the wall.

"Are ye strong enough to stand and hold fast to the sideboard while I open the stool for ye?"

She nodded. "I'll keep my weight on my right leg."

Ever so gently, he lowered her, then stood there watching as if waiting to see if she would topple over.

"Could you get on with it?" She hadn't relieved herself since arriving in this confusing era, and she was about to burst.

With a hurried dip of his chin, he turned to the nightstand, opened its top and side, then moved back to reveal a wooden chair with a hole in the seat—a far cry from any toilet she had ever used. But she'd take it and be grateful that at least she didn't have to squat over a ceramic tureen.

Before she could limp across the distance between her and the seat, he slid his arms under hers, held her tight, and shifted her around to stand in front of the commode. "Pull up yer shift, and I'll ease ye down."

Burning with embarrassment, she did just that. Better to get it over with rather than argue. She would never be able to look him in the eye again. She propped her elbows on her knees and buried her face in her hands.

"Do ye need a basin, lass? Are ye ill?"

"I am not ill—just humiliated beyond belief."

"Why?"

She couldn't believe he actually sounded befuddled, but wasn't about to lift her head to look and see if he was making fun of her. "I just am. Could I have some privacy, please?"

"Aye. Call out when ye are ready to return to the bed."

"I will. Thank you."

Peeking through her fingers, she relaxed a little at finding herself alone. Could things possibly get any worse? She scrubbed her face with her hands. "I bet he doesn't think of me as his precious little ember now," she grumbled under her breath. Leave it to her to find a way to debase herself in the eyes of a hot Highlander whose grumpiness somehow made him even more enticing.

"What was that, lass? I didn't catch it. Are ye ready for help back to the bed?"

"Not yet." She pulled in a deep breath and closed her eyes. *Pee, already!*

At long last, the dam broke, and the deluge echoed like thunder in the large ceramic pot under the wooden seat. She covered her face again. People in her century had probably heard her pee hitting that jug. A great deal lighter and no longer under *that* strain, she glanced all around. When she had stayed with Jessa for a few days in that version of the eighteenth century, old bits of parchment, or rags, or moss, and leaves had been used in place of toilet paper. Surely, they did the same here.

"Bottom drawer of the sideboard, the one closest to ye, has everything ye might need," Gryffe called out as if reading her mind or worse—spying on her.

She squinted at the wooden screen, trying to see through it. Thankfully, from her vantage point, it appeared quite solid and as *private* as its name. The drawer did indeed hold what she needed to finish the job. Since it was old parchment, she let it join the rest of her leavings in the chamber pot.

After latching hold of the sideboard, she pulled herself to her feet, or more accurately, her foot, still not brave enough to put any weight on her left leg. She needed to wash her hands and wouldn't mind splashing some water on her face too. Close enough to one of the tall white ceramic pitchers to peer inside it, she was pleased to find it filled with water. Hopping alongside the cabinet, she better positioned herself to pour some water into the basin and enjoy at least a minimal scrub.

"Ye have to be the stubbornest woman I have ever met," Gryffe said from entirely too close behind her. "Did I not tell ye I would help ye?"

"You said you would help me back into bed when I was ready. I just wanted to wash my face and hands."

"Without falling over?"

"I can stand on one leg without falling over." To prove her point, she scooped up a handful of water and splashed her face. When she opened her eyes, he stood ready with a fresh linen and a sour look.

"Why do ye fight me?" he asked after she took the cloth, patted her face dry, then dried her hands.

"You're a chieftain—not a nursemaid—and I am used to taking care of myself."

As soon as she tossed the cloth aside, he scooped her up, carried her back to bed, and then eased her down into it. Standing over her, he bared his teeth as if about to growl. "A chieftain is all things to those he cares about. Whatever mine need, I become that for them."

She reached up and touched his face, stroking the soft richness of his close cropped beard. She knew she shouldn't, but she couldn't help herself. "Thank you for helping me," she whispered, longing to say so much more but not brave enough to speak her heart. What if she was wrong? What if he wasn't her fated mate—just like he'd said about his mother casting a spell on her. "I know I've been a lot of trouble, and I'm sorry. I'm just...it's...it's complicated."

He groaned with a heavy sigh before pressing his forehead to hers for a brief yet wonderful moment. Then he jerked back and stepped away from the bed. "Sleep, my ember. Sleep and heal."

Unreasonable disappointment crashed through her. "Where are you going? Don't you need sleep too?"

With a hard shove, he pushed his chair back to its place in front of the hearth. "I need to watch the fire for a little while. Those embers dinna present as much danger to me as ye do."

She wanted to argue, demand he tell her how she could possibly be as dangerous to him as a live coal, but she already knew the answer. Because he was just as much a danger to her, even more so. In her case, it was already too late to escape this reality unscathed. When it came time to leave, she already knew she would have to tear herself away, and that was after knowing him for less than a day. How painful would it be after spending time with him for however long it took her to heal and make the trip to Seven Cairns? "You're not the only one hurting, you know." She cringed at her pettiness, but on a deeper level, she needed him to know this wasn't easy for her either. "And if I ever see your mother—"

Hunched over in the chair, he turned and looked at her, his eyes wild and feral, as filled with pain as a beast trying to gnaw itself free from a brutal steel trap. "Once...long ago...a vision came to me. The vision of my *one*. I swore to find her so we would both escape this loneliness."

A fierce, possessive jealousy crackled through Emily like wildfire, even though she had no right. If he belonged to another, then he would never be hers. Plain and simple. She would never share a man and refused to accept the lesser status of the *other* woman. The look in Gryffe's eyes made it clear he would never cease searching for his *one*.

She curled onto her side, facing him as she pulled the bedclothes up over her shoulders and clutched them close. "Why haven't you been able to find her?" She had to be reasonable about this. Maybe it would help her get past this unsettling attraction to him.

He turned back to the fire and stared hopelessly into the flames. "I dinna ken the sweetness of her voice nor her beauty. She came to me in shadow, and hidden in shadow, she has remained."

Hidden in shadow? "How do you know it wasn't some random dream?" Everyone had dreams filled with people they didn't know and couldn't quite remember when the dream was over. Didn't they?

He barely shook his head, squinting at the fire as though trying to peer deeper into the flames. "It was not a dream. It was a vision that hit me with the force of a storm and knocked me from the saddle. As I struggled to regain my footing, I...*felt*...her, as well as saw her, but she was veiled by a dark, swirling mist that refused to reveal her face or let her speak." He shook his head again. "She needed me to save her. I *felt* her begging me to help her." He sucked in a deep breath and let it out with a great sigh. "She is the other half of my soul, and I am hers."

"To feel a love like that and not be able to find her must be—"

"Maddening," he said, then leaned back in the chair and stretched his legs out in front of him, crossing them at the ankles. "Sleep, lass. 'Tis hours before dawn, and ye need the healing that only sleep brings. Elseways, ye'll never get to Seven Cairns and back where ye belong."

Back where she belonged. She wanted to remind him that he'd said she belonged with him, but she clenched her teeth to keep from speaking. No. She refused to beg for anyone's attention. She deserved better. Rolling carefully to keep from hurting her hip, she turned her back on him. Tomorrow—not days from now but *tomorrow*—she would head for Seven Cairns even if she had to crawl.

CHAPTER 6

"Nothing? No sign of her at all?" Mairwen searched each of their downcast faces, looking up and down the line of Weavers, all of them Masters of their particular divinity. Even the Dark Weavers, those in charge of curses, conflict, nightmares, emptiness, and hate, refused to look her in the eye.

"It is as though she never existed." Taskill, Master of the Curse Weavers' ragged, weary appearance gave testament to his efforts in the search for Emily. "I have never seen anything like this in all my eons." He splayed his hands across the glowing map of worlds and realities that floated at eye level in the center of the meeting hall, and slowly rotated it, occasionally enlarging regions as it turned. "We have never lost a mortal before. Never!"

Mairwen reached out and touched the map, lending her energy to it, but the glittering pinpoints that marked the many worlds and eras didn't react. As far as the map was concerned, the mortal known as Emily Mithers did not now, nor ever had existed.

"But the flagstones where last she stood still retain her warmth after all this time," Ishbel said. "Surely, that means something."

"Could the one whose name is not spoken on these hallowed grounds have taken her?" Graine, Master of the Hate Weavers, was a particular admirer of Morrigan, Mairwen's evil sister, but she admired the fearsome Phantom Queen from afar.

"No." Mairwen had sought her sister to discover just that and found Morrigan still in deep mourning for the son from her illicit affair with Mairwen's beloved husband. Carman's cruel sons had destroyed Valor at the same time that they had murdered Mairwen's son, Valan. "If my sister had taken Emily, she would have demanded a proper audience. She feeds on attention and fear."

Keeva stepped forward, holding what mortals perceived as one of their electronic tablets, but was actually the goddesses' Ledger of Infinity. "Do ye wish this meeting of the Council recorded or..."

Mairwen shook her head. "Not yet. I would like to avoid a conversation with the goddesses about losing a mortal—the next fated mate slated to strengthen the Highland Veil—until after we have exhausted every possibility."

Her assistant nodded, darkened the mystical tablet, then retreated to the shadows until needed.

"Is it time yet to notify the Defenders across the realms?" Dream Weaver, Glennis asked.

"No." Mairwen moved to the window and rested her hands on the cool smoothness of the pane. Not only was Emily gone, but the sun had left them as well, leaving them blanketed in the cold, gray dreariness of late November. "Continue the search for the remainder of this moon's cycle. If we have not found Emily by the dark of the moon, we will send out the call then." She pulled in a deep breath and released it with a heavy sigh that fogged the window. "So say Bride and Cerridwen."

"So say Bride and Cerridwen," echoed the Council of Weavers before slowly filing from the room to continue the search.

HUSHED CONVERSATIONS. Soft footsteps. The gentle thump of a carefully closed door. Water cascading down into something metal. Emily slowly opened her eyes and sighed. She was in the same position as last night, turned toward Gryffe's side of the bed—his empty side of the bed. She rolled to her back and stared up at the dark canopy embroidered with silver threads in the pattern of a star-filled sky.

"Good morning to ye, my lady," Inalfi said. "Yer bath is nearly ready. Just a few more kettles by my reckoning. The lads are off to fetch the last of them now."

"Thank you, but all I really need are my clothes from yesterday. Where are they?" Emily rose from the bed and gingerly tested putting weight on her left leg. Her hip grumbled with a bit of soreness, but was loads better. Good. She had a life to get back to. "Inalfi? My clothes from yesterday? And my boots?"

Defiance shouted from the maid as she stood there hugging a bundle of linens and kept her mouth clamped shut.

Emily wasn't in the mood for this. She'd had no tea yet this morning, and yesterday had proven to be a complete disaster that still had her emotions in an uproar. Struggling to maintain control and a reasonable tone, she ambled closer to prove she was fine. "Inalfi—I know you have to obey your chieftain, but I need my clothes, the ones I arrived in, and I need them now." She couldn't very well start across the Highlands in late November, barefoot and wearing nothing but a shift and whatever blankets she took from the bed. But if she had to, she would. For both her and Gryffe's sakes, she had to leave. Today.

The tight-jawed maid, almost comical in her attempt at being stern, stretched as tall as her petite form allowed. "Himself said ye are to have a good, long soak in a hot bath this morning while I smooth out yer bed. Then ye'll be donning a fresh shift and having yer breakfast tray before Grennove and Breenoa come to see how ye're faring."

"I am not *faring* well at all because you refuse to do as I ask."

The bedroom door swung open, and a pair of young men with their eyes downcast hurried inside, each of them bearing large, gleaming black kettles with steam rising from their spouts.

"Add two to the bath and hang the other two over the fire," Inalfi told them.

The lads did as she asked, then moved to stand in front of Emily, bowed their heads, and knelt.

"Lady Emily," Inalfi said, in a pompous, regal tone, "this be Alpip Whistlehide and Ianwin Lightbell. They are more than proud to be the first ones selected by Himself to be yer personal guard and serve ye howsoever ye shall need."

Her personal guard? Why did she need a personal guard? But not wanting to hurt the lads' feelings, she smiled and kept her questions to herself. "Thank you so much, Alpip and Ianwin. I appreciate your service." What else should she say? She had never had a personal guard before?

"We be loyal to the death," Alpip said, then nudged his partner. "Aye, Ianwin?"

"Aye." Ianwin stole a glance up at Emily, then quickly bowed his head even lower.

Bless his shy heart, came to mind. Emily hugged herself, suddenly very much aware that she stood before them in her nightgown with nothing underneath. "Thank you. Let's hope it doesn't come to death."

"Aye," both lads echoed.

"Off wi' ye now. Our lady needs her bath." Inalfi herded them out and closed the door behind them.

"I need my clothes," Emily said. She limped around the enormous copper tub in front of the hearth and turned her backside to the fire, rubbing it to warm it faster. Maybe if she convinced Inalfi that her leaving would be in Gryffe's best interest, that would work in her favor. She lowered her voice in case the Chieftain of Grumpiness had decided to hover in the hallway and eavesdrop. "Himself wants me gone. You know that—right? This glamour his mother cast upon me is causing him nothing but pain. You don't want him in pain, do you?"

Inalfi's eyes narrowed as she gathered more cloths and small chunky bundles wrapped in creamy white parchment. "I dinna believe that. Ye are not like the others Queen Nicnevin sent." She pointed at the steaming bath that was lined with linen and emitting a very pleasant floral fragrance. "In with ye now, lest the water cools too much to do ye any good. I think ye will find Mrs. Thistlebran's oils and soaps verra soothing." She lifted her chin to a stubborn angle as she approached. "Shall I help ye off with yer shift?"

"I will get in that bath if you promise to bring me my clothes." Emily stood her ground.

"I took them to the laundress. She'll not finish with them until later in the day. Maybe not even until tomorrow."

Temporarily defeated and more than a little frustrated, Emily yanked the linen chemise off over her head and stepped into the tub. She had never been self-conscious about nudity and had more important things to worry about than someone seeing her naked. The water bubbled around her as if she were a fizzy tablet for indigestion. It wasn't unpleasant—just unexpected. "Why is the water bubbling as if I'm dissolving?"

Inalfi beamed a self-satisfied smile. "Mrs. Thistlebran's salts pull away ill wishes, curses, and anything else that might harm ye. Sit ye down, my lady. All is well."

Ill wishes, curses, and anything else that might harm me? Settling down into the tub and leaning back against its sloped end, Emily watched the milky white water's effervescing surface gradually calm to a few lazy ripples. "So, I'm curse free now—right? Does that mean Nicnevin's glamour has been neutralized?"

"A glamour is nay a curse, my lady." Inalfi carefully pulled away the parchment wrapped around a thick cake of pale pink soap. She wet a cloth and rubbed it across the bar until a creamy lather frothed around her hands. "A glamour is merely an illusion. It canna harm the one upon which it is placed."

"Good to know." The longer Emily soaked in the comfortably hot water, the lazier and more pliable she felt, which was bad. She had to leave for Seven Cairns. Today. "Thank you for taking such good care of me. I am sorry about getting you yelled at yesterday."

"I should never have left ye." Inalfi gently lifted Emily's foot out of the water and washed it. "I knew better." She lowered that foot and washed the other, pausing to level a scolding glare that almost made Emily laugh. "But I never thought ye would try to leave with a fire spell."

"It wasn't a fire spell. It was a serenity spell. I have trouble focusing and tend to set things on fire whenever I try to use magic."

Inalfi paused in her massaging of Emily's calf. "Everything happens for a reason, my lady. The fire came to keep ye here where ye belong—spell or no spell. It snuffed yer magic."

"*It* did or you did? Gryffe said you could snuff magic, too." Emily leaned forward and bundled her long braids on top of her head so Inalfi could wash her back.

"Forgive me, my lady, I shouldha tied yer hair up out of the way. I didna ken if ye wished it washed or not."

Mesmerized by the deliciousness of having her back scrubbed, Emily closed her eyes and almost let her abundance of braids fall into the water. She caught them just in time. "No. It's clean. Just needs some moisture. What kind of oils does Mrs. Thistlebran have? Any that I could use on my hair and scalp?"

"Aye, I am certain she does." Inalfi moved to wash Emily's arms. "She sent up a fine selection of scents from which ye can choose. They're meant for yer skin and nails, but I dinna see why ye couldna use them for yer hair as well. They're all quite nice."

Even though she was now relaxed to the point of feeling bone-less, Emily didn't miss that Inalfi had failed to address her ability to *snuff* magic. "Explain snuffing magic. What do you do? Douse it like pinching out a candle?"

"More or less. 'Tis somewhat like breathing in the energy afore it can do what it's meant to do." She rinsed out the cloth and soaped it again. "Shall I wash the rest of ye now?"

While she might not be self-conscious about nudity, Emily was a far cry from being comfortable with being bathed like an infant or an invalid. She reached for the soap and cloth. "I'll wash the rest of me, thank you."

"As ye wish."

The mesmerizing effects of the bath somehow seemed to be fading, but she felt far more rejuvenated from this simple act of bathing than she ever had before. It encouraged her to shift to a *Plan B* for leaving for Seven Cairns. "I need traveling clothes, Inalfi. Since mine aren't ready, can you get me some while I finish washing?"

The maid went still, appearing troubled as she turned to look at her. "Traveling clothes?"

"I am leaving for Seven Cairns. Today. It's for the best." Emily hurried to wash, suddenly energized into action. An urgency pulsed through her. Something akin to a very physical premonition or instinct was nudging her to get a move on before it was too late.

Inalfi paused with a wooden chest of quietly rattling vials of oil in her arms. "But ye canna leave, my lady. Ye belong here."

"No, Inalfi. I do not." She lathered her armpits, hoping Mrs. Thistlebran's soap would battle any mustiness that would surely rear its smelly head since her body deodorant had remained in the twenty-first century. "I belong in my time and my reality. My landing here was an accident."

"Everything happens for a reason."

Emily rinsed and stepped out of the tub. "Are you going to help me or do I start across Scotland wearing a nightgown and a bedsheet?"

Inalfi wrapped her in a deliciously toasty length of soft linen and led her to a nearby chair. "I'll not go against Himself, my lady, and ye would do well to listen to him also."

"Exactly what I have told her many times," Gryffe said as he swaggered into the room.

Gooseflesh washed across Emily with a tingling shiver. "You don't believe in knocking?"

"This is my room. Why should I knock?"

"Because I was in here bathing, and a thoughtful host would be considerate of my privacy." She glared at him, fighting the almost impossible to ignore urge to throw herself into his arms. Holy crap, this must be how animals felt when they were in heat.

The maid curtsied, then hurried to fetch the chest of oils and hold it so the chieftain might inspect it. "What scent would ye choose for our lady, my chieftain?"

Before Gryffe could answer, Emily rose from the chair with the linen clutched around her. "*Our lady* is perfectly capable of choosing her own scents, thank you very much."

He gave her a sultry look and almost smiled—almost "The musk for our lady. 'Tis my favorite, and it suits her."

"I refuse to wear oils that come from the glands of a deer." Emily might not be a die-hard vegan, but she went cruelty-free whenever possible.

"Mrs. Thistlebran creates Himself's favorite oil from musk mallow, my lady. 'Tis a lovely plant with a pale lilac flower. The petals remind ye of the palm of yer hand and form a delicate cup when they bloom. Would ye care to have a wee sniff of it?" Inalfi unstoppered one of the vials and held it out. "This batch is from last summer's flowers. The blooms only come between June and August."

Rather than place the poor maid in an untenable situation, Emily waved her forward. "Fine. The musk is fine as long as it doesn't come from a deer or any other animal." She locked eyes with Gryffe. "I can't very well finish dressing with you in the room."

"Of course ye can." He went to the window and stared outside. "I promise not to look."

"Himself never lies," Inalfi hurried to say.

Emily glared at his back, focusing on a spot right between his shoulder blades and willing him to feel her gut-churning mix of frustration and yearning. She wanted to leave the infernal man just as badly as she wanted to stay with him and make him want her as badly as she wanted him. "Tell Inalfi it's all right to either fetch me the clothes I arrived in or others that would be just as good for traveling. I intend to leave for Seven Cairns today."

He slowly turned and scowled at her.

"You promised not to look." She pointed a damning finger at him.

His glower darkened. "Ye canna leave—not when ye canna ride nor walk."

She tightened her hold on the linen around her and limped toward him. "I am a fast healer. Always have been. The pain's nothing like it was. I'm sure I can ride, if you'll loan me a horse."

"And if I will not?"

"Then I'll walk." She moved closer, noting that for every limping step she took, he took one toward her, as if daring her to continue. "I have to leave." She flinched when her voice broke. *Stay strong. Return to what you know.* "I have to leave," she repeated. "You know that as well as I do."

"By horse, this time of year, it could take a sennight or more, and the weather is about to turn."

"I have no choice." She resettled her footing, wishing the linens would soak up the water trickling down her back and pooling with uncomfortable wetness in her crack. But her spine ran deep, and her curves held the cloth away from the slope of her backbone rather than against it. It was hard to stand firm and win an argument when you were cloying wet and wearing nothing but a freaking sheet. She wiggled and reached around to try and dry herself.

"Help yer mistress," Gryffe told Inalfi. "Ye are to see to her comfort at all times, ye ken?"

"Aye, my chieftain."

"Stop yelling at her every time I do something stupid." Emily scolded herself for not concentrating on the argument and ignoring her ever increasing case of swamp ass. After all, she was clean. It wasn't like it was stinky sweat.

"I nay yelled at her."

"Well, you sounded growly and authoritarian."

"I am the authority here." He glared at her, his dark scowl both irritating and enticing. If he was this handsome when he was grumpy, how handsome would he be when he was happy?

"I need traveling clothes," she repeated, returning to the core issue.

Suddenly his glower seemed more sorrowful and sad than angry. He jerked a nod at Inalfi. "Ensure she is dressed in clothing that will protect her from the bitter cold. The sky is heavy with snow."

The maid bowed her head. "Aye, my chieftain."

Then he tucked a finger under Emily's chin and lifted her face to his. She held her breath, both hoping and fearing he was about to kiss her again. "Once ye have dressed and had yer tea, I will transport ye to Seven Cairns the same way I brought ye here. No matter what ye claim, ye are nay hale enough to survive a seven day ride in the weather that's coming. Will that do ye?"

She ached to throw herself against him, hold him tight, and say, *No, I need to stay and make you want me*—but she couldn't, because she didn't understand how she could possibly feel that way. It had to be a trap, a recipe for disaster. "Yes," she forced herself to say. "That will do me."

With a curt nod, he let his hand drop away. "Have Inalfi fetch me once ye have dressed and finished yer breakfast."

Then he stormed out of the room as if unable to leave her fast enough.

Clutching the linens, she pressed her fist tighter against her breastbone. She hurt for him. So badly. Even more than she had hurt for a man she'd once thought she loved, before he had left her when she told him she was pregnant.

～

A SHARP KNOCK hit the door of Gryffe's private solar. He didn't turn from staring out the window behind his desk. It was more than likely just Inalfi, come to tell him that Emily was ready to leave him. He bowed his head, fighting against the lonely, dangerous burn threatening to consume him. "Damn ye, Nicnevin," he said under his breath. "Damn ye straight to hell and back."

The knock came again, thumping louder this time, insisting he acknowledge it.

"Come!" he bellowed.

The door's hinges creaked, then it closed with a quiet thud.

"She is ready, I suppose," he said, keeping his gaze locked on the blanket of gray clouds hanging low with the heavy threat of snow.

"Who is ready?" asked Ferris, second to Gryffe in command of the Highland Defenders and first commander of Clan MacStrath's guard.

Gryffe turned. "I thought ye were Inalfi."

Ferris rumbled with a low laugh that sounded more like the throaty warning growl of a wolf. "Since when do I resemble one of the Fae, especially that tiny maid?"

"She is due to fetch me." Gryffe tipped a nod at the cabinet in the corner. "Help yerself, but mind the smaller bottle in the back—the one with the ruby stopper. Mrs. Thistlebran keeps the spirit cabinet stocked with wolfsbane for unwelcome guests."

Ferris glanced at the cabinet, then shook his head. "I'll stick to me flask, thank ye verra much, in case I've happened to fall on the wrong side of yerself *or* Mrs. Thistlebran."

Gryffe turned back to stare out the window. "Ye've nay fallen on the wrong side of me, old friend," he told the burly guard who could set his shoulder against any mountain and move it, if he so wished. "Ye are one of the few I trust."

"Then tell me what has ye so vexed." Ferris moved to stand alongside him. "I have heard the rumblings, but I prefer the truth from yerself."

"Nicnevin sent another."

"That is not what I heard."

Gryffe hazarded a side-eyed glare at his friend. "Out with it, then. What word has spread through the keep?"

"That this lady is yer elusive *one*. Sent to ye by the goddesses themselves—for the good of the Veil and the good of yer future generations."

Gryffe squared his shoulders and sucked in a deep breath as if doing so would protect him from the claim. "I would know if she was the woman from my vision. Lady Emily is not."

"How the devil would ye know? Ye said yer vision was wrought with darkness and shadow."

"I would know, damn ye."

Ferris shrugged. "Makes me no nevermind, but if this is one of Nicnevin's pets, send her away just as ye did the others. In fact, why have ye not already done so? Ye never hesitated to do so before."

"She was injured." Gryffe resettled his footing like a hen scratching for bugs. "I know well enough that I am considered a hard-hearted bastard, but I'll not send anyone anywhere when they are injured."

"Then why are ye taking her to Seven Cairns today?"

"And how the bloody hell did ye know that?"

"The wolf in me hears everything in this keep. Ye know that well enough." Ferris snorted. "There be many a time when this hearing of mine be more a curse than a blessing. Why do ye think I sleep in the woods on the other side of the loch?"

Gryffe scrubbed his face with both hands. "She is part Weaver and means to return to her proper place through the portal at Seven Cairns." A heavy sigh groaned free of him. "I canna stop her. She is determined to go."

"From the way ye're behaving, seems to me yer lady is not one of Nicnevin's traps."

"She has to be." Gryffe swallowed hard, willing himself to believe that. "'Tis but a stronger glamour this time. Ye know how determined Nicnevin is for a MacStrath grandchild. She loved my father more than any other—or at least, came as close to loving him as is possible for her black heart."

"Why are ye so afraid for this Lady Emily of yers to be the *one*?"

"Because her place in time and reality pulls at her to return. I see the longing in her eyes. I canna compete with what she would be forced to leave behind if she chose me."

"Ye said she was a Weaver. She can visit her time whenever she chooses." Ferris snorted again. "Yer argument makes no sense."

"Her blood is not pure. She might be descended from a Spell Weaver, but her bloodline has diluted so much that whenever she attempts a spell, she sets things on fire."

Ferris tapped on the window pane. "Mighty handy, considering ye need more fires in the winter."

Gryffe glared at his old friend, not in the mood for Ferris's levity. "Did ye seek me out to nettle me or has aught gone amiss that I should know about?"

"I came to warn ye."

Gryffe locked eyes with the man. Their icy blue depths shone with the wisdom and cunning of the man's inner beast—the wolf that sensed before all others whenever Nicnevin was near. "How close?"

"She is in Edinburgh with Roric. With any luck, that sniveling fool will keep her occupied for a while." He slowly shook his silvery head. "But ye know she'll not return to her kingdom without a wee bit of tormenting of yerself." He rolled his shoulders as if trying to shrug free the unpleasantness of his message. "I have come to believe that is how she shows her love for ye."

"Warn the guards and make every Fae in this keep know I will show them no quarter if they give me cause to question their loyalties to me and mine rather than Nicnevin."

"Shall I summon my sons?"

"Aye." Gryffe clapped a hand on his friend's shoulder. "Summon the entire pack. I would be grateful."

"It shall be done." Ferris tipped a single nod and turned to go.

When he reached the door, he paused with his hand on the latch. "Show her ye're worth choosing. Everything happens for a reason, ye ken? She may verra well be the lady of yer vision, and ye just dinna ken it. Give it time."

Gryffe tossed a curt nod in the direction of the door, dismissing Ferris. His friend needed to understand that the matter was not up for further discussion.

As Ferris left, Inalfi entered with her eyes lowered. As one of the Fae and possessing hearing as keen as Ferris's, the maid had likely overheard Gryffe's mandate on loyalty. She offered him a low curtsy as if he were the Unseelie King himself. "Our lady is ready, my chieftain."

"Ye have dressed her warmly?"

"Aye." She lifted her head and gave him a sorrowful look. "Must we let her leave?"

"I canna keep her prisoner, Inalfi—and what good is a love that is not freely given?"

"She is yer *one*, my chieftain," the maid said, her voice pitiful with desperation. "I canna sense a glamour upon her at all. I swear it."

"Nicnevin is sly. Ye know that well enough. How many eras did ye serve in her Court?" He shrugged on his heavier coat over his kilt that he wore over the leather trews he'd donned for the wintry weather. He was not a weak man unused to the bitter cold, but he had endured enough of it during the wars. Why should he suffer more than he already had? He started to belt his weapons across his chest, then thought better of it. The Weavers of Seven Cairns frowned upon any excessive show of force. Instead, he settled for daggers in his boots, his sword at his side, and his pistol tucked through his belt and resting against his hip.

"Our lady is kind, my chieftain," Inalfi said as she scurried along beside him down the hall. With a soft laugh that tinkled like crystal droplets, she added, "She apologized for getting me into trouble."

"Aye, she has a heart, but it is softest for those she left behind."

He lengthened his stride, determined to get this abhorrent task over with and return to the loneliness that was his constant companion.

"It would seem so, my chieftain." The spry maid flew ahead of him and made it to the door before he did. The pity in her eyes shamed him as she opened the door and stepped back for him to enter.

He hardened his heart to the embarrassment, strode into the room, and went mute.

In a burgundy dress of velvet cinched at the waist with a wide leather belt wrapped around her narrow waist twice, Emily stole his ability to reason. Her skirts flared wide as she turned, revealing the knee high, fur-lined boots that would shield her feet from the cold. The rich hand of the supple cloth of her garment caught the light, accentuating her curves. Dark wrist cuffs, wide and embroidered with protective symbols that matched those on the gown's leather breastplate and high collar, complemented her long, slender arms.

"What's wrong?" she asked, lifting her arms and looking down at her skirts. "This should be plenty warm, don't you think? And Inalfi found a heavy cloak to go with it."

"Aye, it will do." How could he tell her of her breathtaking loveliness? How could he tell her that the closer they came to parting, the more his soul crumbled? Nicnevin had truly outdone herself with this particular spell. Its strength was unfathomable. "Inalfi—fetch our lady's cloak so she and I can be on our way."

The maid brought the cloak to Gryffe, then turned and gave Emily a sorrowful bow. "It has been an honor serving ye, my lady. I wish ye the greatest happiness and peace wherever yer travels take ye."

Emily rushed forward and hugged the girl as if she were family. "Thank you, Inalfi. I am so lucky to have met you."

With an awkward nod and wiping her eyes, Inalfi pulled away, then hurried out of the room.

Gryffe braced himself and shook out the cloak, holding it ready. "M'lady."

After she backed into it, he wrapped it around her, breathing her in and immediately wishing he hadn't. Never again would he take in the fragrance of his favorite musk and not think of her. "Button it at yer throat and wrap up tightly," he said, his voice raw and gruff with emotions he would rather not acknowledge. "It's turned a great deal colder than it was when ye arrived."

"I wonder if it'll be just as cold back home?"

Home. She had called wherever she was headed *home.* How could he compete with that? The simple word meant so much more than a house or some sort of abode. It meant a place you were rooted to, a place of safety. It meant a part of your being you had left behind and knew would be there whenever you returned.

"It will probably be cold there too," he said to cover his pain. "Face me, now, and hold fast. I dinna wish to lose ye in the folding."

"In the folding?" She arched a brow, looking entirely too pleased and calm for his liking. Did she have no feelings for him at all? Was she so anxious to be gone from him?

"I fold the distance betwixt here and Seven Cairns. Were I to drop ye, ye would land somewhere in between, and it could take me a while to find ye." Not really. He would find her in the blink of an eye, so attuned he had become to her scent, the sound of her breathing, the very rhythm of her heartbeat. But he couldn't tell her that. He was already so pathetic that his servants pitied him. "Ye dinna wish to be lost in the Highlands, do ye?"

She gave him a strange look. It was almost wistful and threatened to lift his heart. But he shook it off. He was allowing emotion to blind him to the truth and that could not be. He wrapped his arms around her and sadly whispered, "*Septem Cairnēs.*"

As soon as the bitter cold wind stung him with snow, he stepped back, loathing the act of releasing her from his brace. That would probably be the last time he ever held her. "We are here, my precious ember," he said, almost choking on the words. "Open yer eyes."

Her reaction surprised him. Rather than the excitement he

expected, she edged closer, as if afraid. "It looks...different...somehow." She tucked in against his side.

He instinctively wrapped an arm around her and curled her back into a protective embrace, shielding her from the wind. "This is Seven Cairns, Emily. The only Seven Cairns in Scotland." But inwardly, he agreed. It seemed strangely unlike it had been when last he was there.

Clutching the throat of her cloak and ducking deeper into its hood, she squinted against the flying snow. "There's Boyd's. The book shop. Treat Shop. The meeting hall." She perked like a cat that just spotted a mouse. "There's Ishbel!" She tore from his embrace, waving at the woman wrapped in a bulky, dark purple cloak. "Ishbel! Ishbel! My spell went wonky again. Imagine that!"

Ishbel jerked as though startled, then retreated a few steps, almost stumbling in the snow. "Have ye lost yer way, lass? Has the cold made ye unwell?"

Something was amiss. Gryffe could feel it. He knew Ishbel as well. Had met her several times when meeting with the Council of Weavers. She was never so aloof. The Spell Weaver would mother all of creation if given the opportunity. He hurried over to Emily, ready to protect her.

"Ishbel!" Emily pushed back her hood. "It's me. Weren't you wondering what my spell had done this time?" But her smile faded as Ishbel edged away even more, all the while shaking her head.

"Forgive me, lass, but how do ye come to know my name?" Leeriness echoed in the Weaver's tone. "I dinna recall us ever meeting."

"Never meeting?" Emily hitched forward, still moving with a slight limp. "You've been trying to teach me spell casting for nearly a year now. You took me under your wing like an extremely patient mother hen. Ishbel—why are you acting like this? If this is some kind of joke, it's not funny."

The Weaver glanced around, almost seeming afraid. "I am sure ye're mistaken, lass. I dinna ken a thing about...what did ye call it? Spell casting? I am nay a witch. Just a simple weaver." She made a shooing motion while backing away faster. "Off wi' ye now. I'm sure ye've mistaken me for someone else." She gave Gryffe a polite nod, then tapped her temple. "Chieftain MacStrath. Help this poor, confused child, aye? She is a bit *off*, I'd say." Then she turned and fled, disappearing into the largest building on the square and slamming the door shut behind her.

Emily stared after her as if frozen in place by the weather. "Ishbel," she whispered, blinking at the snowflakes catching on her long, dark lashes. "Ishbel—it's me."

Gryffe went to her, uncertain what to do. There was something badly amiss here. He had never felt it before when visiting Seven Cairns as Grand Chieftain of the Defenders. The place felt muffled, oddly coated in something he couldn't quite explain. It couldn't be Nicnevin's doing. Seven Cairns was hallowed ground, forbidden to any magic except for that of the Weavers. In fact, the Unseelie, the Dark Fae, were forbidden to even set foot there. They only welcomed him because of his mortal half and his oath to the Defenders.

Emily turned to him, pleading in her soulful eyes. "How could she not know me? She has been my mentor for the past year. We were…friends."

He slowly shook his head, wishing he knew something hopeful to tell her. "I dinna ken what's amiss here, lass. Could it be she is merely unwell? Could illness cloud her vision?" Ishbel had known him but been especially leery about revealing her identity as a Spell Weaver to Emily. He had seen Weavers behave like that in front of mortals before, but only when trying to preserve the secret of the Highland Veil, Seven Cairns, and the Weavers.

"How?" Emily caught hold of his coat and pitifully tried to shake him. "How could illness make you not know somebody?"

"Come. Into the pub for a bit of warmth." He doubted that a bit of warmth would help, but it couldn't hurt.

With a determined expression, heavily shadowed with fear, she gave him a curt nod. "Yes. Lilias will know me. I've gone to The Fearless Scottie every day since arriving in Scotland—sometimes twice a day for morning tea and supper."

Gryffe tucked her hand through his arm and led her across the square into the warm, cozy pub. He selected a table close to the cheery fire crackling in the hearth. As he helped her into a chair, he noticed her stealing quick looks all around. "What is it, lass? Tell me so I might help ye."

She wet her lips and swallowed hard, her eyes shining with unshed tears. "Even in Jessa's time..."—she twitched an impatient shrug—"the *other* eighteenth century I've been to, Seven Cairns still *felt* familiar. This one doesn't. And Ishbel didn't have a clue who I was. She thought I was crazy. I could see it in her eyes." She straightened, stretching taller and frowning at the bar. "There's Lilias." She forced a smile and waved. "Lilias! Hi!"

The young woman behind the bar smiled back, but it was clearly a smile meant for a customer she had never met. She came over to the table, wiping her hands on the long towel tied to her belt. "Can I be helping ye then, mistress? What'll ye be having? A nice hearty ale to fill yer wame for the long trip home?" She nodded at Gryffe. "And how are ye this blustery day, Grand Chieftain? Looking for a bit of whisky to chase away the bitterness of the cold?"

No amount of whisky could chase away the chill settling deep in his bones. Ignoring Lilias, he watched Emily closely. She had not lied about knowing everyone at Seven Cairns. She knew their names, and her ever increasing panic made it clear she had been close to all of them in her time.

"I need...I need the portal," she told Lilias. "Right away. I have to get back to my time. And Mairwen. I'm sure Mairwen has to be wondering what happened to me."

Lilias backed up a step. Her smiling expression hardened with the strain of keeping it in place. "I have a verra nice port, mistress. I'll fetch ye a glass right away."

"No. Not *port*. Portal. Behind the bar. In your storeroom. I need you to allow me back there. You know it won't work for me without your permission since you're the Watcher for it." Emily rose, pushing back her chair as she stepped away from the table. "Please, Lilias. You may not recognize me, and I can't explain why, but I need you to trust me. Please."

"Ye should go," Lilias told Gryffe. "Take her, Grand Chieftain. Now. Ye ken this is hallowed ground, and her kind is not welcome here."

CHAPTER 7

Her kind? "It's me, Lilias! How can you not know me?" Heart pounding so hard it made her dizzy, Emily kept patting her chest in rapid fire panic as if doing so would coax her soul into chiming in to help Lilias remember. "It's Emily. Special breakfast blend tea with honey, Emily. You've known me for over a year now. Jessa and I rented the cottage on the hill, and once she married Grant, I moved in with Ishbel. Remember?"

Lilias stared at her as if she had never met such a stark raving lunatic in her life, then turned to Gryffe. "Hallowed ground, Grand Chieftain. I am sorry for yer lady's distress, but it would be best if ye took her away." She leaned closer. "She is making me other customers nervous, ye ken? Ye know her kind are not supposed to be in Seven Cairns."

"My kind?" It came out as a shriek, but Emily didn't care. "And what kind is that? You welcomed me with open arms just a couple of days ago. Even told me I was the sister you had never had and always wanted."

Lilias's jaw dropped, and she turned to Gryffe once more, seemingly determined not to speak directly to Emily. "I mean no insult,

Grand Chieftain. I ken well enough yer ancestry, but ye have mortal blood as well and yer oath that makes ye accepted. It's plain to see she is full blooded Unseelie, and ye know that is not allowed. If Mairwen catches me opening the pub to the likes of her, there will be full on hell to pay."

Numbed by this second rejection from someone she considered a close friend, head spinning at the enormity of this unbelievable disaster, Emily sagged back into the chair, hugging herself to keep from shattering into a thousand sobbing pieces.

"Lass—" Gryffe took hold of her shoulders. "Come. Let us return home."

In the depths of her confusion, his deep voice barely made it through, and she had to think really hard on what he had said for the words to even make sense. "Home," she whispered, hugging herself tighter while staring down at the table.

"Aye, my ember. Let me take ye home."

She barely shook her head, and a single tear burned its way down her cheek. "I can't get home. I'm trapped." She closed her eyes and rocked in place, fighting to console herself. A keening wail eked free of her, slicing the air like the clash of forged steel. She would never see her family again. Her mother. Father. Five irritating but totally lovable brothers. And now she had lost the village of friends she'd come to love just as much as family. Uncontrollable sobbing violently shook her.

A strong grip swept her up against a hard, muscular chest, and she vaguely heard *Domus*. Then she was back among the pillows where she had awakened that morning and made such grand plans to return to Seven Cairns to get her life back on track.

From the depths of her misery, she became aware of murmurings, soft conversations swirling all around, but she ignored them. What difference did it make what anyone said? She was lost— forever lost in a place where she didn't belong. No friends. No family. And confusing feelings for a man who had made it quite clear he was waiting for someone else.

"Fetch her some tea and bring Grennove when ye return," Gryffe told someone. He was probably talking to Inalfi, but again, what did it matter?

Emily closed her eyes tighter. Maybe, she should've rushed Lilias's portal and risked the wrath of the powers, the goddesses, or the Highland Veil. She couldn't remember what Mairwen had told her about who or what brought down nine kinds of hell upon those who stormed the portals without permission from a Weaver or the keeper of the portal's key. At least, if she had charged through it and the magic had fried her, she would no longer be in her current situation. At the moment, death didn't seem all that bad of an option.

A warm, callused hand touched her face, making her closed eyes well with more tears that quickly escaped. She opened them to Gryffe. He stared down at her. Unsmiling, but non-accusing. Sorrowful, but not pitying. He merely kept his gaze locked with hers, allowing her to sink into his obsidian eyes as if coaxing her down a dark path that would lead her to the center of his soul. He didn't speak—just tenderly stroked her cheek with the heel of his thumb.

"What do I do now?" she dared to whisper.

"Ye stay here. With me."

"But you don't want me here."

"Ye've no idea of what I want, my ember."

She didn't have an answer for that and was too confused and distraught to try to find one. Besides, what did it matter? What power did she have over anything anymore? She closed her eyes again and turned away, curling into a tight little ball in the middle of the bed, unable to stand what she had become—a helpless wretch wallowing in self-pity. She had only been like this once before. After the miscarriage. She had paid a painfully high price that time for the right to sink into a pit of despair.

But this? She had done this to herself. Stormed Scotland to help her dear friend improve her circumstances, and rather than return to Jersey once Jessa was settled, she had decided to stay on in Seven Cairns and explore her heritage. What an idiot. Once again, she had made the wrong life choice, and now here she was feeling sorry for herself because that choice had backfired. She had never been able to stand whining and wallowing from anyone, and now just look at her. Here she was, refusing to own the fate she had chosen, rise from the ashes, and start all over again. Served her right for being such a sanctimonious, judgy, know-it-all, bossy ass with everyone she had forced her advice on in the past. She'd finally gotten a taste of her own medicine, and damn, it tasted bitter as hell.

"Emily," Gryffe said, his voice gentle but deep and rasping, like the unexpected purr of a tiger. The weight of his hand on her shoulder somehow said so much more than words. His touch told her he was there for her. That she wasn't in this alone.

She closed her eyes and clenched her teeth. *Stop it, you idiot. You just went from the frying pan to the fire. Stop making his politeness more than it is.*

"Emily?"

She pinched the bridge of her nose and willed herself to stop sniveling. "What?"

"Life here with me will nay be so bad."

Fumbling for the square of linen tucked up into her sleeve, she sniffed. "Could we just not talk about this right now? I have a lot to process and need to do it in my own way." If this had been a fairy tale, she would have thrown herself into his arms and let him console her until his heart melted, and he decided it was worth the risk to love her, even if his mother had cast some sort of spell or curse or whatever on them. But this was no damn fairy tale. Fairy tales weren't real.

She had to figure out what to do, how to survive. Somehow, she doubted this version of the eighteenth century needed a social media influencer. She hugged her knees to her chin and tucked her forehead against them. An insistent yearning nudged her, but she flinched away from it. No. Gryffe wanted his *one*, and she wasn't it. The last thing she needed to do was fan the flames of what she felt for him, only to be dumped farther down the road. Been there. Done that. Wasn't about to do it again.

"I have her tea, my chieftain," Inalfi said, but Emily ignored her and remained tightly curled.

"Let me have a look at ye, lass," Grennove said from the other side of the large bed.

Emily gave in to her inner child and pulled a pillow over her head. "Leave me alone. All of you."

"Leave us," Gryffe said, his growling tone sending a shiver along her spine. "Now."

The sound of hurried scuffling filled the room, then ended with a soft thump of the door.

"There is no one here but yerself and I now, lass," Gryffe said. "And I mean to stay and help ye wrestle yer demons until they choose to leave ye in peace."

She pulled the pillow off her head and hugged it to her chest, keeping her back to him. It was better that she not face him. She couldn't think straight whenever she looked into his eyes. "Is there another room I can have?"

"Why?"

She rolled her eyes, knowing he couldn't see since he was sitting behind her on the bed. "This is your room."

"'Tis a big fine room. We can share it."

"So, you can boot me out whenever you find your one? No, thank you."

He caught hold of her arm and rolled her to face him. Eyes flashing with some kind of unholy black fire, he glared at her. "I would never do that to ye."

"You say that now because she's not here." A strange numbness settled within her, right where her heart used to be, and she welcomed it. "I have been thrown away before and didn't much like it. I may make a lot of stupid choices in my life, but setting myself up to be tossed out again is not one of them."

Face flaring red with rage, he bared his teeth and actually

growled, becoming more of a great, dark beast than a man. "Who threw ye away? Who dared treat ye with such disrespect?"

Touched by his protective, righteous indignation, she couldn't even fathom why she had brought it up. She never talked about that time in her life. It was better left to the shadows. Even her family knew the topic was off limits. Why had she spewed out her past like it tasted bad? "It doesn't matter. It was a long time ago."

He pulled her closer and took her hand. "It matters because it hurt ye, and ye still carry that pain. Tell me. Give me the weight of yer misery so it will vex ye no more. My back is strong, my shoulders broad. I can bear yer burdens with ease."

As much as she didn't want to, as much as she knew better, she weakly allowed herself to sink into his gaze. "I swore I would never say his name again. Not after he left me when I told him I was pregnant. I mean to keep that promise to myself."

Gryffe's furious glower hardened even more, if that was possible. His eyes slowly narrowed. "Getting back to yer child—that is what pulls at ye, drives ye to return to yer time?"

She slowly shook her head, allowing the sadness she had carried for the past four years to surface and bloom. She and the sadness had an agreement—it went with her, stayed with her every day, and she embraced it as a painful yet precious memory she would never forget. "No," she whispered. "I can never get back to her, because she is not there." She swallowed hard and managed a shrug. "The doctor called it a miscarriage, but the nurses said stillbirth. And I got to hold her before they took her away. Either way, my daughter didn't live for longer than a few precious hours."

Gryffe bowed his head. "I am so verra sorry."

"So am I. For the rest of my life."

Before she realized what he was doing, he pulled her into his arms and held her. After a tender kiss to her forehead, he whispered, "What is yer dear child's name, my ember?"

No one had ever asked her that before. Her parents and Jessa knew because they had gone with her to order the small, heart-shaped headstone for the grave. "Her name is Cara. It means *dearest.*" It felt so strange to say it aloud.

"An eternal candle shall be lit for her in the MacStrath tombs. I will show ye the place, so ye can visit with her whenever ye like."

The knot of unhappiness and irrational sense of failure she had carried tucked in her heart since losing her child loosened the slightest bit, a shocking first for her. Her entire being warmed, and she breathed easier. The old familiar sadness was still there, but somehow, it was more bearable, maybe even a little bit at peace, as if somehow settled and content. She didn't know why, and she didn't care. For once in her life, she just accepted the relief for what it was.

"Thank you," she whispered, knowing that no matter what happened, no matter if he kicked her out of the keep tomorrow, she would always love Gryffe MacStrath with all her heart. She swallowed hard at the realization, then almost laughed. She had known it for a while now, but this last act of kindness had obliterated her every denial and made her admit it. "You are a good man, Gryffe MacStrath, and I'm so glad you were the one my botched spell chose."

He shifted against her with a heavy sigh. "I am glad yer botched spell dropped ye in Avric's path, as well." Ever so gently, he set her away from him, studying her while slowly shaking his head.

"What?"

"I could always sense Nicnevin's glamours on all the others. Smelled her magic, even. Everyone's mystical energy has a distinct aroma that canna be hidden or disguised. But I canna find it on ye. No trace at all. Nothing but the rich, sweet warmth of yer own essence." The corner of his mouth almost twitched upward, the nearest she had ever seen him come to a smile. "Ye possess the mouthwatering fragrance of Cook's best caramel or warmed honey right as ye mix it with fresh butter, but ye dinna smell of Nicnevin's magic."

"That is because I have yet to have the pleasure of meeting this lovely creature you currently have in your bed."

"Shit!" Emily scrambled backward until she hit the headboard and couldn't retreat any farther to escape the towering column of inky black mist rising up and swirling at the foot of the bed. "It's Morrigan! She's found me! Run, Gryffe! Save yourself."

"Morrigan? I should say not. I am the incomparable Nicnevin, Queen of the Dark Fae, goddess of magic and witches, and beloved mother to this darling boy who always manages to surprise me even though I am all knowing." The roiling mist solidified into a tall, shapely woman dressed in a gown of the blackest silk or some sort of diaphanous veil-like material that clung to her curves. Her flowing black hair was loose and trailed down well past her waist, but was kept at bay by a gleaming silver diadem that rested on her brow and circled her head in a crown of silvery branches. She held her hands aloft and smiled at Gryffe. "I thought this form would be the least frightening for yer lady. Are ye not going to introduce us?"

"Ye said ye were all knowing."

Emily hugged her knees to her chest and tried to stop shaking. This being might not be Morrigan, but she was just as unsettling. "I'm Emily Mithers. From the twenty-first century and a reality that's a great deal more normal than this one."

Nicnevin laughed. "Normal? Normal is a perception, child. Dependent upon the viewer." She swept closer, seeming to float across the floor. "Ye are a Weaver. A Spell Weaver. I smell it in yer blood." She gave a graceful nod. "I am one of yer protective goddesses."

Gryffe stood and blocked his mother's path. "No closer. Remove the glamour, Nicnevin, and leave her be. Ye have caused her enough harm with yer meddling."

The dark goddess glared at him, barely puckering her flawless brow with a faint frown. "I do wish ye would call me *Mother*. Roric does, and it brings me such joy."

"Roric is yer heir. I am naught but yer bastard son. Remember?"

She rolled her eyes, then shifted around him and offered Emily a sympathetic smile.

Emily swallowed hard. While Gryffe and his mother argued, at least they ignored her. She scooted sideways along the headboard, putting more space between herself and Nicnevin.

The Unseelie Queen tipped her head to one side while moving closer. Her dark eyes narrowed, and her smile slowly faded. "I will not harm ye, child, at least not unless ye harm my son. Then I will make ye wish ye never existed."

Gryffe shoved in between them again. "Leave her be."

Nicnevin gave him the look of a mother perturbed with her son. "I just said I would not harm her unless she harmed ye. Calm down, boy. I have never seen ye in such a state." She tucked a finger under his chin and pushed it higher with her astonishingly long black fingernail. As she studied him, her face took on an eerie, pleased with herself glow. "Is she yer one? Have ye found her at long last?"

He bared his teeth and jerked away to escape his mother's touch. "Remove the feckin' glamour, and we shall see."

Emily braced herself. Nicnevin seemed as powerful and narcissistic as Morrigan. If she decided to strip something away, how bad would *that* hurt?

Gryffe's mother gave a long-suffering sigh. "None of my magic rests on this one, my lad." She flattened her hand on his chest, right over his heart. "What ye feel is yer soul crying to unite with its other half. I swear to ye on yer beloved father's grave that I placed no glamour on this child, nor did I bring her to ye. That is the doing of someone else. Either a Weaver, one of the mother goddesses, or the Highland Veil." She turned and eyed Emily. "Lovely creature. I believe they chose well for ye. When do ye intend to make the union official and set to the task of blessing me with a keep full of grandchildren?"

Somewhat relieved that Gryffe's mother seemed appeased and had decided that nothing needed *stripping* away, Emily still wasn't about to let down her guard. "If you didn't put a spell on me, did you put some sort of magical amnesia shield on Seven Cairns?" That even sounded ridiculous to her, but in this reality, who knew? What else

90

would explain Lilias and Ishbel acting as if they'd never seen her before?

Nicnevin's dark brows rose higher, and her lips, plump and painted the same shade as freshly drawn blood, curled with a chilling smile. "Magical amnesia shield?" She laughed, and the somehow icy sound of her mirth made Emily shiver and gather the blankets closer. "What in Hades' name is a *magical amnesia shield*?" Before Emily could explain what she meant, Nicnevin turned to Gryffe and gave him a playful shove. "She surprises me as much as yerself, my precious boy. Well done on finding this one."

"I did not find her," Gryffe said through gritted teeth, "and ye swear on the love ye once felt for my father that ye placed no spell work upon her?"

Nicnevin's mirth faded, but her chilling smile remained, revealing the very tips of her fangs. With the dramatic crossing of her long, thin hands over her heart, she offered him a grave nod. "I swear upon my eternal love for yer father that I placed no magic upon this lady." Then she turned to Emily. "And neither did I meddle with Seven Cairns. That village is hallowed ground, child. I am forbidden from it by the mighty Danu herself." She moved closer, easily nudging Gryffe aside. "Ye do wish to be here, aye? Ye are drawn to my son as he is drawn to ye?"

Emily licked her lips, then caught the bottom one between her teeth and chewed on it. This was the moment of truth. Was she brave enough to risk getting hurt again? And it would be worse this time, since she was completely and totally on her own. She bit her lip harder until she tasted blood. This was a choice, and if she got it wrong again...She swallowed hard and cleared her throat. "I landed here accidentally when I messed up a serenity spell." She twitched a shrug, struggling to scrape up every ounce of courage she possessed. "An ancestor of mine was a Spell Weaver. I am trying to learn, but I'm not very good at it yet. I usually just catch things on fire."

Nicnevin tipped her head and folded her slender arms as if settling in for a long story. Emily was afraid to look at Gryffe.

"I didn't want to be here. At least, not at first," Emily said, avoiding the inevitable by stretching the story out, "and I still miss my family and friends. The thought of never seeing them again breaks my heart—"

"Ye possess Weaver blood, child," Nicnevin said. "Use the portals in Seven Cairns. Ye are but a heartbeat away from those ye left behind."

"They don't know me at Seven Cairns anymore." Emily cleared her throat again, hating the way her voice kept cracking. "It's as though I've been wiped from their memories, and I can't use a portal without permission. Or at least, that's what Mairwen always said."

Another amazingly gorgeous frown settled across Nicnevin's features as she turned to Gryffe. "This is not of my doing, son." Then she turned back to Emily. "But ye nay answered my question, child. Do ye wish to be here *now*? Are ye drawn to my son?"

"No matter what happens," Emily said, "no matter what he does when he finds his *one*, my heart will always belong to Gryffe. I cannot imagine not loving him, and that scares the living daylights out of me because I just met him." Breath held, she ducked her head and stared at her hands, afraid of his reaction. He had always made it clear he would never stop searching for his *one*.

The bed shifted, but she still refused to look up. Instead, she hugged herself tighter. If she didn't look, if she didn't see the rejection and pity in his eyes, then she would be all right and have the strength to get through this terrible day.

"Emily," he whispered.

She kept her gaze locked on her hands. "What?"

"Look at me, lass."

"No."

"Why?"

"Because I am afraid."

"Of what?"

She blew out a frustrated sigh and closed her eyes for good

measure. "I have never handled rejection well, and I handle pity even worse."

His warm hands closed around hers, and he whispered, "I have neither of those to offer ye."

Ever so slowly, she opened her eyes and lifted her head, dismayed when she couldn't read him. He still wasn't smiling, and his eyes had achieved an amazingly dark storminess. It felt like he was pouring himself into her soul.

"What do you have to offer me?" she whispered, bracing herself for his answer.

"Only myself."

"But what about your vision, the one you've been searching for?"

"I found ye or ye found me. Either way, we are one."

She dove into his arms, determined to latch onto this strange fairy tale and hold it so tightly it couldn't break free. He was all she had now, and she dared anyone to try to take him.

CHAPTER 8

The longer he held Emily, the more Gryffe realized what a damned fool he had been. His *one*, the woman of his vision, had been in front of him all along, and he had allowed his dislike and distrust of his mother to blind him.

"Forgive me, my precious one," he whispered. "Forgive me."

"I am most definitely not needed here," Nicnevin announced. "I shall be in the kitchens inspecting the maids I sent over from the kingdom."

Gryffe buried his face in the soft curve of Emily's neck and filled his lungs with the deliciousness of her scent. "Ye have consumed me like a raging fire. I shouldha known ye were my heart's wish."

"Bedelia insisted I had a fated mate. I didn't believe her," Emily murmured as she held him tighter. "Now, I know what Jessa meant. All the powerful feelings she described." Her delicate laugh, like the calming sound of a bubbling stream, shifted her in his arms. "Jessa told me the first realization was so intense it was almost painful. She was right."

He grazed kisses along her sweet skin. "Aye, 'tis almost painful—the wanting. The need to be whole again."

She loosened her embrace and leaned back; her smile soft, almost shy. "Mairwen says fated mates' souls are sometimes separated by those wishing to harm the Highland Veil. They think that if they can keep us apart long enough and make sure we don't find each other in successive lives, that will cause the Veil to weaken even faster. Maybe that's how your soul ended up in this reality—or how my soul ended up in mine."

He cupped her cheek and allowed himself to sink into her gaze. "We found each other now. 'Tis all that matters."

"You're no longer afraid to love me?"

The hesitancy in her eyes pulled at his heart. He leaned in and whispered, "I no longer fear anything other than losing ye. I shall love ye through eternity—maybe even longer if I discover a way to do so." He sealed the vow with the kiss he had longed for ever since the first taste of her lips. The urge to complete their bond, reunite their souls, crackled through him like wildfire.

She clung to him, holding tighter as she hungrily kissed him in return, just as eager to meld their connection, make their union complete.

He lowered her back among the pillows and stretched over her, eager to worship her as she deserved, but everywhere he touched, he felt clothing rather than the perfect silkiness of her skin. "How many feckin' layers did Inalfi dress ye in?"

She treated him to a sultry, almost purring laugh while fumbling with the belt that wrapped around her waist twice. With a maddening wiggle that nearly undid him, she fought to kick off her boots. "You told her to dress me warmly."

"Aye, I did at that." He debated on drawing his dagger and cutting her out of her clothes. Lore, he needed this woman like he had never needed a woman before. He reached down to help her with the straps on her fur lined footwear and came up short. "Ye're wearing trews under yer skirts?"

She gave him a look that made him want her even more. "You told Inalfi the weather was going to be bad." She pushed him away and scooted off the bed. "I know this isn't romantic, but I am about to burst into flames. We need to speed to nakedness and enjoy slow romance later." Tossing her belt to the floor, she backed up to him while tugging on the laces of the decorative wristlets Inalfi had seen fit to have her wear. "Undo me in the back while I work on the front."

"Gladly, m'lady." It was time for the dagger. He drew it from his boot, sliced the lacing, then shoved the heavy velvet gown off her shoulders. "I can bear this no longer." He tossed the knife aside, ripped off her layers of petticoats, tore away her corset, then rent her chemise in two, and tossed the tatters aside.

She slowly turned, wearing nothing but those damn leather trews. "You are very hard on clothes, you know?"

"Aye, verra hard." Her breasts were just as perfect as he had known they would be. "The trews, lass. Off with them as I rid myself of these clothes that separate us."

Eyes smoldering, she kept her gaze locked with his as she unbuttoned the waist, let the trews drop, then kicked them away.

He almost fell to his knees.

"You are still dressed," she said, the sultry throatiness of her voice as exciting as a caress. She smiled and reached for his belt. "Let me help you."

Layer by layer, they tore off his coat, kilt, trews, and tunic until he stood before her as bare as the day he was born. When the tip of her tongue raced across the fullness of her lips, he groaned and pulled her against him, hissing as their flesh finally touched, nothing but skin to skin.

"Take me," she said, with breathless urgency. "Take me now."

"But—" He didn't want her to think him a rutting beast. He wanted to worship her and make her know how he adored her beyond all reasoning, and there was her injury to consider. "Yer bruised arse, m'lady."

"Let me worry about my arse. I need you with an unexplainable —unbelievable—ache. Please—we can go slow next time." She wrapped her fingers around his length and stroked. "Please—now."

He'd heard of the excruciating need in a fated mates' first burn but had passed it off as exaggeration until now. This was no exaggeration. If he didn't bury himself inside her, he would die. He tossed her onto the bed and plunged into her. "Sons a bitches!" 'Twas like being immersed in fire.

"Yes!" She arched and met his every thrust, raking her nails down his back to urge him faster. Squeezing his buttocks, she pulled him in while calling out, "Harder!"

And so he did, pounding with a fury. The inexplicable sensations made him growl. For every sound, every delighted moan Emily released, he roared and drummed into her even faster.

When she dug her nails in and screamed, her ecstasy shot through him like powerful lightning, driving him to the precipice of his own release. He buried himself completely and stayed, pouring into her, reuniting their souls, and melding their bond for the remainder of this lifetime.

After a series of violent shudders, he collapsed, bracing himself on his forearms, as he pressed his forehead to hers, and whispered,

"Heart of my heart,
Soul of my soul,
We reunite,
To never let go.
Blood of my blood,
Bone of my bone,
We two are now one,
Our halves are now whole.
For the good of all,
With harm to none,
So let it be spoken,
So let it be done,
So mote it be."

She laced her fingers in his hair and whispered back, "I love you. So mote it be."

The fire in the hearth roared with fury, crackling and popping as if doused with a bucket of pitch.

Gryffe smiled down at her. "Thank the goddesses, the fire stayed in the hearth."

Her mouth fell open, and she stared at him as if she had never seen him before. Then ever so gently, she touched his lips.

"What, my own? What is it?" He lifted himself a bit, in case he was crushing her.

Tears welled in her eyes and overflowed. "You smiled."

Idly stroking her cheek with his thumb, he almost laughed. "I suppose I did. Is that so shocking?"

"You never smile."

Scooping her up and ensuring he remained buried in her delectable heat, he moved them to his favorite chair in front of the hearth and settled into it with her perfectly astraddle him. He slid his hands along her hips, up her waist, and cupped her perfect breasts. "I never had a reason to smile before. Ye gave me one when we joined our souls."

"I rather like this chair." She adjusted her seating and teased him with a wiggle that hurried him even faster to battle ready hardness.

Leaning forward to kiss her nipples, he slipped his hand downward and stroked the nubbin of her sex with his thumb while arching to encourage her to grind her hips. "There is much furniture in this keep that we must christen."

"What about the servants?" she asked with a groan as she moved with more urgency and leaned into his massaging thumb.

"I shall send them away afore I lift yer skirts and bend ye over the bannister."

She rocked faster. "Sounds delightful. What about the bathtub? We'll need to christen that as well."

He sucked each of her nipples with a deep, slow pull, then teased a trail around them with the tip of his tongue. "Most definitely. And the head table in the main hall."

"The head table in the main hall?"

Her breathlessness fueled his plans for her even more. "Aye, I intend to spread ye out before me and feast on ye till yer cries of delight echo off the rafters."

She rode faster, panting and bucking. "Won't everyone know what we're doing?"

"Everyone will be delighted that their chieftain is pleasuring his lovely wife as much as she pleasures him."

"Pleasuring him," she repeated with a long, low groan, then wet her lips. "Would it please you if I knelt between your knees and tasted you while you sat on your throne? Or do you have a throne?"

"For that, I shall get one."

"Indeed." She caught hold of the back of the chair and ground into him harder, pounding and squeezing with relentless fury, driving him onward to oblivion with her hot wetness. "Oh my," she gasped. "Now!" Her groaning shriek filled the room.

"Aye—now!" He roared and lifted while holding her hips, steadying her and keeping her astraddle as he emptied into her.

She tensed and arched, going still as a breathtaking sculpture while fully giving herself to her shuddering bliss. Then she went limp and melted over him, nuzzling his throat while draped atop his chest. She lay there, barely shifting as her breathing returned to normal. "I never knew it could be like this."

"Neither did I, my own." He ran his hands up and down her back, then comfortably tucked his fingers around the fine round cheeks of her arse. Floating along the haze of spent pleasure, it occurred to him he had never known such contentment existed. "I love ye, my own. Ye ken that, aye? Ye ken this is nay just lust?"

She tucked her face more comfortably under his chin while idly tickling her fingernails through his beard. "What exactly is the meaning of *ken*?"

"To know. Understand."

"Then *yes* to both your questions." She shifted with a deep sigh that worried him.

"Emily?"

"What?"

"What is it? Tell me yer troubles."

"I wish you could meet my parents," she said so softly that he almost missed it. "They would love you almost as much as I do. So would my brothers."

He tightened his arms around her. "We will find a way for ye to see them again. I promise."

She lifted up with another heavy sigh and looked down at him with a sad smile. "Don't make promises you can't keep. I fear that whatever has happened to Seven Cairns is way above our heads and out of our control. You heard your mother."

He trailed his fingers along the line of her jaw and slid them back into her hair. "Will ye be able to be happy here, my love? Will ye be able to embrace a new life with me?"

"I will," she said softly. "But it will take me time. I am going to need even more patience than you've already given me."

"I will give ye whatever ye need."

She leaned forward and treated him to a kiss so tender it squeezed his heart. "In our next life, don't be so hard for me to find, okay?"

He frowned a moment, trying to recall what her word *okay* meant. When it came to him, he gave her another of his rare smiles because he knew it pleased her. "Okay."

She laughed. "It sounds strange when you say it—but I think you could tell me anything when you're smiling, and I'd be so dazzled with your handsomeness that I'd go along with it."

"Ye think me handsome, do ye?"

"Don't fish for compliments." Her stomach vibrated against his, growling like a wee beastie.

"Ye have not eaten today."

She turned somber. "I thought it best to wait until I saw how today went."

He rose from the chair, returned to the bed, and gently placed her among the pillows, immediately missing her warmth when he stepped away. "I shall ring for tea and food. I feel sure Nicnevin has already spread the word about us. They'll nay be expecting us to come down for our supper."

"I don't know whether to be embarrassed or pleased."

But she looked happy and well-sated, so he merely shook his head while crossing the room to the bell pull. "It eases the clan's minds when their chieftain takes a wife out of love and not necessity, especially when I swore I would never settle for a political alliance. All knew I was waiting and searching for ye." He yanked on the braided pull hanging beside the hearth. "Nicnevin will nettle us for a ceremony, I fear, even though we already spoke the binding oath."

With a seductive, lazy stretch, Emily rolled over onto her belly, hugging the pillows and plumping them under her head. She grinned and wrinkled her nose at him. "Are you a momma's boy?"

He snorted, then hurried to pour them both a generous glass of whisky, aching to be joined with her yet again. "Since I dinna ken what a *momma's boy* is, I canna answer that."

She laughed. "I was only teasing, since I doubt very much you do everything your mother wants and would move heaven and earth to keep her happy."

With a whisky in each hand, he climbed into the bed and sat with his back against the headboard. "Come to me, my love." He offered her one of the glasses. "Ye are the only one I would ever move heaven and earth for to keep happy."

As she nestled against him, he allowed himself a contented sigh. "Much better. I ache when I am not touching ye."

"Me too," she whispered, before sipping her drink and snuggling even closer. "And apparently, this *therapy* healed my hip perfectly."

He smoothed his hand up and down the warm silkiness of her back and kissed her forehead, knowing that they would soon set their glasses aside and return to drinking of one another. "I believe this *therapy*, as ye put it, has healed many things."

A purring sigh left her as she stretched and set what was left of her drink on the table beside the bed, then slipped astraddle him once more. "Indeed—shall we heal ourselves some more?"

"Most definitely, my own. Most definitely."

EVERYONE WITHIN THE MAIN HALL, the entire Council of Master Weavers and their apprentices, went still. Each of them, one by one, turned and looked at Mairwen.

She had heard it plainly as well. The Knowing, the energy of the goddesses' combined voices within the Weavers' minds whenever information needed to be shared with one and all, was unmistakable. With a flick of her wrist, she removed her powers from the grand map floating in the center of the large gathering room and sank into a nearby chair. "It would seem Emily has found her mate. Thank the goddesses she is alive and well."

"The goddesses knew," Ishbel said, her voice barely above a whisper.

"It would seem so." Mairwen eyed the others as they gathered around her. "Which of ye took it upon yerself to inform the goddesses about our Emily's disappearance after we all agreed not to do so until we had exhausted all efforts to find her?"

"Really, Mairwen?" Malcolm, Master of the Conflict Weavers stepped forward. "'Tis unlike ye to toss about unfounded accusations like feed for birds." He nodded at the other four Weavers who led the sects of the Dark. "Have ye forgotten that those of my ilk avoid direct contact with the goddesses whenever possible? If anyone did it, it had to be one of your side. Those of the Light always flock to the goddesses."

Mairwen propped her elbow on the chair arm and rested her head in her hand. She was so weary. These past few days of searching for Emily had drained her. Perhaps it was time she stepped down from her position as master over all the Divine Weavers. "I was not accusing," she said without lifting her head. "I was merely inquiring."

"None of us look forward to answering to the goddesses." Shona, Master of the Tranquility Weavers, softly blew into the air, sending a wave of calming energy across them all. "Perhaps Emily called out to them. They have answered a mortal's cry for help before. Not often. But it has happened."

"I noticed they failed to mention where she was," said Taskill, Master of the Curse Weavers. "Think ye it is a challenge from them? One of their damnedable tests to redeem ourselves for losing a mortal in the first place?"

"I dinna ken." All Mairwen knew for certain was that she was weary, and something about this entire disaster made her senses raw. She throbbed with unworthiness. In all their years of finding and uniting fated mates, no reunion had ever been like this one.

"Since our Emily has found her fated mate," Keeva asked while tapping on the screen of her large glass and steel tablet powered more by magic than technology, "shall I tell everyone we are ready to resume joining fated mates? I could have all our matchmaking apps and websites back up and running by the end of the day, and could also remove the barriers from the Dreaming."

"Emily is one of us," Ishbel said in an uncharacteristically snappish way. "She is family, and I will have no part in our next endeavor until I see she is safe and happy. Many in the village feel the same."

Mairwen tipped her head toward the door. "Go, Keeva. I know ye meant well, but ye need to think upon how everyone has been affected by this. The Veil is in fine fettle at the moment. The next bond can wait a bit longer."

Head bowed and cheeks red with embarrassment, Keeva handed her tablet to her brother Killian and hurried out.

It was time to take control and remedy this chaos. Mairwen felt it as surely as if her mothers had nudged her to rise from the chair. She stood, determined to reclaim her strength and fulfill her calling. "Notify the Defenders of every era, every world, every reality. For whatever reason, Weavers could not find her. By the goddesses, it is my hope that the Defenders can."

"If Weavers and all our resources could not find her," Taskill said, "what makes ye think the Defenders can? They are mere mortals."

"Because something has changed now that Emily has found her mate. I feel it."

"And the goddesses?" Malcolm asked.

"I shall seek an audience with them, as soon as they will allow it."

CHAPTER 9

"They do not have to keep doing that," Emily said to Inalfi as they crossed the great hall. It bustled with servants preparing the long rows of trestle tables for the evening meal. As soon as they came within a few feet of any maid or scullery lad, the servant stopped whatever they were doing and bowed low until Emily acknowledged them. "I want to learn everyone's name, but this bowing stuff needs to stop. It's just me. It's not like I'm royalty or anything."

Inalfi eyed her in disbelief, then huffed. "It is not *just yerself*, m'lady. Ye are the chieftain's one, his blessed wife, and we have none of us ever seen him so contented. We wish to serve ye well and honor ye because of that." She leaned in close and lowered her voice. "Mrs. Thistlebran said she thought she saw him smile just the other day. Himself *never* smiles. Especially not when Queen Nicnevin is here."

The strongest sense of *happy* Emily had ever known washed across her. Others had noticed Gryffe's contentment, so it had to be real. That reassured her more than it probably should, but she couldn't help it, especially since she still struggled with bouts of homesickness for family, friends, and even the conveniences of the world she had left behind. It relieved her to know his love for her was just as solid as what she felt for him. This deep connection they shared went both ways, just as it should, even though it was still a little unbelievable. They had known each other for such a short time, at least as far as this lifetime was concerned.

She almost laughed. How many times had she tossed aside a romance book before finishing it, claiming the insta-love factor was too silly to swallow? But this feeling was undeniable. She loved Gryffe completely. From the depths of her soul, she felt as though she had loved him all her life, and all her many past lives too. It was both wonderful and frightening.

"M'lady?" Inalfi cleared her throat, interrupting Emily's inner dialogue.

"Sorry. I am still trying to wrap my mind around everything that's happened in such a short time." She slowly shook her head. "I believed it easily enough when it happened to my friend Jessa, but it's harder to believe now that it's me."

"Love keeps to no timetable, m'lady. It does as it will. Best remember that."

"It most definitely does." Emily paused at an archway to the labyrinth of hallways and looked back at the expansive meeting room with its massive twin hearths, weaponry wall, and tapestries of the clan's more memorable battles hanging from the upper gallery's bannister. MacStrath Keep was impressive, but also easy to get lost in with its many levels, hallways, and multiple turrets. Thankfully, Inalfi didn't seem to mind coming with her until she learned her way around.

Mrs. Thistlebran charged out of one of the hallways, calling out as she careened around the corner, "Lady Emily! Come quick! Queen Nicnevin swears this is meant for ye."

"Swears what is meant for me?" Emily caught up her skirts and ran after the plump housekeeper who moved amazingly fast for a lady of her size and years. "Wait! Mrs. Thistlebran, wait! Tell me what's going on." It couldn't be good if Gryffe's mother was at the center of it. After getting to know Nicnevin better, Emily understood why Gryffe felt the way he did about the Dark Queen.

"She'll not listen, m'lady," Inalfi shouted from behind her. "Not when she is in such a stir."

"This better be a valid *stir*." Emily silently cursed the yardage of petticoats and wool skirts that made something as simple as running a lot more difficult than it should be. But as soon as she chased the housekeeper out into the cold, snowy garden, she was a little more thankful for all the layers.

A line of men armed with spears, swords, and long rifles had something cornered against the farthest stone wall, and whatever it was ripped the air with a loud, feral scream, reminding her of the great wild cats of the jungle documentaries her brothers had always adored.

Nicnevin stood between the men and the animal. She towered over them, stretching herself to a chilling, neck-breaking height meant to back them up and strike fear into their hearts. "Leave the beast alone," she commanded, her voice echoing like thunder. Then she caught sight of Emily and motioned her forward. "It is about time. Grimalkin needs ye to convince these fools she means those of this clan no harm. She has only come to serve ye."

Emily hurried forward, pushing her way through the men. "What is a Grimalkin?" She came up short as she spotted the fearsome beast. Huddled in the corner of the skirting wall was a tiny black kitten with a patch of white shaped like a diamond on its chest. She turned on the men. "You should be ashamed of yourselves. You're scaring that poor little kitten to death."

"Poor wee kitten?" One of the guards, whose name she couldn't remember, sputtered and spat while pointing a spear at the tiny cat. "If Himself catches us letting that Fae panther stay in the garden, 'twill be all hell to pay for certain. Step back, m'lady. Please. I beg ye. Ye must be kept safe for the good of the clan."

Emily shook her head at the man calling the kitten a panther. It looked barely old enough to be weaned from its mother. "Come here, kitty. I know they're scary. They don't mean to be." She crouched, scooped the tiny feline up, and cuddled it close.

The kitten immediately rewarded her with a song of deep, vibrating purrs.

"Come on," she told it, thrilled with the little beastie. "Let's get you something to eat. I bet Cook can spare a saucer of cream or something."

"Inside the keep, m'lady?" Mrs. Thistlebran seemed oddly horrified as she teetered back a few steps.

Suspicions increasing, Emily turned to Inalfi and then to Nicnevin. "What am I not seeing here? Why is everyone afraid of a harmless little kitten?"

Nicnevin beamed at her, appearing proud as a mother hen. "Why, there is nothing amiss at all, Lady Emily. Grimalkin came all the way from the kingdom to stay at yer side and offer ye her protection. She already loves ye, and her loyalty is unquestionable."

Not trusting herself to comment on that obvious half-truth, Emily looked to Inalfi. "Care to comment?"

"Perhaps it would be better if Himself explained." The tiny maid wrinkled her nose as she stepped back with a quick shake of her head.

"What the feckin' hell has happened here?" Gryffe's thunderous roar shook the ground. "Where is my Emily? If any harm has come to her, every one of ye will rue the day ye were born!"

The kitten hissed and growled, balling up tighter in the protection of Emily's arms. "Don't worry, kitty," she reassured it. "He's just a little overprotective."

The cluster of warriors parted and bowed their heads. Gryffe stormed forward, visibly relaxing, when he saw her. But then his attention settled on the cat, and his expression darkened with a displeased scowl. "My own...my dearest love...do ye ken what ye cradle there in yer arms?"

"A kitten." She kissed the top of the tiny black cat's head and was immediately rewarded with louder purring. "Isn't she sweet? Your mother said her name is *Grimalkin*."

"Sweet?" He cut a hard glare over at Nicnevin. "Explain yerself. Now."

The Dark Queen held up a finger and wagged it back and forth. "I did not do this. Grimalkin came of her own accord. She insisted she is meant to serve and protect your Lady Emily."

Gryffe scrubbed his fingers through his beard, scratching along his jawline while scowling up at the heavens. "My love," he said, turning back to Emily, "what ye believe ye see and hold in yer arms, and what we see and believe is there with ye are two entirely different things."

She looked into the kitten's golden eyes. "What is he talking about?"

The little cat squeaked with an adorable kittenish meow, making every warrior in the garden flinch and jerk back another step.

Even more suspicious, Emily turned to Nicnevin. "Drop the illusion."

Nicnevin twitched a nonchalant shrug. "'Tis not my illusion to drop, my lady. Speak to Grimalkin."

"Grimalkin?" Emily arched a brow at the cat. "If we're to be friends, I need to know the truth about you, please."

The dear little creature leapt from her arms and transformed into a monstrously huge black panther, then head-butted Emily's skirts in search of a reassuring pat.

Now she understood everyone's reaction, but was still unable to resist the gorgeous cat. She crouched beside it and pulled it into a hug. "It's going to be so easy to love you, Grimalkin. You're my sweetie. No matter what form you take."

Nicnevin threw back her head and roared with victorious laughter. "It would seem Grimalkin knew all along she would be accepted."

"Don't gloat," Emily told the Dark Fae Queen, making everyone in the garden gasp. Realizing she might've overstepped with the goddess of magic, she softened the advice with a grateful bow of her head. "But thank you for protecting Grimalkin until I could get outside to meet her. I'll need you to teach me about her. What to feed her—things like that. Somehow, I don't think a saucer of cream will be enough."

"It would probably be best that I not teach you about her diet," Nicnevin said as she generously returned Emily's gracious nod. "I will tell you, though, that she feeds but once a Fae year and only within the boundaries of my kingdom—upon her prey that lives there." She cut a sideways look at Gryffe's warriors. "Unless provoked here in Scotland, of course. If anyone threatens ye or my grandchildren once they are born, Grimalkin will be most happy to make exceptions and dine on the entrails of our enemies."

"Eww." Emily scratched the panther under the chin, making the great cat's long whiskers twitch. "Let's try to avoid that here at the keep, okay?"

Golden eyes partially closed in pure bliss, Grimalkin purred louder and slowly moved her head to guide Emily's scratchings to the perfect spot.

"She reminds me of a cat I had when I was little." A wave of homesickness sent the threat of tears. Emily blinked hard and fast to keep them at bay. With the passing days, the sadness came less often, but it still came, and when it did, it hurt. Badly. She swallowed hard and tried to shake herself out of it. "My kitty was named Binxer. She lived to the ripe old age of twenty-two before she crossed the rainbow bridge."

"Crossed the rainbow bridge?" Gryffe asked gently.

She shook her head. "I'll explain later." She was too emotional at the moment to give a lesson in twenty-first century vernacular. She had loved Binxer so very much, as all her family had.

Grimalkin rubbed closer, nudging and purring louder as if understanding her pain and trying to offer healing.

"The heartache again, my love?" Gryffe knelt and wrapped an arm around her. "Cry if ye need to. There is no shame in yer tears."

"I don't need to cry in front of everyone," she whispered, doing her best to sniff them back and concentrate on scratching Grimalkin's sleek head. "They'll think I'm a weenie."

"A what?"

"A weak, whiny person without a spine."

"No one would ever think that of ye." With a flick of his wrist, he dismissed his warriors, hugging her closer as the garden emptied of everyone except themselves, Nicnevin, and Inalfie. Mrs. Thistlebran had taken the opportunity to scurry back inside. Gryffe kissed her cheek. "And now ye not only have a husband who is half Unseelie, ye have one of the kingdoms fiercest beasties pledging to stay at yer side."

"I see my little Binxer whenever I look in her eyes." The tears spilled over, burning trails down her face chilled by the icy wind. She swiped them away. "Sorry. I know you're tired of this. So am I."

"I am tired of nothing. Yer tears simply show me when ye love, ye love hard and never let go. For that—I am grateful because I am blessed to be loved by ye as well."

Grimalkin turned and glared at Nicnevin while barely flipping the tip of her tail.

"What?" the Dark Queen asked the animal.

The great cat rumbled with something akin to a *mouthy* growl.

The goddess of magic threw up her hands. "I dinna ken if it will work or not, but I will offer it."

"You speak *Fae panther*?" Emily asked, silently noting that she had never imagined herself asking such a strange question.

"Of course I do." Nicnevin nodded at Gryffe. "As does he, when he bothers to listen."

Gryffe didn't comment. He simply narrowed his eyes at her.

"Do not think at me in that tone." The Dark Fae Queen shot back a narrow eyed glare of her own.

"You know, it is very rude to leave me out of the conversation." Emily rose to her feet, saddened by the loss of the sweet little kitten, while at the same time enamored of Grimalkin, the powerful Fae panther.

Grimalkin immediately returned to the form of the tiny feline and leapt into her arms.

She turned to Nicnevin. "So the cat can read my mind, too?"

"Rest easy. None of us can read yer mind. Ask my son if ye dinna believe me." Nicnevin nodded at the small beastie. "But Grimalkin can *feel* what ye wish of her. Most animals can. Mortals are simply too dull to realize it."

With her head once again whirling with the strangeness of this world that was like hers but not—Emily scratched the kitten behind the ears and tried to focus on the conversation between the panther and the dark goddess. "What did she want you to try? The thing you said you didn't know whether or not it would work."

"The Dreaming," Nicnevin said. "Ye could visit—"

"Absolutely not!" Gryffe stepped between them. "Ye canna take her there. The place is maddening. It will make her miss her family worse than she already does."

"What is the Dreaming?" Emily stepped around him, still hugging the kitten. If whatever that was would enable her to visit her parents, see her brother, or check in with Jessica, she wanted to give it a try. "Is it something only the Fae can access? Remember, I have a smidgen of Spell Weaver DNA."

The look he gave her told her loud and clear that he was remembering all the fires she had set every time she'd attempted to use magic.

"Do I have to cast a spell to get there?" A blast of cold wind hit her, convincing her this conversation would be more pleasant if they continued it inside, out of the cold weather. "Let's go in, and you and your mother can explain."

Gryffe tipped a leery nod at the kitten. "Ye're bringing that inside with ye?"

"Grimalkin is not a *that*, and yes, she is coming inside. It's cold out here. She might even like a saucer of cream in this form."

He turned and bared his teeth at his mother.

"I did not summon her," Nicnevin reminded in a singsong voice that made Emily cringe. If Gryffe wasn't angry with his mother before, he would be now.

"Grimalkin and I are going inside." Emily took off toward the keep at a determined march. "Come on, Inalfi. You are Fae. You can explain the Dreaming since they're too busy sparring."

"Aye, m'lady." Inalfi caught up and marched alongside her. The way she kept stealing wary glances at Grimalkin made Emily even more thankful that the odd, magical furbaby had chosen her as a bestie. It never hurt to have friends that others respected.

"Now, what is the Dreaming?" she asked Inalfi while attempting to ignore the continued arguing of Gryffe and his mother as they followed along behind them. It was like listening to her brothers fighting over who got the choicest cut of meat at the dinner table.

"'Tis hard to explain." Inalfi wrinkled her nose as if the thought of it smelled bad. "Ye ken how yer dreams often dinna make sense? How anything can happen? Right side up can be upside down, and about the time ye figure it out, it all changes?"

Emily nodded, remembering some of her wilder dreams that even her psychiatrist mother had written down in an attempt to analyze them for one of her many published papers.

"In the Dreaming, ye visit others' dreams where the only control ye have is to either stay or go." Inalfi shuddered. "Oft times, the place can be verra frightening."

"Do the ones you visit know you're there?" One of Emily's greatest worries was that her family had become overwrought because they didn't know what had happened to her. She wanted to reassure them, tell them she was all right, and somehow let them know about Gryffe. While she missed everyone with a vengeance, she hated the thought of making them unhappy and causing them pain. "Could I speak to my mother? Would she know it was me, really me?"

"'Tis hard to say, my lady. She might cling to it with the hope it was truly yerself, but then again, if she nay believes in such things, she might explain it away as just a wishful dream."

That was Emily's fear. Both her parents were extraordinarily pragmatic and down to earth. The only one she might convince was Jessa. If she could get anyone to believe it was her in the Dreaming, it would be her friend who had traveled back in time to find her own fated mate. She nodded to herself while idly scratching Grimalkin's ears and walking faster. Yes. That's what she would do. She would try to visit Jessa and have her explain everything to not only her parents but to the Weavers in Seven Cairns—the Seven Cairns she knew and loved and that knew and loved her back. Maybe then they would find a way to her so she could at least use the portals to visit those she had lost.

Then, life would be perfect.

CHAPTER 10

"Either I go with her into the Dreaming, or she does not go at all." Gryffe stood his ground with his teeth bared and fists clenched, staring down his mother. Emily and Inalfi had gone on ahead, probably heading to the kitchens to get that feckin' panther posing as a wee cat a saucer of cream. "Ye know how dangerous the place can be. I will not have her there unprotected."

Nicnevin rolled her eyes. "I had no intention of simply dropping her in there like a bowl of scraps tossed onto the heap." She patted her chest. "I am going with her. I shall keep her safe."

"The hell ye will."

His mother frowned. "Ye have become most petulant of late. I wouldha thought finding the other half of yer soul wouldha put ye in a better mood."

"It does, except when someone suggests she do something dangerous."

Nicnevin shook a finger. "It was not I, my son. It was Grimalkin."

Gryffe unleashed a growl that did nothing to alleviate the tense knot of worry in his chest. "That feckin' thing. And in my keep, no less."

"She will protect Lady Emily and, someday, yer children. Ye know that."

He decided to debate the Fae panther's arrival later. After all, from the looks of it, Emily had already decided that matter for him. "Be that as it may, *whoever* put the thought of the Dreaming into my dear one's head, there will be no getting it out of her thoughts until she tries it. As I said, I am going with her."

"Fine." Nicnevin shrugged and tossed her hands in the air. "Take the entire clan, if ye wish, but I am sure Lady Emily wishes to go as soon as possible, so make certain everyone is ready by tonight at moonrise." Head held high and her chin jutted even higher, the dark queen swept away as if she had grown tired of her Court and dismissed them.

Gryffe glared after her, clenching his teeth so hard his jaws ached.

"Yer dark-hearted mother makes me arse twitch," Ferris said from behind him. "And was that a feckin' Fae panther yer Lady Emily was toting?"

"According to Nicnevin, Grimalkin chose my dear one. The cat considers herself my Emily's protector." Gryffe turned and eyed his friend. "Hiding in the shadows?"

"I prefer the word *lurking*, and I do some of my best work in the shadows."

"Indeed." Gryffe glanced around, then lowered his voice. "Do ye wish to share yer news here or somewhere more private?"

Ferris tipped his silvery head toward the nearest door to the left. "Best step into the library. Did ye not once tell me ye placed wards in there that keep Nicnevin deaf to what is said?"

"Aye. Come." Gryffe led the way, an ominous sense of dread taking root in his gut and squeezing like a poisonous vine.

Ferris swaggered into the room after him and closed the door. He studied Gryffe for a long moment before joining him in front of the roaring fire in the hearth. "The Weavers—"

Gryffe held up a hand. "I know. Their frantic whispers reached my ears as well."

"Be it yer Emily they search for? Is she their *precious mortal* that must be found at all costs?"

"I dinna ken." He paced the width of the massive room lined with floor to ceiling bookshelves, and then he halted and scowled at Ferris. "Ye would not have known the place had ye been with us that day. It was Seven Cairns—yet somehow—it wasn't."

"What do ye mean *it wasn't?*"

Gryffe shook his head. "It looked the same and all the folk knew me, but they nay spoke as the close friends and allies they have always been in the past. Their words were stilted. Formal. Devoid of all emotion." He resumed pacing, beating the air with his hands as he walked. "And even though my Emily knew their names, called out to them with the heart of a friend, they denied knowing her." He halted again and slowly turned to face his friend. "They thought her an Unseelie and demanded I take her away."

"Seven Cairns is hallowed ground. Forbidden to the Unseelie."

"Aye, I know." Gryffe raked a hand through his hair. "The only reason they suffer my presence is because of my father and my oath to the Highland Veil." He shook his head again. "But Emily has no Fae blood. Weaver ancestry? Aye, that she has, but nothing from the Fae—be they light or dark."

"And that was before the two of ye spoke the binding oath?" Ferris widened his stance and folded his arms across his broad chest, appearing as perplexed as Gryffe.

"Aye. At that time, if she could have gone through the portals, she would have left me."

Scrubbing the stubble of his day's growth of beard, Ferris cringed as if the wonderment of it all pained him. "There is no way Nicnevin, even as powerful as she is, there is no way she could have spelled the entire village of Seven Cairns and the Weavers. The goddesses blessed that land in the beginning—eons ago—it protects those upon it."

"Aye, and any glamour Nicnevin might have attempted to place on Emily to hide her from their minds would have fallen away as soon as we stepped inside the borders of the village."

Ferris appeared even more pained. "This stinks of a higher power meddling. Ye ken that, aye?"

"Aye, and where they have meddled once, I fear they will meddle again. They have been known to take away just as quickly as they give." A feeling of helplessness, the not knowing, raged through Gryffe. "They will never take her from me," he said with a low, guttural growl. "Not her nor any of our children. Never."

Ferris took hold of Gryffe's shoulder and squeezed. "Whatever ye need from me, ye have it. Aye?"

"Aye." Gryffe appreciated his old friend more than he could ever put into words, and he knew Ferris knew that. "Come into the Dreaming with us tonight. Nicnevin put it into Emily's head as a way of visiting her loved ones, and there'll be no peace now until she attempts it."

Ferris's lips curled back in a distasteful sneer. "I hate the Dreaming, and so does my wolf."

"I would never ask it of ye if I didn't fear I would need ye."

Ferris nodded. "I'll be there, old friend."

"I thank ye."

With a formal nod, Ferris went to the door. "I shall return at moonrise."

"Aye—to moonrise."

INALFI ADJUSTED both the front and back ties of Emily's corset.

"You're actually loosening them?" Emily sucked in a satisfyingly deeper breath. "Usually, you yank them so tight they cut me in half."

The studious maid gave her a scolding look. "If yer stays are not tight, they do little to support yer lovely figure, my lady." She caught hold of the bottom edge of the corset and tugged and shook it, settling Emily's *parts* more snugly into the increased space. "But the Dreaming is...different. Yer ability to move is more important than uplifting yer bosoms."

"That sounds ominous." Emily stepped into the dark blue over-skirt Inalfi held out, then wiggled to straighten the layers of petti-coats beneath it before the maid buttoned the waistband in the back. "If I need to be able to move, perhaps I should wear the clothes I wore when I arrived here in this time." The more she heard about the Dreaming, the more she wondered if using it as a way to contact Jessa was wise. That momentary cowardice made her shake her head. No. She would not be a chicken. She had to at least try to let everyone know where she was and that she was all right. With a nod at the trunk beneath the window, she resettled her footing as if about to charge into battle. "Everything's in there, isn't it? Fetch my stuff. All of it. Hiking boots and underthings too, please."

Inalfi went still, her pale blue eyes narrowing as she eyed the fullness of Emily's skirt. "That is not a bad plan, my lady. Those clothes from yer time are scandalous the way they cling to ye, but ye would be able to run, jump, and roll with more speed and accuracy." She wrinkled her nose. "But Himself might not be pleased."

"Himself will only fuss a little, then I'll fuss back, and he'll give in because he'll know I'm right." Emily glanced back over her shoulder and smiled at the great black panther stretched across the bed. "Case in point right over there."

"Himself gives in because he is besotted with ye and willna deny ye anything as long as he knows it willna hurt ye." Inalfi grunted as she hefted open the thick lid of the wood trunk trimmed with brass and leather. She rooted around in it, then returned with the clothes and boots bundled in her arms.

After helping Emily remove her corset, skirt, and petticoat, she backed away with the eighteenth century garments hugged to her middle. "On with yer things, my lady. I know ye dinna need my help to don them."

"They're not that bad, Inalfi." A happy sigh escaped Emily as she pulled on her favorite panties and sports bra. She had missed the ease and comfort of her twenty-first century garb. After wiggling into the snug, black tank top she always wore as another layer during workouts, she slipped on the fleece-lined leggings that had been her mainstay. "These are my old friends. I wore them all the time back home."

"I thought this was yer home, my lady."

Emily paused before slipping on her chunky cable knit sweater, suddenly guilty about the quiet but impossible to miss hurt in Inalfi's usually sparkling tone. "Well, of course, this is my home—now." She tried to shake off not only a silly sense of guilt but the strange sensation of having somehow betrayed Gryffe by referring to somewhere else as home. "It's just a figure of speech. A lot easier than saying I wore them all the time in the reality I came from in the twenty-first century. See? So many more words. I don't want to sound like one of those people who love to listen to themselves talk." And yet here she was babbling. Why? Why did she feel so guilty about that one little slip?

Doubt. The word filled her mind and took her back to a conversation she'd once had with Jessa before that terrifying battle with the Morrigan that had nearly cost Jessa her life. Doubt had caused that. Doubt was a dangerous thing when it came to the magic of Scotland.

Inalfi remained subdued, turning aside to put away the skirt and petticoats. Her deafening silence made Emily feel even worse.

Snatching her old hiking boots up from the floor, she crossed the room to the bed and sat beside Grimalkin. The great cat trilled out an affectionate welcome, rolled over onto her back, and nudged Emily with her head. Emily paused long enough to scratch the softly rumbling feline under the chin while trying to think of a way to make Inalfi feel better. But she couldn't. Once something was said, it was impossible to snatch it back—kind of like trying to unring a bell.

She settled for a despondent sigh while pulling on her socks and lacing up her boots. "Will you be coming to the Dreaming with me?" she asked the cheerless maid.

"Coming with ye?" Inalfi looked as if she had just been asked to assassinate the chieftain. She clutched Emily's heavy wool cloak to her chest like a shield. "Oh no, my lady. I canna go to the Dreaming."

"*Canna* go or would rather not go?"

Once again, Inalfi studied her, as she often did, Emily had noticed. It had occurred to her on more than one occasion that she was kind of like some sort of science project for the Fae maid—like growing an unknown substance in a Petri dish to see what it turned out to be.

"I canna go, my lady," Inalfi said. "I have the bloodline of a commoner."

"What?"

"Only those of the royal court or their descendants may travel through the Dreaming and visit the worlds and times the Highland Veil separates."

"Then how am I supposed to be able to get in there? I am a mortal with no Fae blood at all."

"But ye have bonded with Himself, the son of Queen Nicnevin—and ye have the divine blood of a Weaver in yer ancestry. Did ye not say yer grandmam was a Spell Weaver?"

"My great great grandmother was a Spell Weaver." Emily finished tying her boots, then pulled her cellphone from her pocket. "I won't be needing this." She tossed it onto the bedside table, then arched a brow at Inalfi. "You've seen how talented I am when it comes to magic. How many times have you gone running for the water pitcher to put out the fires?"

Inalfi lifted her chin higher and assumed a lofty demeanor. "Not that many. And they've not been nearly as bad as they were. I think ye are improving...somewhat."

"I still wish you could go with me. You are kind of like my safety net here."

"Safety net?" The maid gingerly scooped up the cell phone, holding it at arm's length between her thumb and index finger as if it were either dipped in something nasty or might explode. "Is that good or bad?" she asked as she placed the phone back in the trunk and slammed the lid shut before it escaped.

"A safety net is a good thing. You explain things to me and help me fit in so I don't have to embarrass myself by asking Gryffe."

Inalfi smiled and bowed her head. "I can but try, my lady. Yer happiness brings all of us joy." She slid her focus to the great cat purring beside Emily. "Yer Grimalkin can go with ye. Her kind guard the Fae Court and go anywhere they wish."

"You want to go into the Dreaming with me?" Emily asked the panther that was lazily flexing its front paws as if kneading biscuits.

Eyes barely open, Grimalkin yawned, revealing her lethal set of fangs. Then she trilled another purring meow and closed her eyes completely. Her kneading paws slowly went still, and her purring faded, as she drifted into a deeper sleep.

"I'll take that as an affirmative," Emily told the napping cat. Still unable to assess what time it was by the length of the shadows on the floor, she nodded at the window. "When exactly is moonrise?"

"When the moon takes the sun's place in the sky," Inalfi said with a rueful look.

"Yeah...I suppose that title was pretty self-explanatory. Sorry. I guess I'm nervous." Emily hopped off the edge of the bed and went to the door. "I'm going to find Gryffe. Do you want me to take Grimalkin with me, or are you all right with her in here?" She had noticed Inalfi always gave the cat a wide berth.

"Take her, if ye dinna mind." Inalfi sidled away from the bed while keeping her gaze locked on the beast. "I'll get better with her. I swear, I will. I need but a wee bit more time."

"She is a big cat. I understand completely." Emily made a kissing sound to rouse the lazy panther from its nap. "Come on, Grimalkin. Let's find Gryffe." The feline remained sound asleep. She opened the door. As soon as the hinges creaked, the ebony beast leapt from the bed with her ears perked and the tip of her tail twitching.

As they walked down the hallway, Emily noticed the large panther made a soft huffing grunt with every fluid step of her graceful march. It made Emily smile as she trailed her fingers down the cat's broad head and muscular shoulders. Even on all fours, Grimalkin's back was even with Emily's hip.

"You sound like a steam train chugging along," she told the cat.

Grimalkin answered with a long, low, almost clicking growl that sounded more affectionate than threatening.

"I wonder where Gryffe is? He was lagging back so I wouldn't have to listen to him and his mother spatting." Emily found it perfectly natural to think out loud to the furry shadow walking at her side. But it surprised her when Grimalkin responded with a perky trilling and took off at a faster trot.

"Hey—wait!" Thank heavens she had changed into her old clothes that were better suited to chasing after a determined panther. She loped after the great cat, following it down the spiral stairs to the main floor and into the great hall. The clansmen and servants filling the room went unnaturally quiet before several gasped and even a few shrieked as the great cat moved among them. Grimalkin halted, lifted her head, then sniffed the air, her gleaming black nostrils flexing in the torchlight.

"It's all right," Emily told one and all, wondering if they would even hear her since they were frozen either in shock at the sight of her strange clothes or in fear of the Fae cat. She decided to go with the cat theory. "She won't hurt you. She's helping me find Gryffe...uhm...I mean...the chieftain." My, my, didn't she sound efficient and ready to accept the responsibility of helping her husband lead the clan? "Does anyone know where Himself might be?"

"Library...my lady," one of the nearest servants said, a lad who squeaked like he was trapped in the throes of puberty. As he pointed in that direction, he bobbed his head so many times, it was a wonder he didn't fall over from dizziness.

"Thank you." Emily patted her leg. "Come on, Grimalkin. He's in the library."

The panther gave her a disinterested glance, then sauntered

closer to the nearest table, causing those sitting on the benches beside it to scatter.

"Grimalkin—come along now. You're scaring them, and that's not nice."

The cat poached an entire joint of beef off one of the platters before returning to Emily's side.

"So Nicnevin lied about you only eating when in the Fae kingdom?"

Grimalkin flipped her tail and purred while proudly carrying her treat with her head held high.

"Come on." Emily headed for the library. She'd be having a word with Nicnevin. While she already loved the great black cat, she couldn't have those of the clan living in a constant state of terror. When she reached the door, she knocked.

"Come!"

She pushed open the door, then stepped back, allowing Grimalkin to enter first. "Why don't you go over there by the hearth to eat?"

The cat complied, flopping down on the flagstones with a satisfied grunt as she started ripping the meat from the bone.

"Apparently, your mother was slightly mistaken about Grimalkin's eating habits," Emily said as she joined Gryffe at the window.

"And that surprises ye?" As soon as she drew near, he wrapped an arm around her and pulled her close.

Hugging herself against him, she rested her head on his shoulder. "I love how you do that. It always makes me feel safe."

"Do what, my love?"

"Always hug me close whenever I'm near."

"The touch of ye comforts me. Yer warmth feeds my soul." But even though his sweet words were like a caress, he sounded distracted.

"What's wrong?"

He shifted with a heavy sigh, faintly fogging the window in front of them. "I dinna like the thought of ye risking the Dreaming. 'Tis not a pleasant place, nor is it safe."

She could *feel* his concern as plainly as the beat of his heart. It both filled her with the contentment of being well and truly loved and also made her sad. "I need to try to speak with Jessa. She is the only one I know for sure who will believe it's really me and tell everyone else that I am all right."

He took hold of her by the shoulders and stared into her eyes. "And are ye, my love? Are ye truly all right?"

She stared back at him, unable to answer right away. He knew. He felt her doubt. "I love you," she whispered.

"I love ye as well, but that is not what I asked."

"I will be all right. Eventually." She wouldn't lie to him. He always deserved the truth. "Besides—I can't go back. Remember?"

"But if ye could?"

She shook her head. "I can't so there's no reason to even wonder about it."

Sadness shouted from him. "If ye could go back, ye would. Ye would leave me."

"No. I would not." And she wouldn't—she would just visit home once in a while and then come back. *Home.* She had done it again. Referred to somewhere other than here as home. "I cannot imagine my life without you. You have to believe that."

He cupped her cheek, tenderly grazing his callused thumb back and forth across it. "I believe ye've yet to give me the entirety of yer heart. There is a part of ye held back. A part of ye that longs for all ye once knew and would love to know again. A part of ye does not belong to me...and maybe never will."

Sliding her hands up his chest and around his neck, she hugged him tighter than she had ever hugged him before. Rising on tiptoe, she pressed a kiss to his ear before whispering, "I love you. You have to believe that."

His arms tightened around her, and he buried his face in the crook of her neck. "I never truly lived until ye came into my life, and without ye, I would cease to live once more. Ye are the lifeblood of my heart. The air in my lungs. The bread to my soul." He drew back and stared into her eyes again, fiercer this time. "And never will I let anything or anyone take ye from me—not yer past life and not even death."

She shivered. Not from a chill, but from the fury in his eyes and the fire in his tone. He wasn't threatening. He was making an oath. An oath as precious and sacred as their binding vows. She felt it surge through her like an intoxicating drug. She framed his face with her hands and gave herself over to his powerful, dark gaze. "I am yours forever and beyond. Know that."

He closed his mouth over hers, kissing her with such intensity that her knees went weak. He caught her up, booted a table off the rug in front of the settee, and lowered them both to the floor. "These feckin' clothes are nay as easy as tossing yer skirts up out of the way." He rumbled with a low, frustrated growl while kissing a trail along her collarbone and running his hands across her.

Just as electrified with the impossible to ignore urgency to achieve a full joining, she took hold of the waistband of her leggings and panties and shoved them down to her boot tops. "Let me on my knees," she said with desperation. This need to have him inside her was more powerful than their fated mate binding. She shoved at him when he didn't listen. "Back up and let me on my knees."

"Knees," he repeated as if trapped in a spell. He shook his head and brightened. "Aye, on yer knees."

As she rolled to her knees, she whipped her sweater off over her head, then went to all fours. "Hurry, Gryffe—I need you more than I ever have before. Take me!"

And then he was inside her, filling her to perfection. She groaned and rocked back against him, meeting him thrust for thrust. "This time is different—I need—I need—" She needed blessed oblivion.

He pounded faster, rutting into her with the same urgency that was setting her ablaze. Grabbing hold of her hips, he pulled her back harder, growling with every delicious slap of their flesh.

Excruciating bliss exploded through her with wave after wave of wondrous sensation. She may have screamed, and he may have roared, she really didn't know, and definitely didn't care. Gryffe had given her what she had needed so badly—even better than usual, which was impossible to imagine. As the tsunami of pleasure ebbed, she swayed forward and collapsed, grunting as he slumped across her.

"Feckin' hell. Are ye all right, love? I nay meant to crush ye." He rolled to one side, taking her with him, and spooning his body around hers.

"I have never been more all right in my life," she said, barely finding the energy to speak. She closed her eyes and hugged his arms around her. "I love you. Really and truly, I do"

He tightened his embrace. "I love ye as well, my precious ember. Sleep for a while in my arms now, aye? We'll be needing our strength for tonight."

"Tonight," she repeated, struggling to remember what tonight was...and then it came to her and made her sad. Maybe the Dreaming was a mistake. Maybe it was another wrong choice. She squinted her eyes shut even tighter and breathed Gryffe in. His familiar, comforting scent spiked with the essence of their loving calmed her, lulled her back to where she needed to be. She would hold tight to Gryffe while in the Dreaming, she silently vowed to herself. Gryffe would make everything all right.

CHAPTER II

Gryffe longed to sweep his precious Emily up into his arms, carry her to their bedchamber, and never let her out again until she got this foolish notion of visiting the Dreaming out of her head. But he couldn't. To do so would hurt her, and that, he would never purposely do. As he had told her before their frantic lovemaking in the library, he knew there was a part of her heart she would never give him. He sensed it like something ominous lurking in the shadows, and he hated it. But he would not prevent her from trying to make peace with that part of herself that longed for her home. He clenched his fists so tightly his knuckles popped. She might long for her other life, but never would he let her leave him. Never. He would find a way to follow her to the ends of the earth—no matter what earth they found themselves on.

He let his narrow-eyed gaze drift across Emily, Ferris, Nicnevin, and that damn Fae panther, Grimalkin. They had gathered in the center of the broad battlement atop the north tower of MacStrath fortress. Not only was it the highest point of the castle, but the one most open to the sky and the moon—a great help when it came to successfully crossing the breach into the Dreaming.

Emily's nervous fidgeting betrayed her fears that had almost reached the brink of terror. He saw it in her eyes and ached to take advantage of it to dissuade her from continuing this dangerous endeavor. But that would not be fair to her. Not after he had agreed they would go.

Ferris looked ill at ease, Nicnevin was pleasant and calm enough to be even more infuriating than usual, and the useless beast that refused to leave Emily's side occasionally gave a bored yawn while looking around and slowly flipping the tip of its long black tail.

When Emily slipped her hand into Gryffe's, he bowed his head and fought the urge to roar that they would not go and for everyone to leave the battlements.

"What do we do now?" she asked with the quiet innocence of a child.

Before Gryffe could explain, Nicnevin clapped her hands, shattering the midnight sky with lightning. "We cross!"

Fetid air slid across his flesh, changing to the cloying wetness of cold mud as the Dreaming's border swallowed him. Emily's hand slipped free of his grasp, throwing him into a panic. He burst out of the disgusting barrier that kept the mystical place within its boundaries and turned to dive back in after her, but the wall went solid. Such was the way of the Dreaming. You might enter it at your own will, but you only leave when the Dreaming releases you. "Emily!"

Ferris emerged farther down the way, growling like his wolf and shaking like a wet dog casting off the rain. Nicnevin followed him, ever smiling.

Gryffe attempted to re-enter the barrier where they had stepped through, but again, the wall resealed, forbidding his exit. He spun about and bore down on his mother, grabbing her by the throat. "Where is she? What have ye done with her?"

Nicnevin's eyes flared wide. The scent of her fear goaded him onward. He tightened his hold on her long, slender neck. "I will kill ye, if ye have harmed her. Ye know I can do it. Yer blood in my veins gives me that power."

She wet her lips and flinched with a failed attempt at swallowing. Her delicate throat swelled and flexed within his grasp. "I did nothing but pull everyone into the Dreaming," she said, her voice cracking with the effort. "Set Grimalkin to searching. She will find her."

With the dark queen still in his grasp, Gryffe glanced around the formless clearing that held them. "Grimalkin is gone as well. Neither of them made it through with us."

"I dinna ken, my son," Nicnevin said, her quiet voice revealing she too feared the worst for Emily. "I swear I have no knowledge of what happened to either of them." She tried to swallow again and flinched harder, her face reddening. "But know this, if Grimalkin is with her, she will be safe from anything the Dreaming might attempt."

"Emily!" Gryffe bellowed into the void, making the pale gray mist surrounding them swirl into eddies that spiraled out as far as the eye could see. But only silence answered. He shook his mother again, not caring that she was growing ever weaker. "I have always known ye to be cruel and black-hearted—especially as far as I am concerned—but why would ye do this? Why, when ye have beat my ears raw with yer nagging about me taking a wife and siring an heir?"

"I swear on my eternal love for yer father that I had nothing to do with any of this." The sadness in her eyes was almost convincing. "Why else would I suffer yer enraged hold when I could easily shapeshift and escape ye?"

There was that. He let his hand fall and turned away, bowing his head, frantic to solve this damnedable puzzle and find his beloved Emily. Her hand had slipped from his while they were within the barrier. Was it possible the Dreaming had rejected her even though she was a royal Fae's mate and also possessed the ancestry of a divine Weaver? "Think ye she remained at the castle? Could she have been denied entry?"

"Ye were holding her hand, aye?" Nicnevin frowned at the now sealed barrier as if examining it for cracks.

"Aye. Her hand slipped from mine after the border swallowed me."

"After and not before. Ye are certain?"

Her expression made his heart drop. The hope that Emily had remained at MacStrath fortress crumbled into dust. "Aye. After. She is not back at the keep. Is she?"

His mother sadly shook her head. "No, my son. I am sorry." She turned and swirled a hand through the mists that shielded all the dreams until they decided which of them to visit. "She is here. Somewhere."

"If we dinna find her, she will not know how to get back." Gryffe drew his sword for no other reason than it made him feel better to slash and stir the surrounding mist.

"We will find her," Ferris said, baring his teeth as he drew his sword as well. "I hate this feckin' place. It toys with anyone fool enough to wander across its borders."

"The goddesses created it to preserve and protect the mortals' dreams so they might study them. It does what it does because that is all it knows." Nicnevin meandered deeper into a bank of swirling gray fog. "Emily's instincts should help her find her way to dreamers she would know." She turned back and gave Gryffe a pained look. "As long as she is able to remain calm and listen to her heart. A great deal depends on yer precious one, and how well she can control her path and choose wisely."

"She has been so heartsick for those she left behind." He closed his eyes and rubbed his forehead, trying to recall the names of those his precious one missed the most. Other than the Weavers they had seen at Seven Cairns, he knew she missed her parents and brothers, but couldn't bring any of their names to mind. "Jessa. Jessa is the friend who was like a sister to her. She told me Jessa might believe it's really her because she too traveled back in time to find her fated mate—except her timeline remained in her reality."

"'Tis a shame that Weavers do not dream," Ferris said. "Even the Dream Weavers have no dreams of their own. They only manipulate the dreams of others." He arched a brow. "Glennis and Gillespie are the Master Dream Weavers. If they happen to be in here, they could help us find her."

"We are wasting time." Raw urgency and dread pounded through Gryffe, setting him on edge even more. "How do we find Emily's Jessa? If we find her dreams, maybe Emily will be there."

"What does she look like?" Nicnevin asked.

Gryffe shook his head. "I dinna ken."

His mother's scowl darkened with hopelessness. "Is she like our Emily? Not from Scotland. Possesses an accent unlike any we have ever heard before?"

"I dinna ken," Gryffe said in a rasping, despondent whisper. "All I know about the woman is her name, that Emily loves her, and she has three wee bairns that Emily loves as well."

"A mortal woman with three wee bairns." Nicnevin released a heavy sigh. "That does not exactly narrow the search all that much, but it is all we have, so it is a place to start. Do ye ken if she is Emily's age?"

He scrubbed his face again. "What the hell do ye think?"

Nicnevin's brows arched higher. "I shall take that as a *nay*. Come, my warriors. Let us begin our search for females with bairns. Keep that thought foremost in yer mind so the Dreaming will part the mists and show us the way."

"Gryffe?" Heart pounding so hard she almost couldn't breathe, Emily crouched as low as she could, cowering in the shadows of some dimly lit room she had never seen before. How had she ended up here? The last thing she remembered was a strange pulling that had yanked her away from Gryffe.

The cold emanating from the slate floor surrounded by walls of chiseled stone blocks made her shudder. Had she landed in a dungeon? A single torch stabbed into a crude black iron bracket on the opposite wall did little to light the place. Its flames crackled and hissed, occasionally sending ribbons of dank smoke upward. The thing smelled like the greasy black tar that pavers used to patch potholes back in Jersey.

Fur brushed against her hand, making her bite her tongue to keep from shrieking as she skittered away from it. Then the black shadow opened its golden, glowing eyes, and she realized it was Grimalkin. She threw her arms around the great beast and hugged it. "Thank goodness, you're here," she whispered.

Grimalkin didn't purr or respond. Instead, the panther lifted her nose higher and huffed the air.

Emily took that to mean they needed to be quiet until they figured out where they were. She started to rise, but the cat caught her by the wrist, pulled her back down, then leaned against her until Emily sank deeper into the shadows and bumped into the wall. Apparently, the Fae panther wanted her to stay hidden. That concerned her even more. She glanced down at her creamy white sweater, which didn't exactly blend into the shadows. In fact, it almost glowed like a beacon. As much as she hated to lose its warmth, she ripped it off over her head, wadded it up, and tossed it into an even darker corner across the room. With her black tank and leggings, she now blended in with the darkness a lot better than before.

Sliding her hands along the wall behind her, she stood. Grimalkin scolded her with a soft growl.

"We can't hide here forever," she whispered. "I have to find a way out of here."

The loyal beast head-butted her leg in what appeared to be grudging agreement. Keeping to the shadows, Emily sidled along the wall, searching for a door, a window, anything—she would even settle for something as simple as a hole big enough for Grimalkin to squeeze through and see if it led to anywhere promising, even if the panther had to shift to her kitten-sized self.

After passing her discarded sweater *twice*, Emily realized there was no way out of the strange room. Or at least, none she had been able to detect. How the devil had she gotten in here, then? When she looked up, there was only blackness. She couldn't decide if it went on forever or if someone had taken it upon themselves to paint the ceiling. Inalfi's conversations about the Dreaming came back to her. "Is this someone's weird dream we've stumbled into?"

Grimalkin backed up against the wall, pushed off at a hard lope, and launched herself skyward.

Emily held her breath, her feelings mixed. She didn't like being left behind in the stone box, but if Grimalkin could find a way out, she was all for it. But the cat landed back on the floor, gracefully alighting on all fours.

"At least you tried."

The panther grumbled with a low growl, pacing around the room, glaring at the walls.

Emily joined the cat and slowly turned in a circle. If this was someone's dream—or more like someone's nightmare—then it wasn't real. Right? It might *feel* genuine enough to the one dreaming it, but that didn't mean it had to be real to her. At least, she hoped that was one of the rules of the Dreaming. She was sadly uneducated on that particular subject. Maybe, all they had to do was decide to walk out?

"It can't be that easy," she told the panther as she retrieved her sweater and pulled it back on. The place was getting colder by the minute. Inalfi had mentioned the need to be able to move fast, and duck and roll, but the Fae maid had also admitted to never being here. Maybe you only had to do those things if you *believed* something might harm you.

Gryffe had been leery about the place, too, and Ferris hated this strange dimension. The only one unfazed by whatever the Dreaming might be was Nicnevin. Gryffe was half mortal. Ferris wasn't exactly mortal since he could shapeshift into a wolf, but he claimed to have a few mortals in his ancestry. Perhaps the secret that Nicnevin had failed to share was that mortals and those like them struggled with believing and listening to their intuition rather than whatever was right in front of them. If a person *saw* something, they tended to believe it was real. It would be hard to *see* and actually *touch* something, yet convince yourself it wasn't there at all. It would be even harder to convince yourself it was only an illusion created by someone else's dream.

"So, none of this is really here—right?" she asked Grimalkin.

The cat looked up at her, slowly blinked, then started purring. Loudly.

"I'm taking that as a *you hope I'm right*." Now. What to do about it. She had to admit that convincing herself to just walk through those stone block walls would be no easy feat. Especially, when she had just reinforced their existence in her mind by sidling around them while searching for a door. It would be mentally easier to walk through them with her eyes shut, but how would she know when to stop? She eyed the panther. "I wish you had a collar or leash or something. I could close my eyes, and you could be my seeing eye cat, since you seem to agree that none of this is real." She was counting on the Fae panther being able to suspend her beliefs and rely on instinct a lot easier than she could. But she was afraid that if she simply walked along with her hand on the beast's back, it might slip off. Then she'd open her eyes and be back right where she started. "I could hold on to your tail."

Grimalkin growled and curled it out of Emily's reach.

"It was only an idea."

The panther caught hold of her sleeve and tugged, then eyed Emily, waiting.

"That could work." Emily shrugged the sleeve out past her fingertips so Grimalkin could get a better grip. She closed her eyes and clamped her free hand over them to keep from reaching out to *touch* the wall that wasn't really there. "I hope I'm right about this."

She almost told the cat to go slowly, so if she was wrong, she wouldn't hit the wall too hard. But if she went into this with *that* mindset, she would definitely fail and hit the wall that wasn't really there. Maybe. The idea was almost too hard to swallow. She had to believe, had to convince herself that Grimalkin was going to lead her to anywhere but here.

"Give me a minute to get my head straight." Ishbel's advice about concentrating on her calming vision to help her focus came to mind. "We're going to the beach, Grimalkin. Smell the brine? Hear the gulls? Feel the warm breeze?" Emily relived every sound and sensation from the last time she had lounged on that sandy beach, lazing away the day. She was there. "Lead on, my friend. Let's walk across the sand and find some seashells."

Forcing herself to walk with confidence and not shuffle forward in fear that she might hit something, Emily envisioned the white sandy beach, lifting her nose to breathe in the tropical flowers in bloom. The sweet fragrance of frangipani, ginger Thomas, and liana fragante filled the air, making her smile and breathe deeper.

Then the tug on her sleeve ceased, and the beastie leaned against her. Emily peeked through her fingers. "It worked!" Well...it sort of worked. They were no longer boxed inside a stone room with a single stinky torch. Now, they were on a narrow dirt path with scrubby green grass growing along its edges. For some inexplicable reason, it felt as if it was a path winding up the side of a mountain. It was hard to tell, since the area was blanketed in fog. But it smelled wet and earthy. Familiar. A slow smile lightened her heart. This area smelled like Scotland after a rain. Maybe this was a misty mountain top she had been on before. It didn't matter. At least this dream was more open and less like a dungeon.

"I wonder who this dream belongs to?" She started up the path, not knowing why she went that way; it just *felt* right.

Grimalkin padded along beside her, obviously more relaxed but alert.

"I have *been* here before, Grimalkin. I *feel* it."

The panther huffed, then resumed her usual chugging grunt that matched her smooth, liquid gait.

Laughter not too far ahead made Emily stop and listen harder. One was deep and rumbling, and the other was—Jessa! Emily would know that snorting giggle anywhere. She broke into a run. This was her chance to connect with *home*. Rounding a pile of boulders shaggy with moss, she halted so fast that Grimalkin ran into the backs of her legs and nearly knocked them out from under her.

Jessa and her husband Grant were having an obviously romantic and very naked swim in a secluded Highland pool fed by a gorgeous waterfall. Emily bit her lip and retreated, backing around the enormous pile of mossy stones, hating to interrupt them. Of course, Jessa's dreams would be something like this. With triplets under a year old, she and Grant probably didn't have many opportunities like this anymore.

Emily crouched and wrapped an arm around Grimalkin's shoulders. "Now what do I do?" she whispered. "She is having such a nice dream."

The panther flicked her ears and glared at her as if she had lost her mind. And maybe she had lost her mind. This might be her one chance to connect with Jessa and get word to everyone else that she was fine and still trying to find a way back. That thought brought her up short again. *Still trying to find a way back?* Did she really mean that?

"Only for a visit," she hurried to say out loud, running from the guilt of even having the thought. With a heavy sigh, she bowed her head and rubbed her eyes, willing herself not to cry. She missed her *world*, her family, her friends—everything. That didn't mean she loved Gryffe any less. It just meant she needed both. "Why can't I have both, Grimalkin? Why do I have to sever all ties to everything I have ever known?"

The cat looked away and stretched out on the ground as if concluding they would be there a while.

Still unsure but unwilling to stay there squatting on a tightrope of indecision, Emily leapt to her feet and bounded around the boulders. "Jessa!"

But they were gone, and ever so slowly, a pale gray mist was rolling in, eating up the peaceful scene of the Highland getaway. Emily blinked as the fog swirled around her, returning her to a place of nothingness. She had blown it. Missed her chance to speak with Jessa through her dream. One of the babies had probably cried out for a cuddle or a nighttime feeding. It could be hours before Jessa went back to sleep, and maybe even longer for her to dream. Emily had always heard that not everyone dreamed every time they slept. It could depend on the level of exhaustion, and as a mother of triplets, Jessa had to be exhausted, even though she had all kinds of help.

"What a waste—and all because I couldn't make up my mind." Emily slowly turned in a circle, looking all around. She rubbed her arms, wrinkling her nose at the chilly dampness of the air. "It's like I'm trapped in a storm cloud now. Everything's all gray and fuzzy."

Grimalkin rose up out of the mist, stretching and yawning. She snorted and sneezed, making the fog swirl and ripple like water.

Filled with hopelessness and teetering on the verge of tears, Emily swallowed hard and started walking. What else could she do? Maybe she'd stumble into someone else's dream, someone she knew. Or even better, maybe she would find Gryffe. Or he would find her. And they could leave this unholy plane and return to his keep.

"Home," she forced herself to say. She never referred to Gryffe's stronghold as home or jointly theirs, mainly because it wasn't. Or, at least, it didn't feel like it to her. It was a safe place, a loving place, and Gryffe was there, but if she was honest with herself, when she thought of *home*, MacStrath Castle wasn't it. "Mama always said wherever your heart is, that's your home. I love Gryffe with all my heart. What is wrong with me?"

Grimalkin made one of her kittenish trilling noises that didn't quite fit with her current extra large size.

They wandered through the fog for what felt like hours, but who knew? Maybe they had only been wandering for minutes. Emily decided that time wasn't the same here. This was some eternal, foggy anteroom of hell. Nothing else was real here but her and Grimalkin. And Gryffe.

She plopped down onto the ground, propped her elbows on her knees, and dropped her head into her hands. Where was Gryffe? The man who had sworn he would never let her go? She rubbed her eyes and sniffed back the threat of tears. Maybe he had been taken away because she didn't deserve him.

"Bullshit." She sniffed again, refusing to beat herself up. "I do deserve him. I am just having commitment issues because the cost is so high."

Grimalkin meowed like a housecat.

"Do not do that," Emily said. "You have no idea how confusing it is to see you in all your greatness eke out a meow that belongs to a two pound kitten."

The massive cat nudged her head under Emily's arm, purring as she pushed. Then she bit a fold of Emily's sweater and tugged.

"What?" Emily pushed the panther away. "Let's just sit here a while. Okay? I'm tired and feeling sorry for myself. Let me have a little bit of a pout, and then we'll get back to looking for Gryffe and a way out of this place."

Grimalkin grumbled with a low, throaty growl, bit into the sweater again, and pulled harder.

"Stop! You're going to ruin my sweater, and I can't get another one like this." And then the tears bubbled over, fueled by the gutwrenching homesickness that always simmered just below the surface. "Dammit!" She wiped her eyes but cried even harder. "I am not a spoiled brat, you know, I'm just close to my parents. And even when I didn't see them for a while, we talked almost every day, and if not every day, at least once a week. They have always been there for me. Always. And my overbearing brothers. And Jessa. And after I moved to Scotland, Ishbel and Lilias from Seven Cairns." She sobbed harder, covering her face with her hands. "And now I'll never see any of them ever again. I miss them so much. I wish I could go back and hug them all tight—tight enough to never let them go. I'm not used to being so alone."

"Ye're nay alone, lass. Ye have me."

She jerked her head up from her hands, her heart leaping, but then it plummeted at the pain in Gryffe's eyes. The pain she had put there. He had heard her babbling. Every. Last. Word.

He angled his chin higher, but sorrow slumped his shoulders and lent a rawness to his voice. "I wish I were enough for yer happiness, Emily. I am sorry."

When she opened her mouth to explain, he shook his head and held his hand for her to take. "Come. Nicnevin and Ferris search for ye as well. We must let them know ye are found, and that we can exit the Dreaming if it will release us."

CHAPTER 12

Ferris handed Gryffe a glass filled with a generous amount of whisky. "What will ye do?"

"I dinna ken."

"But ye are fated mates. Ye spoke the binding oath."

"*I* spoke the binding oath." Gryffe sipped his drink while keeping his gaze locked on the fire crackling through the logs in the fireplace. "She told me she loved me and repeated *so mote it be.*" His heart had soared at the time...but now?

With a weary groan, Ferris lowered himself into the depths of the other leather chair angled in front of the hearth. "I wonder if the two of ye are not fully bound, then? Do the both of ye have to repeat each word of the vow?"

"Again—I have no knowing about all the feckin' intricacies and rules the powers set for us. All I know is that I felt the binding as soon as I spoke the words, and even stronger when I took her that first time." He shook his head. "I thought she felt the melding, too, but more often of late, it's as though something pulls her away from me." He swirled the golden liquid in his glass, almost mesmerized by the firelight glowing through it. "And then I heard her in the Dreaming. The loss in her voice. The loneliness." He swallowed hard, trying not to choke on the knot of pain threatening to cut off his wind. "She would leave me, if she could. The only reason she is still here is because she is trapped."

Ferris growled and shook his silvery head. "I dinna believe that. I have seen the way she looks at ye—and heard the two of ye in the throes of passion from clear across the loch."

"Satisfying lust does not prove love." Gryffe tore his focus from the fire and turned to study his friend. "Ye ken that well enough. How many times have ye told me that not a single one of yer sons' mothers were yer true fated mate?"

"Perhaps not everyone has a fated mate." Ferris tossed back the rest of his drink and rose for another.

"That is not what the goddesses say," Gryffe said with a wry snort. "Feckin' immortals."

"At least Nicnevin's gone back to the kingdom." Ferris returned but sat on the edge of the seat with his forearms resting on his knees, leaning forward as if about to leap into the fire. "One less worry for ye to deal with, I reckon."

"Aye. One less worry." As if he would grant room in his heart and mind for any worry other than Emily not loving him with all of her being. "Do ye mean to stay here at the keep for a while?"

"If ye wish it."

"I wish it."

"Then it shall be so."

～

"Where is he?" Emily asked.

Gryffe had escorted her to their bedchamber upon their return from the Dreaming and disappeared, slamming the door behind him. She observed Inalfi closely as the maid bustled around the room, tending to whatever endless duties she always did. Knowing the maid hid her thoughts and feelings poorly, Emily counted on

Inalfi's input to help her figure out a way to make things right. She had wounded Gryffe just as surely as if she had stabbed him in the heart with a jagged blade, and that had not been her intent.

The Dreaming had reduced her to a sobbing, babbling mess, spouting an exaggerated rant that needed to be ignored. In time, she would adjust to this reality, and accept this place as home. If not, she would learn to live with it. After all, what choice did she have? The only thing she knew for certain was that she truly loved Gryffe, and she needed him to understand that she loved him above all else. "Inalfi? Where is Himself?"

The maid didn't turn and look at her as she usually did whenever speaking. Instead, she kept her gaze locked on the open drawer of the dresser. "I believe Himself is in his solar, my lady, entertaining Commander Ferris."

Her back against the headboard in the middle of the abundance of pillows that Gryffe loved, Emily hugged her knees and chewed on her bottom lip, ruminating about the mess she had made by succumbing to a bout of overly emotional homesickness. But in her defense, even though Gryffe was like the last missing piece of her personal puzzle, that didn't mean her feelings about her family and friends could just be flipped off like a light switch. She wished he could understand that, but even more, she wished he would give her a chance to explain.

She scrambled out of the bed. "I am going to go talk to him. Don't wait up." She could change out of her twenty-first century clothes and into her nightclothes all by herself.

"Ye will not be able to enter the solar," the maid called out before Emily even reached the door.

"What's that supposed to mean? Has he placed guards at the door to keep me out?"

Inalfi finally looked up from the stockings she was rolling into neat little wads and tucking into the drawer. "Wards, my lady. Not guards."

Emily stared at her in disbelief. "Wards? As in...like...magical stuff that blocks evil? He thinks I'm evil?"

"Ye wounded him, my lady. Mortally so."

"You think I'm evil, too." Emily could see it in the maid's eyes. Gone was every last ounce of affection, admiration, or friendship that had ever been there, replaced with chilling disdain.

Defeated and now even more isolated, Emily hissed out a heavy sigh, but she had to admire the girl's loyalty to her chieftain. "I suppose I can't really blame you. You only tolerated me because he ordered you to—I am really sorry, Inalfi."

She snatched up her hiking boots from where they were drying on the hearth, put them on, and yanked the laces tight while reviewing her dwindling options. It was time to go. She didn't know where, but she couldn't stay here. Everything was falling apart, and she had ripped the proverbial seams wide open all by herself—yet again. She should've handled things better. If she bundled up and got far enough from the keep to protect it from harm, she could work on her spells until she shot herself somewhere else. Hopefully home. At least if she started any fires, they would stave off the cold, wintry weather. She had lost her cloak in the Dreaming, so she pulled the extra blanket off the foot of the bed and tied it around her shoulders.

After a long moment of staring at the angry maid still rolling stockings and shoving them in the drawer, she decided just to leave without saying anything more. In Inalfi's eyes, she had betrayed and unnecessarily hurt Gryffe and damned if the petite little firecracker wasn't right. She swept out the door and charged down the hallway.

Grimalkin loped after her and shook the place with a thunderous roar, the likes of which Emily had never heard the cat make before. She spun around and pointed at the panther. "If you want to come with me, then come, but no more of that noise. All right?"

The monstrous beast roared again, baring her fangs as if warning that she was about to attack.

Gryffe exploded into the hallway with his sword drawn, appearing ready to unleash the powers of hell. His eyes narrowed when he caught sight of her. "What is this? Why are ye not in yer nightclothes? In bed?"

"Do not talk to me like I am a child up past my bedtime." She gathered the heavy wool blanket more regally around her, fighting to gather up every last shred of composure she could pull together. "I wanted to come talk to you, but it came to my attention you had placed magical wards around your solar to keep me out." She wouldn't rat out Inalfi. The loyal Fae maid deserved better than that.

"I shall be heading to the watchtower," Ferris said as he sheathed his sword and passed behind Gryffe, shoving around him to disappear into the nearest stairwell.

Gryffe just stood there, glaring at her with a dark, unreadable expression. The muscles in his squared jaw flexed enough to make the dark richness of his closely trimmed beard seem to ripple in the hallway's torchlight.

She jutted her chin higher, determined to stay strong and be the voice of reason. "Well?"

"Well, what?"

"Can we sit down and have a conversation? Clear the air between us?" She needed him to say *yes*. He had no idea how badly she needed him to agree, and to really listen and forgive her for being such a sentimental, sobbing mess. "Please?"

He pulled in a deep breath, making his broad chest swell even broader, then he sheathed his sword, bowed his head, and motioned for her to enter his sanctuary.

"Don't you have to deactivate the wards or something?"

With a weariness and sorrow that pulled at her to comfort him, he slowly shook his head. "There are no wards, my precious one. I would never block ye from coming to me. Not ever."

So, Inalfi had lied. Wasn't that lovely? With the now quite smug panther at her side, Emily drew in a deep breath of her own and entered the solar, or the chieftain's lair, as she had come to call it because the room was unmistakeably male from its dark wood paneling, rich leather furniture, to its weaponry and shields on the

walls. Suppressing a nervous shiver, she went to the pair of sump-
tuous chairs in front of the massive stone fireplace and took a seat.
Grimalkin stretched out on the hearth and promptly went to sleep.
Apparently, her roaring fit had worked as she had wished, and now
she was going to celebrate with a nap.

"Would ye drink anything?" Gryffe asked as he closed the door.

Not normally a drinker, she wondered if a glass of wine might
help level out her nerves. "Do you have any wine or something not as
lethal as whisky?"

"Aye."

She clenched her teeth and blinked against the sting of tears. No.
She would not cry even though every word he said, every manner-
ism, screamed of his despondency and pain. She swallowed hard
against the knot of emotions making her throat ache and locked her
gaze on the fire, determined to sit in this room until he understood
and realized she loved him, and that her desire to reunite with her
family didn't diminish that love in any way, shape, or form.

"Yer wine, my lady," he said in a voice so soft and dear she almost
melted.

"Thank you." She hazarded a sip, pleasantly surprised with its
delicate fruitiness and the lack of a hard alcoholic burn. Without
looking at him, she idly ran a finger around the rim of the glass while
concentrating on the golden flames dancing across the popping and
hissing logs. "I found Jessa's dream. Grimalkin and I did."

"Aye?"

"But it disappeared into the fog before I could talk to her. I
figured one of the babies probably woke her. I guess maybe that's
how the Dreaming works."

He didn't comment.

She took another sip of the ruby liquid, parsing it out to make the one
glass of wine last forever. "When you found me, I was upset because I
had missed my chance to let her know I was all right, so she could relay
that to my family and friends." She risked a glance at him and wished she

hadn't. Never had he seemed so...so... Her heart swelled with an inde-scribable ache for him. The fire set his strong, solemn profile aglow as he sat there staring at it, clutching his glass of whisky propped on the wide, padded arm of the chair. "Whenever I get upset and finally disintegrate into a sobbing session, I say stupid things that are better off ignored."

Without looking her way, he heaved a great sigh. "Ye long for yer family. For yer world. If ye were nay trapped here, ye would have left me long ago and never returned. Ye as much as said so in the Dream-ing." Ever so slowly, he dragged his gaze from the fire and settled it on her. "Where ye wish to go, I can never follow. I belong to this world and can never live in another, other than through a portal to a different Seven Cairns or viewing those worlds or times through the Dreaming. Even then, I must stay within Seven Cairns' borders or cease to exist. Only females may travel freely among the planes sepa-rated by the Highland Veil because they are the life bringers—the divine mothers." He eyed her as if seeing her for the first time. "I believe the reason ye find yerself trapped here is because ye have denied the entirety of our bond. I can think of no other reason why the goddesses would not allow ye to leave this place. The Veil needs the strength of our union—our strong, complete union. Not just a few broken pieces."

"I do not want to leave here."

"Dinna lie to me, love." He returned to staring at the fire and sipped his whisky.

"I am not lying. I don't want to leave this place. Not permanently. I simply want to see my family and friends. Be able to visit them once in a while. Jessa is allowed to visit twenty-first century Seven Cairns whenever she wishes." Holy cripes. She sounded like a petulant teenager, and she hated herself for it.

Gryffe sat there, silent as a stone.

She had to make him see. "You have known I was homesick, and you said you understood. Why is this hurting you so much now?" She pointed at the fire as if it were a portal to her world. "Just because I want to visit them doesn't mean I don't love you. I would always come back. Always."

"On the day of my birth, Nicnevin left me here. Never to return. Never to see if I lived or died. She claimed she left because she had foreseen my father's death in an upcoming war and could not bear to live through that and experience it firsthand. That war did not take place until I was a man grown and strong enough to wield a sword at my father's side. Only recently did she reappear in my life for reasons only known to herself. I never expected to meet the woman who bore me. Not ever." He took another sip of his whisky, then slowly shook his head, his gaze still locked on the fire. "I understood yer missing those ye loved, mourning them, and yer way of life before ye came here. But as the days passed, yer mourning, that *homesickness* as ye call it, took ye over with the relentlessness of a demon determined to possess ye completely and steal ye away. I tried to ignore it, hoping our love would someday be enough. From what ye said in the Dreaming, I now fear that will never be." He shrugged and bowed his head. "I canna force ye to commit fully to all that we are and might become. All I can do is resign myself to yer leaving as soon as ye find a way to do so."

She was at a complete loss. She had never felt so loved and adored, nor so abandoned and confused in all her life. Setting her wine on the table, she scooted back deeper into the chair and pulled her feet up after her. Arms around her knees, she cocooned herself in the blanket. "Have you never said something you wished you hadn't when your emotions took hold of you? Something that could easily be misunderstood?"

"No."

She blew out a heavy sigh. "Then you are a rare beast indeed."

Grimalkin lifted her head.

"Not you. Him."

The massive cat yawned, then went back to sleep.

"I am sorry your mother abandoned you." She wished her psychiatrist mother were here. Mama would know what to say to help him realize that just because the first woman in his life had tossed him aside, that didn't mean every woman would. "Just because she did that doesn't mean I am going to abandon you."

He took a long, slow sip of his drink, then scowled straight ahead, narrowing his eyes as if his thoughts pained him. "Ye say ye would never abandon me, yet once ye returned to yer world, time would slip through yer fingers, and ye would be gone from me for far longer than ye ever intended—maybe even a lifetime."

Emily went still as the hard, bitter truth hit her. How many times had she *meant* to call her mother, only to put it off until far longer than the *once a week* she had faithfully committed to had flown out the door? She'd lied to herself in the Dreaming. Yes, she was close to her parents, but she wasn't always the dutiful daughter who called them regularly like she should. Time slipped away. Just like Gryffe described.

She had been the same with Jessa, but it hadn't been as much of a crisis because Jessa did it too. Each of them got busy with *stuff* that ate up the hours, the days, sometimes even the weeks. Whenever they finally got back together, they apologized to each other, laughed it off, and promised to do better—but then, they never did. Was that her? Was that the way she really was? Was Gryffe right to be so convinced that she would leave him and never return? The only answer that came to mind was a sadly shameful *yes to all the above.*

"I am sorry," she whispered as a tear burned its way down her cheek. She remembered whenever Jessa put her off that the waiting had felt like forever, but when she put Jessa or her parents off, it felt like only a few minutes had passed. *Pining away* her mother had called it when scolding her for not calling and making them worry. What a terrible way to show someone just how little they mattered.

She wiped her eyes with the back of her hand and curled into a tighter ball of despondency, staring at the fire, her mind surprisingly still and at a loss for a solution. Trying to leave wouldn't make things any better, and yet, neither would staying. And even though she'd not found a way to reconnect with her loved ones and her world, something told her that from this day forward, he would never let down his guard. He would always be waiting for her to leave at her first opportunity. The waiting would squat between them like a greasy black poison.

Damn, she loved him like she had loved no other. Then a realization hit her, sowing a hearty dose of misgivings that made the wine in her stomach churn. Gryffe loved her with an intensity that bordered on the obsessive. He'd often whispered in the darkness, after their loving, that their fated bond was all consuming and burned with a fury. Yes, she loved him too, but didn't live in constant fear of losing him. Was something wrong with her? Or was it because she had learned to wall a part of herself off, protect that little piece of herself so she could nurture herself back into being just in case...Had her long ago abandonment and then the loss of the baby taught her to shield herself at all costs? Holy cripes, was she that big of a hypocrite? Judging him for allowing the abandonment by his mother when he was born effect his life now?

Damn, I wish Mama was here to analyze me and tell me what to do.

It all comes down to trust, her mother had once said. *Love is easy. Trust is the tricky part because it makes you vulnerable.*

And there it was in a nutshell. She loved Gryffe with all her being, but she didn't trust him not to hurt her as she had been so badly hurt before. Yes, she was a hypocrite. Judging him for his abandonment that made him hold her tighter, while using her abandonment to keep him at arm's length. What a pair of fools. Both were afraid of being hurt again, and only Gryffe was the brave one willing to take that chance and fully commit. Or at least, he had been willing to fully commit until overhearing her pitiful rant. She had to let go and trust him or be miserable. It was her choice, and she heard those words in her mother's voice. A warmth at that realization rushed through her. *Thanks, Mom.*

She rose from the chair and pushed her way into his lap, curling up with her head on his shoulder. After an awkward moment of hesitation, he wrapped an arm around her and pressed a kiss to her forehead.

"I am sorry I hurt you," she whispered.

He didn't answer, just shifted with a heavy sigh, then took another sip of his whisky. But he kept his arm around her, even hugged her a little tighter. So there was that.

"I don't ever want to go to the Dreaming again," she said and meant it. Maybe someday the Weavers would find her. Maybe not. Either way, it was time for her to learn to trust and to fully commit. "Not ever," she said, hoping it would nudge him into responding.

"Aye, 'tis a terrible place," he finally said, "better left to the Dream Weavers and the immortals."

This conversation, this clearing of the air between them, was not going as she had wished. Apologies weren't making any headway with him, and sitting in his lap had done little to convince him that she really was sorry. A possibility, a way to prove she was ready to fully commit, and he was really and truly stuck with her, came to mind. "You said Nicnevin would want us to have a ceremony even though we already took the binding oath. Right?"

He took another slow sip of his whisky, tempting her to take the glass away and set it aside. "Aye."

"I think a ceremony is a good idea. Even though you and I know we are bound, it would be an outward display to show everyone else." She held her breath, counting his heartbeats as she waited for a response.

He started to lift his glass, apparently realized it was now empty, then set it on the table beside his chair. "Ye want a ceremony?" His leeriness and disbelief was impossible to miss. It stung, but she refused to give up.

"Yes. I want a ceremony—not some big elaborate something that costs a lot of money or uses resources we shouldn't waste since winter's setting in. But something where everyone could come and see that we mean it."

"See that we mean it," he repeated.

She pushed herself upright and looked him in the eyes. "I do *mean* it, and this time, I am not holding anything back. I know I love you. I just have to learn to trust you, and a ceremony would be a good kickoff."

"Kickoff?"

"A good start. A beginning. An affirmation."

His dark brows slowly drew together, furrowing his brow. Genuine confusion filled his face. "Why would ye not trust me?"

"Because the last time I trusted a man, I got pregnant, and he left me." She hoped that was a flicker of realization in his eyes—the realization that she feared being abandoned just as much as he did, but simply handled it differently.

"And that mistrust made ye protect yerself and hold on to the safety of family and friends ye might never see again."

She allowed herself a heavy sigh of relief before snuggling against his chest once more and resting her head on his shoulder. She was suddenly very, very tired. "Exactly."

The hollow ache under her breastbone, the heavy knot of worry she had carried since spelling herself into this place was still there, but maybe now that she knew it for what it was, she could deal with it like an annoying case of heartburn—at least until she finally worked through everything and moved on. And work through it, she would. After all, the choice to be happy or miserable, whatever her circumstances, was hers to make.

CHAPTER 13

E mily slowly rose from the depths of a lovely, delicious sleep and became aware of Gryffe's warm, callused hand resting low on her bare stomach. His fingers were splayed wide as if to keep her from floating up into the night, and every now and then, they would gently flex in a caress meant to be tender so as not to wake her.

The candle on the mantel had burned out so the only light in the room was that of the full moon peeping in through the window. Its light shone across the bed, setting them both aglow with an eerie blue-white luminescence. He whispered something, or at least, she thought he did. He was so quiet, and she was still so delightfully lethargic from their make up sex that she didn't know for sure.

"Did you say something?" she asked, speaking softly in case he was asleep, and she had imagined him talking.

He kissed her shoulder and whispered, "I think we made a bairn."

Still so nicely groggy, she kept her eyes closed and smiled. "If we didn't, it wasn't for the lack of trying." He had masterfully re-energized her in the solar with kisses that had kindled *all* her fires. After they'd christened every piece of furniture in that room, he had carried her back to the bedroom, and they'd blessed every level spot, and a few not so level spots in *that* chamber as well. "But we won't know for a while. My time is not due for at least another week or so." And she wasn't looking forward to it since what she had seen of feminine products in this century was appalling.

He shifted, propping up on his elbow to peer at her. "Yer time? Ye mean yer courses?"

"Uhm...yes." Seems like she remembered Jessa calling them that after living in her eighteenth century for a while. "And my timetable is fairly reliable." Well, at least it always had been, thanks to the dedication of taking her pills every day, but she'd been without her prescription since arriving here. Surely, she wouldn't be likely to get pregnant right away. The thought both excited and terrified her. Her last pregnancy had broken her heart. "Did you have a dream or something that made you think that we'd started a baby?"

He frowned down at her, his scowl handsome and somber in the moonlight. "Can ye not hear the wee one's song? Feel its soul stretching and dancing, even?"

So comfortably warm and contented that she never wished to move, she closed her eyes again. "Snuggle closer and go back to sleep. It was a dream."

"Hmmpf."

She smiled at the indignance in his growly huff. "Have I insulted you, my chieftain?"

"We started a bairn this verra night, and ye refuse to believe me."

He was entirely serious. She heard it in his voice. "Is this a fairy thing?" she asked, then inwardly cringed. "I mean...a *Fae* thing?"

He lovingly placed his hand on her stomach again. "I dinna ken. I only know what I know, and I know I hear new life in yer womb—the life of our child."

The excitement and depth of his sincerity made her heart ache and swell with more love than she had ever felt before. She pulled him down to rest his head on her chest and laced her fingers into his hair. "I love you more than you will ever know," she whispered, "and I hope what you say is true—but if it is, I am afraid, and you know why."

He shifted and pulled her into a comforting, protective embrace. "Our bairn is strong and will have met yer sweet Cara before coming to us. All will be well, my love. I swear it."

She hoped he was right. With all her heart, she hoped he was right, because other than him, she had no one in this time and place that she could lean upon and trust to get her through this should something go wrong. Inalfi had lied to her, and she had trouble getting past that.

"Ye dinna believe me," he said softly. "I hear the doubt whirring through ye."

"Overcoming fear is kind of like eating an entire elephant. At one bite at a time, it takes a while to finish it off."

"What is an elephant?"

"An enormous animal that is about three times the size of your horse."

"Ahh."

"And I have no one here other than you—not that you're not enough—but I have no *female* friends. No one to talk to. Like you have Ferris when you need to talk to someone to work through your problems."

"Ye have Inalfi. As yer personal maid, ye should be able to speak with her about anything. She considers yer confidence sacred."

She clenched her teeth, unwilling to *tattle* through implication any more than she already had. Inalfi's current behavior stemmed from loyalty to him. Something for which the maid should not be punished. "Let's just go back to sleep. I'm sure you're right. It'll be fine. I'll just make a point to mingle more with the women of the clan. I am sure I'll make friends." She sounded like a nervous kid trying to fit in at a new school, for good reason. She had met several ladies of the clan, but they all seemed leery about getting too close to the chieftain's *one.*

He rolled away from her, left the bed, and lit a fresh candle on the mantel. Then he stood at the foot of their bed, magnificent in his nakedness, and gave her a stern look. "Tell me. Now."

"Tell you what?"

"Ye ken verra well *what*. We will not be sleeping until ye tell me what has happened between yerself and yer maid that makes ye unable to look upon her as not only a servant but a confidante and companion."

"Nothing has happened," she lied and immediately regretted it because his glower darkened.

Arms folded across his irresistible chest, he paced back and forth at the foot of the bed like a war general planning a major attack. "Would ye care to answer my question again, my love? Preferably with the truth this time?"

"Inalfi is very protective of you. As she should be." There. Maybe that would satisfy him.

"Protective how?" He jutted his chin higher, studying her with a look that made her nervous. His head slowly tilted to the side, and his eyes narrowed. "When ye came to find me in my solar, ye mentioned wards set to keep ye out. Who put that worry into yer head?"

She tugged the covers up to her chin, rolled over onto her side, and adjusted her pillow. "Come to bed. I'm cold."

"Inalfi lied to ye, and now, ye dinna trust her."

Doing her best to hide any reaction to his irritating accuracy at reading her, Emily closed her eyes and wiggled deeper into the pillows. "Come to bed."

Suprisingly, he did just that, sliding under the covers and curling his warmth around her. "At first light, I shall have her removed and returned to the kingdom. Grennove's assistant, Breenoa, can attend ye until we find a maid better suited to serve ye."

"No."

"No?"

"No—I don't want her punished for being loyal to you. She was angry with me for hurting you in the Dreaming. Just leave her alone." Unless Inalfi didn't want to be her maid anymore? Maybe she didn't like her. Maybe she never had. The young Fae woman had often struggled with understanding her. "I'll ask her if she wants to go. If she does, then she can go of her own free will. Not because she's fired."

"Fired?"

"Dismissed."

"Ahh." He kissed the back of her shoulder. "Why do ye care about what the maid wants or needs? Especially after she lied to ye?"

"Because she is a person. She matters."

"She does not matter when she betrays ye and causes ye to feel even more isolated."

"Give me a chance to work it out with her. Please?"

He curled tighter around her and kissed her shoulder again. "On one condition."

"What?"

"I will be kept informed."

"I promise." She wiggled back against him and hugged his arms tighter around her. "Now, go to sleep."

EVEN BEFORE OPENING HER EYES, Emily sensed something was wrong— or at least, very *different*. Without moving and doing her best to appear still deep in slumber, she listened and reached out with her senses as Ishbel had tried to teach her so many times. She had never managed it that well before. But this time, she fully intended to conquer the elusive ability.

Rustling. The rustling of purposeful steps. It had to be Inalfi bustling about the room. She always came in after Gryffe rose and went out to do whatever he did so unbelievably early every morning. But there was something else.

Emily centered herself by counting her slow, deep breaths, then envisioned the bedchamber, searching it with her inner sight as well as what made its way to her ears. The hushed yet sharp thud of drawers, the abrupt click of the wardrobe's door, and the hurried thump of the water pitcher tattled on Inalfi's current frame of mind. No surprise there. Although how the maid couldn't possibly know that her chieftain and his lady had set things right—Emily's cheeks flushed hot. There had a been a few times where they had gotten *very* loud. The entire keep had to of heard them *making up*.

She didn't relish the idea of speaking to Inalfi and asking her if she wanted to leave, but if she didn't do it first thing, Gryffe would do it for her. Rather than open her eyes and start the day with that unpleasant task, she kept them shut and continued sweeping the room with her senses. Was she procrastinating? Yes. But only for a little while.

Then an odd brightness caught her inner eye. It was beside the window, but there wasn't sunshine beaming into the room. That was impossible. That window faced the west. And the faint tinkling of metal against porcelain—a spoon in a teacup, maybe? Ishbel would be so proud of her for getting this far without giving up and popping open her eyes.

"Our lady will wish to bathe this morning," a lilting voice, the voice of a woman, said. "But tell the lads to bring plenty of cool water along with the hot. Too hot of a bath will not be permitted for our lady in her condition."

Emily almost gave herself away with a groan. Apparently, Gryffe had put the word out that they were expecting. Was he really that certain? More importantly, was he accurate?

"Aye, m'lady," Inalfi said in a subdued tone. "I shall see to it immediately."

My lady? Emily couldn't remember Inalfi addressing anyone but her that way. The bedchamber door creaked, then thumped shut.

"She is gone now, Lady Emily," the unknown woman said, her lilting voice made even more musical with amusement. "And she does wish to stay, if ye so choose to allow her to do so."

Holding the bedclothes to her chest to hide her nakedness, Emily pushed herself up in the bed and scooted back against the headboard. The unexplainable light she had sensed was the woman sitting at the table in front of the window. Even though her apparel was an overskirt and jacket of wool dyed in subdued tones of burgundy and gray with a fichu of white at her throat and lacy white cuffs peeping out of her sleeves, the lady emitted an inexplicable luminance. Maybe it was her silvery blonde hair or the otherworldly creaminess of her complexion, but she seemed to *glow*, for lack of a better word.

"Uhm…" Emily inwardly cringed at her lack of hospitality, even if this was her bedroom that the stranger had invaded. "Since you already seem to know who I am…uhm…who are you?"

The woman laughed, her gleaming smile as sparkling and filled with light as the rest of her. "Forgive me, m'lady. I am Tayda, the Bright. Sent by the beneficent Queen Nicnevin to be yer lady-in-waiting. Formerly, I was a courtier for the beloved queen and pleased her greatly. Her Majesty felt I might bring ye the same comfort and companionship I provided to her."

"It's a pleasure to meet you," Emily said, trying to sound polite and grateful even though she smelled a rat—a rat named Gryffe. Apparently, he had been quite busy not only informing one and all that they might be expecting a child, but also telling his mother that Inalfi had lied, and his wife needed a friend.

Tayda swept toward her with a steaming cup of something that smelled as delicious and tempting as her favorite caramel iced frappuccino from the coffee shop back in Jersey. "Here ye are, m'lady. A special blend I developed long ago. 'Tis one of my favorites."

"Thank you." Emily accepted the cup, breathing in the steamy fragrance that took her back home and made her smile. "It smells wonderful."

Tayda offered her a graceful nod before returning to her seat at the table. "I know ye heard my request for yer bath. I thought it might refresh ye after yer eventful night in the Dreaming and then yer return home to beget the next prince."

Emily choked, coughing on the sip that had gone down sideways. "Beget the next prince?"

"Oh dear. Forgive me." Tayda rushed to her, took away the cup, and rubbed her back. "Do ye need a basin?"

Clearing her throat, Emily shook her head. "No...no...it just went down the wrong pipe. Thank you. I'm fine now." She tried to assume a calm she didn't feel. "Did Gryffe tell you we had made a prince?"

"Oh no, m'lady. As soon as the wee one took hold in yer womb and sang his song, all of Fae heard him and rejoiced that Prince Gryffe had fulfilled the prophecy rather than Prince Roric." She glanced around as if to ensure they were truly alone. "None of us much cares for Prince Roric. He is always so petulant."

Emily stared at the woman, completely at a loss. "I am sorry. I'm going to need a little more information here. Gryffe never said he was a prince. In fact, I believe he mentioned that Nicnevin had chosen Roric as her heir—not Gryffe."

Tayda waved away the words with a laugh that sounded like the clear pinging of fine crystal. "Oh no, m'lady. Queen Nicnevin must bow to the Unseelie prophecy that has always been and always will be. Whichever of her sons found his fated mate first and sired a child, *that* son is heir to the throne of the Dark Fae and his son—or his daughter—is the next prince or princess." Tayda gave Emily her drink once more and pulled a chair closer to the bed. "Children are rare for the Unseelie. 'Tis why our kingdom is sadly dwindling. When yer precious child awakened in yer womb, we all heard him." She smiled. "At least, we believe it is a wee prince. His soul's song was strong like the roar of a mighty beast." She leaned forward with a conspiratorial look. "But I heard the brightest laughter along with that roar. Who knows? Maybe a wee princess decided to come along as well, to ensure her brother behaves."

"Oh my." Emily decided not to try another sip of the drink, fearing she would choke again in case Tayda had any more bombshell revelations. "So, the Fae really can *hear* a child? Even as early as conception?"

"Of course." Tayda looked at her as if amazed that there was ever any doubt.

Trembling, Emily set her drink aside and hugged herself. "A baby."

"Aye." With an understanding nod, Tayda seemed to glow brighter. "Prince Gryffe is more pleased than I have ever seen him. He actually smiled."

Inalfi entered the bedroom, commandeering the lads carrying not only the bathtub but the steaming kettles as well. When she turned and spied Emily, she flew to the side of the bed and dropped to her knees. "Please forgive me for lying to ye, m'lady. I swear it will never happen again."

Uncomfortable with such an overt apology, Emily waved for the maid to stand. "It's all right, Inalfi. You only did it because you were so angry with me for hurting Himself. I know how loyal to him you are."

Eyes still downcast, Inalfi stood there wringing her hands. "I was still wrong to behave so poorly, m'lady, and I am sorry. May I please stay and serve ye?"

"Of course you may. As long as that is what you wish to do. I don't want you to stay if you're not happy here."

"Fate indeed blessed our prince with such a fair minded lady," Tayda said. "Would ye not agree, Inalfi?"

Bowing her head lower, Inalfi backed up a step to include Tayda in her groveling. "A most fair minded wife indeed, m'lady, and I am blessed to have her as a mistress."

While Emily appreciated the apology, the excessive laying it on made her shudder.

"Our lady is chilled," Inalfi said with a snap of her fingers at the lads. "Hie yerselves with the rest of that water. Now!"

Relaxing back into the pillows, Emily breathed a sigh of relief. There was the Inalfi to whom she was accustomed.

Tayda smiled and nodded while reaching for Emily's cup. "Another, m'lady?"

"That would be lovely."

EVEN THE STING of sleet and snow didn't faze Gryffe as he strode along the path atop the skirting wall. He was as warm and contented as if lounging in front of a roaring fire. His precious Emily had committed fully to their bond. If she hadn't, their beloved bairn's soul never would have taken root in her womb so early in their marriage. He almost smiled, silently thanking his father for such determined virility in siring bairns because the Unseelie struggled with procreation and the continuance of their race. Excitement thrummed through him like the wildness of a storm crashing waves against the shore. A wee bairn. His and Emily's child. How would he ever find the patience to wait all those months to hold the babe in his arms?

Eyes narrowed against winter's blasting tempest, he looked out upon his lands as he strolled, then came to a halt and frowned. That light skimming along the base of the mountains—he had only seen such a light once before. A Weaver was coming, the most powerful Weaver of all, from the brightness and hue of that beacon. That did not bode well for this auspicious day. A day when Clan MacStrath and the Dark Fae should know nothing other than celebration. The only time a Weaver, and most especially *this* Weaver, ever traveled past the boundaries of Seven Cairns was if something was terribly wrong, so wrong that the Highland Veil risked falling.

"Ferris!" Gryffe moved faster toward the battlement facing the ridgeline. "Ferris!"

"I see it." Ferris stepped out of the storm's white haze. "'Tis the old one, for sure. Her scent rides on the winds."

"Triple the guard. Whatever news she brings canna be good."

"I already have," Ferris said. "Think ye she comes for yer lady?

From everything shared with us, it seemed as though Lady Emily was their lost mortal."

"And yet none of them knew her when I took her to Seven Cairns." Gryffe bared his teeth, glaring at the light coming ever closer. "They broke her heart that day. I will not give them another chance to put her through such misery, especially not now."

"We canna refuse her entry. Ye ken that as well as I."

"I know." As the light drew ever closer, it split into two glowing orbs. Gryffe tightened his fists, popping every knuckle. "Two feckin' Weavers and one of them, Mairwen. I will not allow them to take her." He turned to Ferris and thumped his chest with his fist. "Even if I must rescind my oath and position as Grand Chieftain of the Defenders. Nothing matters but my Emily and our bairn."

Ferris bowed his head. "I understand."

"More importantly, do ye support me?"

"Aye, I do. Without question."

Gryffe bared his teeth at the orbs, willing them to feel his protective fury. If need be, he would call down the forces of the Unseelie to protect his own. For the first time in his long life, he was thankful for his ancestry. The Dark Fae were renowned warriors.

CHAPTER 14

"What if she refuses?" Ishbel asked quietly as they floated over the rugged, snow covered land, safe from the storm while enclosed in their crystal orbs. "And I still say we shouldha simply folded realities and stepped into their entry hall. Ye know they see us coming, aye? I spied them atop the skirting wall. They have tripled their guard, and knowing the chieftain, the army of the Dark Fae could very well be upon us before we know it."

"And that is exactly why we did not fold our realities and enter MacStrath Castle without warning. We have mishandled this from the verra start and must do better—for Emily's sake and out of respect to Grand Chieftain Gryffe." A sense of despondency filled Mairwen as they drew closer to the fortress. The goddesses had made her see just how poorly she had managed this holy task—all because she had been so overwrought about the loss of her son and the extension of her husband's sentence in Danu's prison. Lúnastal had sorely failed their vows because it had been he who summoned Carmen the witch's sons to the stronghold in hopes of escaping. Their own son's blood was on her husband's hands, and she would never forgive him for their precious Valan's death. As far as she was concerned, their vows were permanently severed, and Lúnastal was as dead to her as Valan.

Ishbel cleared her throat, then squeaked in surprise as the rising wind caused them both to bounce and skitter to one side. "What if she refuses to come with us?" she repeated.

"Bride and Cerridwen said she must come with us for her own safety."

"For her own safety? What does that mean? Is Morrigan afoot? Has Nicnevin turned dark enough to be dangerous to Emily or the Veil?"

With a wave of her hand, Mairwen urged their protective enclosures to skim toward the castle even faster. "The goddesses informed me I would fully understand when I am meant to understand. I assume the same holds true for yerself." That was a lie, but it was all she felt comfortable saying for now.

"If anyone has hurt our Emily—" Ishbel took the lead, her orb now spinning with an angry red glow.

Mairwen understood. However, what Ishbel didn't know or understand was that they were to blame for Emily's misfortune and soon to be misery. They had failed this special mortal by not finding her fated mate first, and blocking the two of them from each other until their next incarnation—an incarnation that would hopefully include neither Weaver blood nor the blood of a Dark Fae in their reborn bodies.

Under no circumstances must a Weaver ever bind with an Unseelie. The goddesses forbade it because only a Weaver's blood possessed the strength to nurture and heal the nearly sterile Unseelie and enable them to procreate. The Dark Fae, while not entirely evil and only a minor threat to the Highland Veil, had caused more trouble across the planes and realities than their existence was worth to the goddesses. Their race needed to die out by natural attrition—so said Bride and Cerridwen and even the mighty Danu herself.

The mother goddesses had decided, in all their mercy, not to war against the Unseelie and destroy them outright. They knew the race's infertility would eventually complete that task for them. In Mairwen's mind, mercy had nothing to do with it. The goddesses were afraid to confront the Dark Fae. They were afraid the Unseelie would turn even darker and actively join the side of chaos and evil that was attempting to take down the Veil. The temperamental Fae of the shadows were just as fearsome and strong as the Morrigan. It would not bode well if they became allies and joined forces with the evil one.

The tall wooden gates of MacStrath Castle slowly swung open as they reached the skirting wall. Once inside the bailey, Mairwen allowed their crystal enclosures to disappear like morning mist touched by the sun.

The winter wind gusted, shoving and pelting them with ice and snow as if to tell them they were not welcome here. Mairwen understood that better than anyone. Emily had bonded with her fated mate. Securing such a bond could at times be a Weaver's most challenging and rewarding task, but separating them—that was nie on impossible and not a task to be relished. But Cerridwen and Bride had left her no choice. The union between Emily and Gryffe had to be severed before they succeeded in creating a child.

Bowing her head against the wind, she gathered her cloak tighter around her throat and led the way into the keep. The immediate warmth and the loss of the wind's cold, forceful shove nearly knocked her off balance. She pushed back her hood and swallowed hard.

Grand Chieftain Gryffe's icy scowl raged with dark fury, leaving no doubt that she and Ishbel were not welcome. She offered a graceful nod, knowing it would not be accepted. "Thank you for allowing us entry, Grand Chieftain."

He stood in front of his chair on the dais at the head of the room, stance wide and hand resting on the black hilt of his mystically lethal Unseelie sword that she knew for a fact he rarely carried. He sneered at her. "As if I had a choice but to allow ye entry."

"One always has choices." She swallowed hard again at the bitter taste of the lie. If one always had choices, she would not be here to sever Emily's union. "We request an audience with Emily Mithers."

"There is no Emily Mithers here." He added a rumbling, low growl and bared his teeth like a cornered beast. The warrior clansmen lining the walls of the cavernous meeting hall did the same, aiming their venom directly at her and Ishbel. Then an ominous silence fell, and the loyal kin returned their focus to their chieftain. Gryffe squared his shoulders. "There is only Lady Emily MacStrath, my wife, this clan's lady, and the mother of my child."

"They haven't been together that long," Ishbel whispered through the Ether, attuning her words so they would only reach Mairwen's thoughts, and the rest of the Weavers would be none the wiser. "How can our Emily already be with child? He is half Unseelie. It should be difficult for them to conceive. Did ye not tell me that must not happen?"

"Hush, Ishbel!" Mairwen thought back at her. "I canna reason with a crowded mind." Forcing a pleasant expression and another nod, she focused on the chieftain. "The mother of yer child? Ye were bound but days ago. Surely, ye have not been blessed so quickly. Forgive me, grand chieftain, but ye must be mistaken."

"Have ye forgotten my ancestry, old one? Ye ken as well as I that as soon as a bairn's soul takes root in the womb of the one we love, the Unseelie hear the child's awakening song."

Knowing the goddesses would not be pleased, Mairwen struggled to keep the situation from devolving further. All life was sacred —even a child born from a Weaver and Unseelie union. "We must speak with her, Grand Chieftain. Her safety depends upon it. So say the goddesses."

"Her safety depends on me." Gryffe jutted his chin higher. "And I assure ye, no harm will ever come to her while I live and breathe." He slowly approached, descending the steps of the dais as if preparing to mow them down with his great sword of darkness. "Yer kind cut her to the quick when ye rejected her at Seven Cairns. I shall not give the two of ye the opportunity to hurt her again." He tossed a harder scowl at Ishbel. "That one there hurt her the most when she backed away from my precious Emily on that day. Treated her as if she were the lowliest of the low."

"Liar! I would never reject my Emily." Ishbel shoved forward as if ready to fight the chieftain with her bare fists.

Taking hold of the Spell Weaver and pulling her back, Mairwen stepped ahead of her, studying Gryffe and searching for signs of deception. "When did ye bring our Emily to Seven Cairns? Someone would have fetched me. I would have felt her presence."

"Not but a day or so after her arrival here. No one in Seven Cairns knew her. Lilias even asked me to take her away. Accused her of being full-blooded Unseelie and not welcome in the pub because it upset the customers."

At a complete loss, Mairwen slowly shook her head. "Full-blooded Unseelie canna cross into Seven Cairns. The wards would never allow it. The only reason you yerself can enter the village is because of yer vow to the Order, and yer father's blood that dilutes the Unseelie's darkness in yer veins."

"He speaks the truth, Mairwen," Emily said from the archway to the right of the dais. "I didn't see you that day, but I saw Ishbel, and she didn't know me. Acted like I had the plague or something. And Lilias acted as if she despised me."

Mairwen's heart fell at the subtle golden glow floating around Emily's middle like a protective halo to guard the new life in her womb. Only another Weaver would be able to detect the telltale change in Emily's aura that guaranteed Gryffe had not been wrong. His beloved Emily was with child, even though her stomach was as flat and trim as the day she disappeared from Seven Cairns.

"It is true," Ishbel whispered through the Ether.

"Be quiet," Mairwen whispered back.

Emily moved to Gryffe's side, and he pulled her closer, drawing his sword for good measure. "My wife is safe with me, old one. Yer kind failed her twice—once by letting a spell tear her away from all she had ever known and loved, and twice by rejecting her. Ye will not be getting a third opportunity to break her heart and fail her again."

Mairwen stared at the pair. The goddesses would not be pleased, and whenever the mighty ones had their wishes denied and cast to the winds, disaster and discord always struck. But if she could convince Emily to return to their world, the child could be hidden and kept safe. The Weavers could guard the secrets of its ancestry with their lives.

But the longer she eyed Emily and Gryffe, the stronger her sense of right and wrong and moral justice balked at that solution. The ancient mothers were not always right or reasonable. Why should their wishes always be granted? Her dreams and wishes had been dashed many a time. And these two hadn't been bound for long, but their union had been strong enough to start a new life. That in and of itself made Mairwen know deep in her heart that Emily and Gryffe needed to be told the truth so they might decide what course of action they wished to take to not only protect each other but to keep their child safe as well.

"Would ye kindly grant us an audience with the both of ye?" she asked. "In private—and might I add that the safety of yer child and yerselves is at risk if ye dinna hear Ishbel and myself out."

Gryffe glared at them for a long, hard moment before turning to Emily. "It is yer decision, my own. But know that I am ever beside ye —no matter what ye decide."

With an anguished look, Emily rested her hand on his chest and looked into his eyes.

Mairwen knew then and there why a child had come to them so quickly. The bond between these two had already grown stronger than most. No wonder the Highland Veil had hummed with such vigor for the past several days. She should have known then that this task would be no simple thing. "Emily? What say ye? I swear it is of the utmost importance. While I admit the Weavers failed ye in many ways, never have we lied to ye."

"Is that so?" Emily said with a wry smile. "You've been known to get pretty creative with the truth at times. I was there for Jessa—remember? In fact, I seem to remember you admitted to lying when you told her you didn't know Grant."

There was that, and leave it to Emily to remember it. Mairwen bowed her head. "I am not lying this time, Emily. Never would I lie when it comes to the safety of a child."

"I cannot lose another baby," Emily said so softly that Mairwen almost didn't hear her.

"We must talk with the both of ye then, child," Ishbel said. "We dinna wish for anything to happen to yer precious wee one either."

Emily looked at Gryffe again and barely nodded.

Keeping his arm protectively around her waist, he tipped a curt but meaningful look at the guard standing off to the side. "Bring them to my solar," he said, then he and Emily disappeared through the archway behind the dais.

"Follow me," the guard instructed.

"Warn the others," Mairwen said to Ishbel through the Ether. "They must not speak a word to the goddesses or any of the Defenders about where we are or what we are doing."

"So shall it be," Ishbel replied as she fell in step behind Mairwen.

Gryffe had never seen himself as one who could take the life of a Divine Weaver with his deadly Unseelie blade—until now. If Mairwen or Ishbel caused his precious Emily any additional distress, he would send their heads back to Seven Cairns in one wagon and their bodies in another. He stood beside his precious one after escorting her to one of the chairs beside the window.

She patted the chair next to her and mouthed, *sit.*

He barely shook his head, then turned as Ferris showed Mairwen and Ishbel into the room. He pointed at the cushioned settee in front of the bookshelves, not caring if he seemed rude. "Seat yerselves and state yer case."

Something thudded against the solar's closed door, then it flew open and banged against the wall. Grimalkin entered, announcing her mood with a thunderous roar before hissing at Mairwen and Ishbel. Then she placed herself in a protective stance in front of Emily.

"This is Grimalkin," Emily told Mairwen and Ishbel. "Nicnevin said she came to me from Fae because she felt it her calling to protect me."

"A Fae panther," Ishbel said, appearing suitably impressed.

Mairwen eyed the beast with a leery expression. "There is no loyalty or unconditional love like that of a Fae panther."

"Why have ye come?" Gryffe asked. This was not a time for pleasantries or visiting. "What is yer claim regarding my Emily's safety, and I assume, the safety of our precious bairn?"

"The goddesses have anxiously awaited eons for the Unseelie to be no more since their ability to bring forth children has all but left their race," Mairwen said. "King Roric was reported to be the last born to them, but there was a rumor he possessed no Unseelie ancestry at all. It was said yer mother saved him from the mortals' home for foundlings." Mairwen's eerily blue eyes glinted with her knowledge of the ages, making Gryffe's skin crawl. "The Weavers validated that rumor, and discovered ye were actually the last child born to the Unseelie."

That had to be a lie, but flashes of Roric's weaknesses and lack of magic throughout his life made Gryffe's gut churn with uncertainty. He stepped forward, moving in front of Emily. Grimalkin rose and stood beside him, softly growling at the Weavers. "I ken well enough that the Unseelie are the dark ones. Prone to wicked mischief and even cruelty at times, but humans are much the same. What gives the goddesses the right to do their damnedest to ensure the Unseelie cease to exist? What gives them the right to threaten the lives of my fated mate and our child?" The Weavers had yet to come out and say that was the true reason for their visit, but he saw it as clearly as if Mairwen had thrown it in his face.

"The goddesses would never harm a child," Ishbel said, but her expression was anything but reassuring.

"No, they would just keep him or her locked up like an oddity at the zoo. Right?" Emily pushed around Gryffe. "No one is taking my baby. No one." She trembled with what smelled like rage. "I thought the Weavers, especially you two, were my friends, my extended family in Scotland. But it appears those of Seven Cairns are nothing more than the goddesses' dogs, ensuring their dirty work is done. I thought you served the Highland Veil? I thought protecting the worlds and joining fated mates was your calling?"

"It is..." Mairwen bowed her head, her shoulders slumping. She turned to Ishbel. "I can make no argument against her words, against a mother's love for her child, against the bond of mates fated to be united. She is right in all she has said."

Ishbel slowly shook her head. "I agree, Mairwen. Never did I think I would live to say it, but the mothers are wrong this time. How can they ask this of us? To take Emily away from her mate and back to her time? Ye know they will demand we surrender the child as soon as they hear its first cries."

Gryffe drew his sword, making the metal ring with a deathly howl as he pulled it from its sheath. "No one is taking Emily or our child. I will call upon the powers of the Unseelie kingdom to join the warriors of my clan in battle against anyone who tries. We will even stand against the mighty Danu herself if need be."

"The goddesses forget that I know their weakness," Emily said, tipping her chin higher to a proud angle. "They are just like Morrigan. They cannot exist if they are not remembered. Believed in. They feed on the thoughts, prayers, and offerings from their precious mortals that they treat like pets. But if those mortals cease to believe and turn them into nothing more than fairy tales..." She wrinkled her nose at Gryffe and offered an apologetic shrug. "Sorry—not fairy tales—but myths and legends. Powerless fantasies, then the goddesses will cease to exist. If they don't leave me and mine alone, we will see to it that no one in this reality, and any other reality I can portal to, ever believes in them again. We will protect the Highland Veil because it protects us. But we will not acknowledge the goddesses' existence if they insist on treating all of creation like their personal breeding ground for lab rats. The Unseelie have as much right to exist as any other race. From what I have seen of them, they are no worse than humans, and we all know what humans are capable of."

Gryffe wasn't certain what *lab rats* were, but caught the gist of his dear one's speech. He thumped the hilt of his sword to his chest. "So let it be spoken. So let it be done. So mote it be."

Nicnevin shimmered into being at his side in her silver and black battle regalia. Her armor devoured any light attempting to make it gleam. Just as suddenly, her personal guard, clad in their war armor, with their softly glowing swords and spears of ebony at the ready, stood at attention along the walls of the room.

"No one threatens my son," Nicnevin said, her voice echoing with the ferocity of a mother's love. "The goddesses might wish to take another count of the Unseelie forces. Our numbers may have dwindled from the elder age of long ago, but we are still many and strong —and we stand united."

For the first time in his life, Gryffe appreciated having his mother at his side. "We will honor our oath to protect the Highland Veil, and I might also add that we wish the Weavers no harm." He strode forward until he stood directly in front of Mairwen. "But I know yer bloodline, old one. I also know yer story and yer pain. Ye understand these things lessen my trusting of ye. Are ye willing to give me yer blood oath? Yer allegiance to me and mine? Or must we declare war against the goddesses here and now?"

As Mairwen rose from her seat, the years seemed to drop away from her, making her appear more vital, stronger, and filled with life. With her gaze locked in his, she held her hand to Ishbel. "The crystal athame, Ishbel."

He sensed Emily at his side as Ishbel rose and produced the Weaver's hallowed blade used in healing, binding, and for initiates seeking to become Defenders. The dagger suffered nothing but goodness and truth. It consumed those seeking to do evil or turn to darkness with lies.

With the blade pointed upward, Mairwen nodded first at Emily, then at Gryffe. "Give me yer hands." Her eyes flared wide with surprise as Nicnevin stepped forward and held out her hand as well.

"I will not allow my grandchildren to believe I did not offer my blood for them," she said, glaring at the Weavers, daring them to deny her this right.

The athame started glowing with a blue white light as though it knew what was about to happen. It hummed even louder and shone even brighter as Mairwen sliced her palm, then cut Nicnevin's, Emily's, and Gryffe's. She held out her bleeding hand, opening it so the other three could hold their wounds over hers and add their blood to hers. Once their blood was mixed, she shared it with them, adding it to the cuts across their palms. Then they joined their hands in unity, pressing their palms together and allowing the blood to stain the floor.

"By our blood, we are bound through all eternity," Mairwen said, "Unseelie, Weaver, and mortal." She bent and touched the tip of the crystal knife to the dark crimson spot on the floor. "A blood oath, a hallowed vow to protect Clan MacStrath, the Unseelie race, the Weavers of Seven Cairns, and above all, the Highland Veil. So let it be spoken. So let it be done. So mote it be."

"So mote it be," Emily and Nicnevin echoed, but Gryffe remained silent.

The old one dared to meet his gaze as she squatted with the knife tip dipped in the blood of their vow. "Grand Chieftain?"

"I want my children and my children's children included in this vow. I want it spoken—not merely implied by mentioning our clan, the Unseelies, or the mortals." He would not bend on this. The wily goddesses were known to find every loophole when it came to breaking vows.

Mairwen nodded and tapped the knife against the floor three

times. "This blood shall also protect any and all children of Grand Chieftain Gryffe and his beloved Lady Emily—and their children's children down through eternity. So let it be spoken. So let it be done. So mote it be." The bloodstain shimmered, seeming to grow and breathe with the addition to the original vow.

"So mote it be," Gryffe said, then fisted his wounded hand tighter so more of his blood would fall and join that on the floor.

Emily did the same. "So mote it be."

CHAPTER 15

Emily drew the heavy shawl closer around her while sitting on the ledge of the large bay window of her sittingroom—a room Gryffe had ordered tailored for her in an astonishingly short amount of time, for when her sanity needed to escape the United Kingdom of Scotland's alternate eighteenth century.

Another winter storm howled across the land, bringing more snow, ice, and bitter cold. A heavy sigh filled with sadness escaped her. Even if Gryffe transported her to Seven Cairns, and she portaled through to the twenty-first century, it was doubtful she could book a flight home for the holidays since the weather was probably doing the same there. And it usually did. That was one thing she had noticed when first arriving here. The weather was the same across the realities. Perhaps nature didn't have time to juggle things any more than it already did.

"I promised Mama and Papa I would be home for Christmas." She scraped the shape of a heart in the thick layer of frost coating the glass, then drew a jagged line through it, breaking it down the middle. Even though a fire roared in the hearth, the room still possessed a noticeable chill. "They are going to be so upset with me. I've disappointed them again."

"Lady Emily, come away from there. Sit here by the fire where it's warm." Tayda gently tugged on her, as if coaxing a toddler or an elderly patient away from the edge of an abyss. "Mairwen and Ishbel swore to have yer Jessa speak with yer parents, so they would not worry. From all ye have told me about Lady Jessa, I am sure everything will be fine. Come spring, ye can visit with all of them in Seven Cairns before the blessed wee one comes this summer. The prince said so, remember?"

Hearing Gryffe referred to as *the prince* still took some getting used to. Emily wondered if they'd made a new enemy in his step brother Roric since the truth of that ancestry had become known. Hopefully not. They didn't need any more enemies than they already had. Besides, Roric still ruled the mortal kingdom of Britannia here on this plane. Hopefully, that would be enough for him.

"My lady—Please?"

To pacify Tayda, Emily rose and meandered closer to the hearth where Grimalkin was stretched her full length in front of the fire.

"Would ye like to paint, perhaps?" Tayda paused by the shelves filled with brushes, parchment, and palettes of dried pigments only needing water to come to life. "Or are ye of a mind to continue yer yarn work? Forgive me, but the word ye called it escapes me."

"Crochet." That activity had brought Emily some comfort, not only bringing back the many happy memories of learning the stitches with her grandmother but also by doing something useful. She had already made several pairs of baby booties in various neutral shades since she didn't know how accurate Gryffe was about insisting she carried a son, and then Tayda smugly argued she carried a son *and* a daughter. With her abs as muscular and flat as always and only a few days past what should've been the onset of her menstrual cycle, she struggled with hoping against hope that she really was pregnant. Believing in the unbelievable was still a work in progress for her. But she'd get it. One way or another, she would get it.

She crouched down beside Grimalkin and scratched the great cat under her chin. "It's a restless sort of day. I can't explain it, but I *feel* like something is about to happen. It's like the air is stretched too tight and about to snap."

Grimalkin rolled to her back, exposing her belly for a good scratching.

"Yer fine cat there would sense if something was wrong, my lady." Tayda fetched a basket from the table beside the door. She seated herself with it in her lap, pawing through the many different colors of yarn within it. "Come see these newest shades the dyers sent up for yer inspection. These threads are quite lovely—maybe ye could make blankets for the wee ones' cradles?"

Emily rose from the floor, ignoring Tayda, and returned to the window. There was something out there making a noise that sounded so familiar—but not. A calling of her name, maybe? A voice she hadn't heard in a very long time, but it was outside in the storm. "Do you hear that?"

"'Tis nothing more than the song of the wind." Tayda held up a skein of yarn. "See here, m'lady. Is this not the prettiest shade of green? 'Tis like meadow grass during the first warming of spring."

Uneasiness washed across Emily, taking her closer to the frosted pane. The broken heart she had scratched into the frost was gone, replaced by a large eye shedding a tear. She stepped back, her vague uneasiness changing to an ominous sense of doom. "Is Gryffe back yet?"

Tayda didn't answer, causing Emily to turn and discover herself alone in a bleak, empty room she didn't recognize. *Don't panic.* Hands fisted against her middle, she swallowed hard and forced herself to pull in a deep breath and then slowly exhale. Shock and fear turned to irritation, that quickly flared into rage. She was so done with being manipulated by forces outside her control.

"I am really getting tired of this shit!" she told the glaringly bright emptiness of the place.

"Allow us to reset ye, child," said a trio of women's voices that echoed as if they were talking inside an empty bucket to try to sound even more ominous. "All will be well, and ye willna recall a thing—all yer painful memories will be gone."

"No."

"No?"

Emily slowly turned, eyeing the area that suffered from a complete lack of color. "No, is my final answer. Is that not plain enough for you?" She had a pretty fair idea of whom she was dealing with, but couldn't tell for sure. She'd never studied pagan religions and their gods and goddesses all that much. She only knew them from a book about Scottish legends she'd read back at Seven Cairns and her firsthand experience with the vile Morrigan. "Put me back where I belong. I promise you'll regret it if you don't. I know you know about the blood vow."

Laughter filled the air like soft music. It was not taunting or cruel, merely amused. "We dinna mean ye harm, child. We merely offer ye relief from the pain of yer past and protection from the pain of yer future."

"Everyone has pain. That's what makes us who we are. How we use it makes us stronger." Her mother had told her that once. Right after the miscarriage. Emily had thought it sounded pretty hokey back then, but now? Now, not so much. She finally understood the truth of it. Everything she'd been through, everything that had touched her—be it good or bad—had prepared her for now. Prepared her to fight. "Your offer is weak for those who call themselves mothers," she told the voices. "Would you choose to forget your children just because they caused you pain? I never want to lose the memory of holding my sweet daughter in my arms. Send me home. Now."

"Why should we?"

"Why shouldn't you?" She could play their stupid, cryptic games just as easily as they could. "I'm just a mortal, remember? Gone from the earth in the blink of an eye by your standards. No wonder you don't care about us. We don't live long enough for you to get attached. We're like goldfish that you continuously flush down the toilet."

Deafening silence filled the strange formless space, making her stick her fingers in her ears and swallow hard to pop them. "Gryffe will come for me. So will Nicnevin."

"Ye should have never bound yerself to him, child. Him and his kind bring nothing but sorrow."

"The same could be said of many *kinds* that populate the worlds. That doesn't mean any one kind is better than the other or deserves a better shot at surviving."

"Ye dinna love him."

"You are wrong about that, and you know it."

"We created ye. We created him. We ken well enough who ye should love and who ye should not."

"My heart tells me who I love—not you or any other myth or legend."

"Ye canna bear this child."

"I can, and I will." Emily jutted her chin higher. How dare they threaten her baby.

"Ye canna bear this child—and live. Ye will never survive the birth."

"Is that your latest scare tactic?" She refused to flinch or show any weakness. "You're going to have to do better than that. I don't fear you, but you should fear me."

"What harm could ye possibly bring to us?"

"Disbelief. I have learned not to believe in just anything." Emily turned in a slow circle, then stopped. The disconcerting whiteness, the inability to tell the walls from the floors and the floors from the ceiling of the room made it hard to keep her balance. It was like floating in a bank of clouds. "If no one believes in you, you cease to exist. Have you failed to notice I refuse to even say your names, even though I know who you are? The Dreaming taught me that. What I *believe* in is real. What I don't believe in—is not."

"Ye are but one mortal of millions and millions."

"But how many mortals from my original time truly believe you are anything more than a myth? I know some worship you, but not nearly as many as there once was, or as many as I am sure you wish there were. What would happen, how many fewer still would believe in you, if Jessa and I concentrated on erasing your names from history? How would that affect your believers in the future?"

"Ye will not survive the birth of this child."

"All that matters is that my child lives. Gryffe will be an adoring father, and I am sure Nicnevin will be a doting grandmother." Already feeling more certain that all would be well, Emily stood taller. "If I can't see my babies in this life, then I shall see them in the next."

Whisperings, the disjointed hissing of words flowing fast and frantic, flittered through the eerie whiteness like annoying gnats, buzzing to be noticed.

Emily strained to capture the words, understand them, and decipher the goddesses' plot. Time to poke the bear and make them roar so she could hear them. "I thought you three were supposed to be the good ones. The ones devoted to the strength and continuance of the Highland Veil? From what I have seen so far, you are little better than Morrigan. Yours is just a more subtle form of evil manipulation."

Silence fell, but they weren't gone. She could *feel* them fuming. Time to poke them again. "The one true God, the Supreme Creator, the Great Spirit, put the Highland Veil in place, didn't He? What does that make you three, then? Fallen angels or something just *claiming* to be goddesses so mortals will notice you and give you the attention you seek like toddlers tugging on their mother's skirts?"

"We could make ye no more at this verra minute," the trio of voices said, still speaking as one.

Emily nodded and squared her shoulders. "You could—but you

won't. What's your angle? You're afraid of something. What is it? I know you're afraid of being forgotten, but there's something else too. I smell it."

"Sleep until ye learn some respect!"

~

"PLEASE OPEN YER EYES, MY LOVE." Gryffe barely touched Emily's face, watching her long dark lashes, longing for them to flutter and give him hope.

But she remained as still as she had been when Lady Tayda and Grimalkin had sounded the alarm and brought everyone to the sitting room where Emily had collapsed.

Nicnevin hovered close on the other side of the bed. "This is no sickness, my son. The mothers pull at her. See how she keeps her hands closed into fists and her jaw strong and tight? Our Lady Emily battles them. Hold fast to her and give her yer strength."

"They will not take her from me." He gently brushed her dark mane of wild curls back from her face. She had undone her braids for him, revealing an abundance of long, silky coils that he couldn't resist. He leaned forward and pressed a kiss to her forehead, lingering to breathe her in and will her to feel his love. "Fight them, my dear one. Fight yer way back to me."

"I never realized the mother goddesses bore the Unseelie so much hatred and prejudice." Nicnevin settled into a chair close to the bed, perching on the edge of its seat. Her scowl puckered even harder as she shook her head. "We are dark, that is undeniable, and full of mischief that sometimes turns wicked. But for the most part, those we visit our cruelty upon, earned it." She released a heavy sigh, then offered him a sad smile. "She holds tightly to the child and protects it. Hear its song?"

"Aye, I hear the wee one singing." Gryffe rested his head on Emily's middle and closed his eyes, drinking in the light airy song, as tender and lilting as a gentle breeze making a leaf dance across the grass. Then another song joined in, a different melody that harmonized with the first. He sat up straight and stared at his motionless wife. "Lady Tayda was right. There are two."

Nicnevin leaned forward and rested her hand on Emily's shoulder. "A good omen, indeed. She is stronger with a pair of Unseelie bairns in her womb." She patted Emily's hand. "Fight on, my fearless daughter. We are with ye."

She rose, rounded the bed, and brushed a kiss to Gryffe's cheek. "I will see if the Weavers have arrived yet. Their strength will help her, too."

He nodded without taking his gaze from his precious wife. The soft click of the door told him it was just himself and Emily warring against the unseen forces that kept her as still and lifeless as a corpse. He took her cold hand in his and slowly shook his head. "I dinna ken why they have done this to ye, my love. I've bent to their every feckin' whim in service to the Highland Veil." He kissed her hand, then pressed it to his cheek. "Even the Unseelie have left them be for the most part. I dinna understand it."

"It is Emily herself who worries them, my chieftain," Mairwen said from the doorway. She came closer, her silvery head barely tipped to one side as she studied Emily. "It is Emily's bloodline they fear."

"Fear?"

"Aye." The matron went to him, rested a hand on his shoulder, then took Emily's hand out of his and held it. "Her great-great grandmother was the most powerful Spell Weaver ever to exist." She gently squeezed his shoulder. "And do ye know why?"

"Just tell me, old one. I am too weary for more games." Gryffe tensed, bracing himself for whatever Mairwen was about to share.

"Because she is like me, grand chieftain." Mairwen took her hand away from his shoulder, but kept hold of Emily as if determined to keep her from drifting away. "Emily's great-great grandmother Esme was born from Cerridwen's forbidden tryst with the Seelie king of the Seventh Realm. As a babe, Esme was ordained a Weaver and taken to the hallowed grounds of Seven Cairns to protect her from the Seelie queen's jealous rage."

Gryffe stared at Mairwen, fighting to come to grips with what she had just said. "Ye are telling me my Emily possesses no Weaver blood in her ancestry—"

"Oh, she has Weaver ancestry because Esme fully embraced and became a Weaver—much as I have," Mairwen said. "But yer Emily also descends from Cerridwen, the mighty Seelie king of the Seventh Realm, and some extraordinary mortals."

"Has Cerridwen no heart, then? No caring for her own?" Gryffe rose, ready to call down the fickle goddess and demand she face him in battle. He pointed at Emily. "She is of her blood. The bairns she carries are of her blood."

"The bairns she carries are also of the Unseelie," Mairwen said so quietly that a chill raced across him. "It is the strengthening of the dark ones they fear. This will be the first time Seelie and Unseelie become one."

"The Dark Fae are no worse than the goddesses themselves are." He pushed away from Mairwen and paced the width of the room, no longer able to remain still. Pointing at Emily, he bared his teeth. "We would never do this to our own blood, and the Unseelie kingdom was overjoyed when they heard the wee ones' songs at their creation."

Mairwen seated herself in the chair beside the bed and gently arranged Emily's long, dark curls across the pillows. "I make no defense of the mother goddesses. They cost me my child and my mate. My only allegiance is to the Highland Veil and joining fated mates in search of their other halves to keep the Veil strong and the realms separated. Only the Veil has kept its purity and goodness throughout the ages."

"Tell me how to steal her back. Tell me how to reach them."

The old one's heavy sigh weighed down his hopes. "If they have taken her to the in-between, there is no way for us to get to her.

"Like hell." Gryffe paced faster, opening and closing his fists.

"There has to be a way, and I mean to find it. Even if it means waging war against the Highland Veil itself."

Mairwen gasped. "Dinna speak such blasphemy!"

He pointed at his wife. "All that matters to me is her—her and our bairns. If the goddesses force my hand, I will fully embrace the darkness of my Unseelie blood and make all creation pay."

A flash of light blinded him. He shielded his eyes from the painful whiteness, struggling to regain his sight so he could protect Emily. The ground beneath his feet felt solid, but everything else was misty white nothingness. He blinked hard, then held up his hand and stared at it, thankful he could see once more. His ears itched with buzzing whispers that made him wait for a horde of midges to swarm down and feast on his flesh.

"Are ye cowards, then?" he shouted into the void.

"Gryffe?"

His breath caught in his lungs. That voice. The voice he feared he would never hear again. "Emily!" He squinted harder, trying to see through the fog. "Where are ye, my love? Talk me to ye."

"I am close," she said, "because every time you speak, the clouds swirl. Talk so I can follow the movement."

"Are ye injured? Have they hurt ye in any way?"

"They kept trying to make me sleep, but I told them I didn't believe in their powers, and it worked. I stayed awake. I haven't heard from them since."

The pride in her voice made his heart sing. "They canna stand against the likes of ye, my own. Ye are too canny for them."

She stepped into view, arms outstretched, swimming through the mists. "Gryffe!"

Catching her up in his arms, he crushed her to his chest, burying his face in the sweet softness of her hair. "I shall never let ye go, my love. Never."

She clutched him just as tightly. "I don't know how you got here, but I knew you'd come. I told them you would."

"Maybe that is how I got here—yer belief that I would."

She leaned back and smiled up at him. "I will always believe in you. Always."

"This cannot be," said a trio of voices, rumbling with distant thunder.

Gryffe drew his Unseelie blade while keeping Emily safely tucked against his side. "This is as it should be, whether ye wish it or not. My wife. My bairns. Do ye truly wish me to wage war against ye? Against the Highland Veil itself?"

"The Veil?" The voices wavered, trembling with barely controlled panic. "Ye are the Grand Chieftain of the Order. Ye would go against yer vows to unleash evil against the Veil?"

"What do ye know of vows? What do ye care?"

No answer came, confirming he was right.

"My Emily and I are bound for all time. Leave us be and all will be well. Fight us on this, and we will wipe yer names from history and erase yer existance from every realm. No one will remember ye. Ever."

"I told them that too," Emily whispered ever so softly. "So far, it hasn't worked."

"Believe," he told her just as quietly, giving her a rare smile. His precious woman loved his smiles. He had no idea why, but if it pleased her, he would do his best to do it more often.

Cutting through the mists with his softly glowing blade, he bared his teeth at the unseen goddesses. "Ye make yerselves out to be so much better than all others. Ye claim to be holy and good. And yet, ye do this to one of yer own, her and the bairns, treating them like an unwanted mongrel's pups ye intend to drown to rid yerself of them —much as ye did Esme and Mairwen."

He knows echoed over and over throughout the nothingness, growing louder, then fading away only to grow louder again.

"What are you talking about?" Emily asked in the faintest whisper.

"I will explain later," he said just as quietly. Raising his voice and his sword, he continued, "Send us back and trouble us no more.

Leave our descendants alone as well, and we will keep the truth of my wife's ancestry secret. All will continue to believe her the descendant of a Spell Weaver. But if ye dinna return us, Mairwen will share with one and all that Emily descends from Cerridwen and King Zeerin, the Seelie king of the Seventh Realm, and therefore, our children are of Seelie and Unseelie blood. Both light and dark. Both sides united for the first time ever."

"Ye canna tell the truths if we keep ye here. We would be better served to keep ye prisoner."

"Mairwen can share yer truths, and if ye take her, she has left a sealed text with each of the Weavers to be opened upon her disappearance."

"There is no way ye could have arranged that!" the voices said, squalling like a rising storm. "We took ye afore ye had time."

"Nay, my pompous goddesses. It would seem ye are not so all-knowing. Mairwen spoke to me in my thoughts as the irritating witch is wont to do. She assured me this would be done. She knew it would be the only way to make ye listen—since ye wish yer indiscretions kept secret." Gryffe threw out his chest with pride. He had forgotten how satisfying it felt to fully connect with his dark side and create a lie so stunning he almost believed it himself.

Nothing but silence filled the eerie void of foggy brightness.

"Something's about to happen." Emily wrapped both arms around him and hugged him tight. "I feel it. The air...stings."

Sword at the ready in one hand and his other arm around her, Gryffe braced himself. It wasn't the air that stung. 'Twas the goddesses building fury.

And then their howling wails shattered the mist, louder and more piercing than any banshee could ever hope to be. The place shook with their rage, making Gryffe wrap both arms around Emily and hold fast while trying not to drop his sword. She buried her face in his chest and held on to him just as tightly.

At least if they died now, they died together.

CHAPTER 16

T he familiar softness of his bed cradled him, or at least it felt like his bed. But before Gryffe dared to open his eyes and reveal his consciousness, he breathed in the scents of the surroundings to make sure. The faint acrid hint of wood smoke came to him. The old leather upholstery of his chairs. Fresh linens. But best of all, the alluring sweetness of Emily's perfume, his favorite scent of musk that he always asked her to wear. All this dared him to believe the goddesses had truly sent them home, and this wasn't some sort of trap. He cracked one eye open, then opened them both to the cozy bedchamber, dimly lit by a few sputtering candles on the mantel and the tables beside the bed. Contentment washed over him as he gathered Emily closer, spooning his body with hers.

She sleepily hummed her approval and snuggled back against him, treating him to a contented sigh that reminded him of the cooing of a dove. "We're home at last," she said in a breathy whisper that thrilled him. She had finally claimed this place as home.

"Aye, my love. Home at last, indeed." He kissed her shoulder, then raised up and frowned down at her when she flinched and drew away. "What is it, my own? Did I hurt ye, somehow?"

She twisted and tried to touch the back of her left shoulder. "It's sore right there. Like a bad scrape. Can you see anything? I don't remember falling, and they never made physical contact with me."

"Let us see." Mairwen and Grennove the healer spoke as one as they stepped out of the shadows.

"Holy cripes!" Emily squeaked so hard she choked and reeled into a coughing fit.

"What the devil is wrong with the two of ye?" Gryffe demanded of the women as he rubbed Emily's back to soothe her. "Hiding in the shadows of our bedchamber?"

"Forgive us, grand chieftain," Mairwen said, her sarcasm unmistakable. "But if ye recall, the last time we spoke, yer wife was as still and cold as the dead. Ye joined her, ye stubborn fool. We have watched over the two of ye, waiting for ye to either return to us or move on to the next life." She motioned to Emily. "Turn this way, child, so Grennove and I can have a look at what's paining ye."

"Wait." Gryffe took the candle off the bedside table and held it high. "I shall be having a look at my wife's injury first."

The candle's glow revealed a mark similar to one that only a rare few had ever received from the mothers. The sign of the triple goddesses. A waxing moon, a full moon, and a waning moon. All three touching. The symbol of the triple goddesses: maiden, mother, and crone. But this tattoo was rarer still in that the full moon portrayed within its roundness, the tree of life, its many roots mirroring its spreading branches, symbolizing the interconnected-ness and unity of all things and the cyclical way of life. He had only seen this particular version in ancient books, and he struggled to remember its significance.

"They marked ye, my love," he said. The brand they had placed upon her, imprinting it in stark black, had been cut deep into the flesh of Emily's shoulder. It was an open wound that would take a bit of time to heal.

"They placed their mark upon ye as well, my chieftain," Grennove said. "I have a salve that will ease the pain and help the both of ye heal all the quicker."

The old healer eyed him with a look he couldn't read.

"Speak yer mind, Grennove. Ye've never been one to hold yer tongue before."

"Mairwen?" Grennove turned to the Weaver. "Ye ken more about these things than I. Perhaps ye should explain the truth of that mark. I dinna wish to dishonor it with misunderstandings."

Mairwen peered at him, her startling blue eyes narrowing. Then she turned and pulled at her tunic, baring her left shoulder. "I wear the same label," she said. "The sign that proves I am a direct descendant of the mothers."

"But I am not," Gryffe argued, rolling his shoulder as if the thing could be shrugged off his flesh.

Emily pushed herself up to sit among the pillows and gingerly leaned back against the headboard. She hugged the bedclothes higher to hide her nakedness and raked a hand through her wild hair. "So it's true, then? What you said when they held us captive? It wasn't just a bluff about my great-great grandmother?"

"Ye told them ye knew of the secret? All of it? My ancestry included?" Mairwen stared at him in open-mouthed wonder.

"Aye, I also told them ye'd left sealed texts with every detail of the secret to be opened if ye ever disappeared from our presence." He grinned. He couldn't help it. "I told them ye had given a copy to every Weaver in creation. I also shared that if they didna leave me and mine alone, we would see them forgotten across the ages and every realm—and we would also wage war upon the Highland Veil itself."

"And they believed that lie? Me safeguarding myself with sealed texts?"

"Of course they did. My dark side proves useful at such times." He offered a nod. "But I would advise ye to make that lie a truth—for yer own safety. I dinna think that place where we were would be bearable for an eternity."

"It most definitely wouldn't be." Emily rolled her shoulders and flinched again. "So, is this mark proof that they accepted our demands to leave us alone, or does it mean war?"

"That mark is their vow to protect ye as one of their own," Mairwen said, but her scowl hardened with a fiercer glower. "Even yerself, my grand chieftain, because ye fought so valiantly for yer mate. But dinna trust them. They are as fickle as any human. More often than not, their only concerns are for themselves rather than the goodness of others."

"So, they'll leave us alone now?" Emily asked.

"They should," Mairwen said. "But remember, it was they who brought ye here and shielded ye from us only to try to rip ye apart once more."

"About that," Nicnevin said, her expression a bit sheepish as she shimmered into view.

"Has my feckin' bedchamber taken the place of the great meeting hall?" Gryffe scooted back beside Emily and hugged her close. "And which one of ye stripped me down afore putting me to bed like a bairn?"

"I believe ye already know the answer to that," Nicnevin said as she sat on the edge of the bed. "If not, I sorely misjudged yer intelligence." She offered an apologetic tip of her head. "I thought it time to confess. Now that everything has come to pass so beautifully."

"Ye brought her here, and then ye lied about it." Gryffe stabbed his finger in the air, pointing at his mother. "I knew it was yer doing. I knew it."

"The mother goddesses never would have allowed yer fated mate to come to ye because of her ancestry," she said quietly. "I had no choice."

"Ye knew about her ancestry as well." He pinched the bridge of his nose and rubbed the inner corners of his tired, gritty eyes. "And ye thought not to mention that?"

Nicnevin shrugged again. "I had heard rumors—nothing substantial, you understand. I didna wish to cloud yer reasoning with such things in case they held no truth."

"We have been manipulated into marriage and parenthood," Emily said, directing her words to him alone. But she didn't sound angry or filled with regret. She seemed almost...contented. "So, are we expected to do stuff like this to our children so they know how much we love them?"

The uncertainty weighing so heavily on his heart slipped away, leaving him in peace. He gifted her one of his rare smiles and kissed her forehead. "I suppose so." He shot a sideways glance at his mother. "We shall have to consult with the expert on manipulation."

"Absolutely, my darling daughter, and never fear," Nicnevin said to Emily, "I shall be most happy to help."

"Feckin' hell." Gryffe scrubbed his face. "She'll have our daughter fully turned to the dark side afore we know it."

"I thought we were having a son?" Emily arched a brow at him. "Or are you admitting that Tayda was right? We're getting one of each?"

"Aye, one of each."

"I see."

Something in her tone raked across his senses, pleading for help and comfort. "Leave us," he told everyone in the room. "My dear one and I have much to discuss."

"I shall go to make the salve," Grennove said. "Fresh is best for those markings. We dinna wish to fade them."

"I shall help with the herbs," Mairwen said. "This time of year, fresh herbs are rare as hen's teeth."

"I suppose I shall just go," Nicnevin said, and promptly disappeared.

Gryffe turned to Emily. "What is it, my love? When ye first awakened, ye were at peace—but now?" The way she stared at him, pensive and hesitant as though afraid to speak, alarmed him even more. "Please, Emily. Tell me."

She stared down at her hands in her lap. "I know they were just trying to manipulate me, but..."

He held his breath, waiting and worrying about what the

mothers he had once admired had done to put such fear into his own. "But?" he gently encouraged.

She twitched a shrug, then flinched and squirmed, gingerly rolling her shoulder. "Damn. I keep forgetting about that until I hit it."

He laid his hand atop hers. "What did they do, my own? What did they say to ye?"

Head bowed, she released a heavy sigh. "The babies will live, but I won't."

Terror shot through him, rending his heart in two. "What?"

She lifted her head, chewing her bottom lip with a nervous frenzy. "They said I won't survive the birth."

"They lied. Ye will survive. I will not think otherwise, and ye should not dwell on it a moment longer. Ye ken well enough I refuse to allow ye to leave me." Emotions throbbing into a choking knot in his throat, he gathered her close and kissed her forehead. "Both yerself and the wee ones will be well," he whispered. "I swear ye will be finer than fine."

She hiccupped, a sure sign she was struggling not to sob. "I told them all that mattered was that the babies lived. I told them you would love them enough for both of us, and Nicnevin would spoil them rotten." She sniffed, fighting back the tears. "I also told them I didn't believe what they said." She hugged him tighter and whispered, "If I don't believe, then it can't happen. Right?"

"Absolutely, my love." But he didn't feel the words. The fear of losing her was too strong, too stubborn to release him from its icy grasp.

"Mairwen and Ishbel will help me fight them, too. I know they will."

"We will all fight them," he reassured. "Nicnevin has taken a keen liking to ye. She would protect ye with her life." A strange warmth filled his heart. One he had never felt for his mother—not ever. "As soon as the weather eases up, we'll shift to Seven Cairns. I dinna wish ye out and about when it's so bloody cold. It canna be good for yerself or the wee ones."

She nestled her head on his chest and hugged him even tighter. "That's fine. I'm just so happy to finally be home."

He swallowed hard and closed his eyes tightly. Since when did feckin' tears dare to show up in his eyes? 'Twas shameful! "I am glad we're home as well, my own," he said, struggling to keep the roar of emotions out of his tone. "More glad than ye will ever know."

CHAPTER 17

Scotland had finally gifted them a day balmy enough to suit Gryffe and convince him to keep his word to shift them to Seven Cairns. Under no circumstances would he allow Emily to ride a horse, and that was fine by her. If they shifted, she would have more time to visit with everyone and make that long overdue video call to her parents. She dreaded that call, because she had to keep them in the dark about most of the things in her life while at the same time apologizing for disappearing off the face of the earth with no warning. But Gryffe and even Nicnevin had sworn to help her convince her parents that all was well and normal in her new path as a wife and soon to be mother happily living in Scotland with her clan chieftain husband.

"Ye'll soon feel the quickening, m'lady." Inalfi beamed and fluttered about like an overjoyed butterfly while helping Emily dress. "I canna pull yer stays nearly so close as before. The wee ones are growing."

Emily smoothed her hands down her slightly thicker middle. It was still too early to feel the babies' movement, but the *sensation* of new life was unmistakable. "I can't wait until they start kicking."

Grimalkin leaned against her, purring so loudly that the vibration nearly shook her.

"Yes...you're coming," she told the spoiled panther. "Gryffe finally agreed."

The great cat yawned and flexed its long whiskers as if pleased with the news that she too, would soon be transported to Seven Cairns.

"Are ye ready yet, my own?" Gryffe entered the bedchamber, stealing her breath away with his appearance.

"Well, aren't you amazing?"

He smiled, melting her even more. "I thought to dress in my finest to meet yer parents and give them my oath to always protect their daughter and grandchildren."

His black coat, broad at the shoulders and narrow at the waist, accentuated his alpha male physique to the nth degree. He wore his colors proudly with his kilt pinned to his shoulder with the MacStrath crest. His close fitting breeches and tall black boots gave off pirate vibes and tempted her to ask Inalfi to leave the room so her husband could take her up against the wall. He created an insatiable hunger within her that made her greedy for more.

He moved closer, tipped up her face up to his, and teased her with a sexy, lop-sided smile. "When we return, my love," he said in a husky whisper. "If we give in now to what we crave, we will never get to Seven Cairns."

She allowed herself a heavy sigh and stretched on tiptoe to steal a kiss. "I hate it when you're right."

With a smug tilt of his head, he wrapped his arms around her. "Ye must hate it all the time, then."

Unable to refrain from rolling her eyes, she motioned Grimalkin closer. "We're ready to shift whenever you are, my chieftain."

"That feckin' cat," he muttered before nodding. "Hold fast, my own, and keep yer hand on yer wee guardian."

She buried her fingers in the short black ruff at the back of Grimalkin's neck. "Ready."

"*Septem Cairnēs.*"

A flurry of wind gusted around them, making Emily close her eyes. When she opened them, she smiled. Gryffe had landed them directly in front of the pub. She gave him a quick kiss. "You are perfect."

"Was there ever any doubt, lass?"

"Emily!" Lilias exploded out of the pub, running at full speed with her arms open wide. "I have missed ye so much!"

"You know me this time! You know me!" Emily caught the pub owner up in a tight hug and swayed back and forth with her. "You have no idea how good it feels to be recognized."

Lilias set her back and gave her the saddest look. Tears gleamed in the pixie-like woman's eyes. "Mairwen told me about that, and I couldn't believe it. I am so sorry. I couldn't see ye as ye truly are. I saw...something else."

"From the sound of your voice, I don't think I even want to know what you saw." Emily pulled Lilias into another hug. "It doesn't matter now. Everything's all sorted—as the English say."

Lilias playfully shook her. "Ye best be talking like a Scot, lass—not an English." She gave Gryffe a look Emily didn't quite understand. "We have a surprise for ye. Are ye ready?"

"Uhm...I guess so." She had thought she'd be the one dishing out the surprises today by telling everyone about her pregnancy. She smoothed her gown more snugly across her middle and turned sideways. "Apparently, you already know?"

Lilias laughed, then tipped a nod at Gryffe. "Of course we know, lass. That one's pride roared the news of yer wee ones across the realities."

Emily gave Gryffe a look she knew he would understand. "You couldn't let me tell a few people?"

"Ye get to tell yer parents during whatever that magic is ye spoke of. I merely told everyone else."

"About that," Lilias said as she looped her arm through Emily's.

"We've set up what ye need for yer call right here in the pub. The signal's better and all."

"I thought you said your signal was worse?"

"We got a new provider...uh...service for the internet. 'Tis much better. Even Keeva thinks so."

"That'll be nice," Emily said even though she wasn't all that keen on getting scolded in public. She felt certain her mother would have a great deal to say, and she deserved every bit of her parents' angst. "Is it okay if Grimalkin comes inside? She's well-behaved."

Lilias leaned to one side and eyed the Fae panther quietly sitting behind Emily. "She knows not to attack unless ye give the order, aye? Even if someone makes sudden moves?"

"Sudden moves? What sudden moves?" Emily turned and looked at the pub. Near as she could tell, there was very little going on inside, so there couldn't be that many customers at this hour. The breakfast folks should already be gone, and the lunch crowd wouldn't arrive for an hour or so. "I promise Grimalkin won't react unless I'm threatened."

Lilias's smile seemed a little strained—which was unusual, but Emily shrugged it off. The large Fae panther tended to have that effect on some people.

"Come, my own. Time to speak with yer parents." Gryffe rested a protective arm around her. "Dinna be afraid," he whispered. "All will be well."

"I hope so." She knew they'd be so relieved but also angry, confused, and frustrated. She loved them so very much and prayed she could make them understand that she was truly happy.

As they entered the cozy pub, she waved at Lilias's brother Lyal behind the bar. With a small teapot, a plate of shortbreads, and a cup neatly arranged on a tray, he met them at their table, set the items down, and gave her a big hug. "Welcome back, Lady MacStrath. I've yer favorite tea ready."

"Thank you, Lyal." She thought about switching seats, since

she'd ended up with her back to the door and facing the window, but the laptop was already at her spot, so she stayed put.

"I'll fetch ye a whisky, Grand Chieftain," Lyal said.

"Good man." Gryffe kept his gaze locked on Emily, and she couldn't figure out why.

"What's wrong?" she quietly asked when Lilias went back behind the bar with Lyal.

Both of his sleek, dark brows arched higher. "Wrong?"

"Yes. Wrong. You're on edge."

"I am about to meet me wife's parents. Is that not enough to put a man on edge?"

"I suppose you have a point." She powered up the laptop, signed on, and clicked the link to make the video call. It jingled and jangled like it always did while attempting to connect, but her mother never picked up. "I know it's early there, but she's always up by six. She thinks sleeping in is one of the seven deadly sins."

"Does she now?" Gryffe said, sounding distracted. He kept craning his neck as if trying to see behind the bar.

"What are you doing? Trying to admire yourself in the mirror back there?" She couldn't resist teasing him. It helped allay her own nervousness.

"Excuse me, m'love. Lyal needs something." He rose and hurried away, disappearing through the door behind the counter.

Emily tried to wave Lilias over, but she disappeared through the door after him. "Well, good heavens, is something on fire back there or something?" Shaking her head at their strangeness, she turned back to the laptop and tried to get the call to go through again. Disappointment and frustration filled her. Had her mother had an early meeting or something? Had she missed her? "Where are you, Mama?"

"Right behind you, dear."

Emily held tight to the table and tried to remember how to breathe. "Mama?" she repeated ever so softly.

"Turn around and see, Emily."

After a deep breath and a hard swallow, Emily pushed back her chair, slowly rose, then whirled about and split the air with a scream. "You're here!" She pulled her much shorter mother into an enormous hug and gave in to the happy sobs that refused to be denied. "I missed you so much. It's so wonderful to see you."

"Oh, my baby girl. I have missed you, too." Mama hugged and patted and hugged some more. "I was so worried about you, Emily."

"Do I not get a hug too?" Emily's father asked. "I am here too, you know."

"Papa!" Emily's shriek made Grimalkin growl and move to her side. "No, no. It's all right," she told the cat. "These are my parents, Grimalkin. Never ever hurt them. Okay?"

The panther flipped her tail and sat back on her haunches.

"Quite the pet you have there, daughter," her father said as he hugged her more gently than she'd hugged her mother. As she stepped back, he smiled down at her middle. "Twins, I hear. Who is your OB/GYN? I would like to have a word with him or her and ensure they are worth their salt."

"We can talk about that later," Emily said, hoping to dodge the question permanently. She pulled Gryffe closer. "From the way you two are acting, I take it you have already met my wonderful husband?"

"You mean the man who stole you from us?" her mother said with a condescending sniff.

"Aye, that would be me," Gryffe said, jutting his chin to a more defiant angle.

"He stole my heart," Emily said, then pressed both hands to her stomach. "And gave me babies that he already loves and cherishes. I am so happy, Mama, and also so sorry for worrying you and Papa. Can you please forgive me? Can we put it all behind us?"

Mama's eyes welled with tears that quickly overflowed, streaking her usually flawless makeup. "You're giving Papa and me grandbabies to spoil. How could we not forgive you?"

"Walk with me, young man, so I can see if you're worth *your* salt," Emily's father said to Gryffe with a gruffness that did not sound real.

"It would be my pleasure, Mr. Mithers," Gryffe said, then turned to Emily. "As long as ye've no objections, my own?"

For some inexplicable reason, Emily got the impression that all this had somehow been rehearsed. Everything was too neat—too tidy. Her instincts tingled with the strange undercurrent of *something* in the room. "What's going on here?"

Gryffe and her parents failed at assuming an air of innocence. "Yer father wishes to speak with me. 'Tis only natural he do so to put his worries about his daughter to rest."

She folded her arms across her chest and eyed them. "You expect me to believe that?"

"Emily," her father said in a gently scolding tone. He gave her the *it's time to straighten up and be serious* look. "Your mother needs to speak with you. I have decided to be a coward and visit with your husband while she does so."

"Be a coward?" Emily stared at him, unable to believe that of her father. "You're not afraid of anything, Papa. What are you talking about?"

"The only thing I fear in this life is disappointing my little girl." He kissed her forehead like he used to do when she was little, then hurried and left the room with Gryffe before she could say anything else. She turned back to her mother and braced herself. "Okay. What's going on? You two aren't getting a divorce, are you?"

"Absolutely not," her mother said. "I am entirely too old to start training another one, and I abhor living alone. Well...as alone as I could possibly be with your five brothers constantly running in and out whenever they're in need of a home-cooked meal." She pointed at the chairs around the table. "Sit. Your tea is getting cold, and you do remember you need to limit your intake of caffeine while pregnant and when breastfeeding—yes?"

"Yes." Emily took a seat but didn't pour any tea. She'd worry about that after she heard what her mother had to say. "What's going on, Mama? Papa looked—strained."

Her mother fidgeted with her bracelet of multi-colored beads, twisting and rolling the beads between her fingers. "When we thought we'd lost you, we realized that we'd not prepared you properly."

"Prepared me properly?"

"Been honest with you so you would be aware and able to defend yourself."

Emily slowly shook her head and leaned back in the spindle chair that was so worn, it cradled her like a hammock made just for her. "I have no idea what you're trying to say. Can you just come out and say it?"

"Papa and I are not your biological parents."

A spinning sensation crashed across Emily, threatening to make her vomit. She closed her eyes and pulled in deep, deliberate breaths. "Could you ask Lilias for a cool cloth, please?"

"Here ye are pet," Lilias said. "I had one at the ready. Thought ye might need it. Shout out should ye need anything else."

"Thank you," Emily said, struggling not to throw up her dignity. She pressed the cool damp cloth to her face, then to the back of her neck. She swallowed hard, wincing at the bitter bile burning the back of her throat. "If I get through this without puking, it'll be a miracle."

"Breathe, Emily. Deep and slow. In through the nose and out your mouth. It's the hormones—and the shock. I am sorry. We should've told you years ago."

Closing her eyes, Emily bowed her head and held the washcloth to her throat. "How old was I when you got me?"

"Days." Her mother released a heavy sigh, holding a hand to her chest as if she struggled to breathe. "Your birth mother left you there in the neonatal unit. You were such a tiny little thing. I held you in the palm of one hand."

"How?" Emily couldn't speak in full sentences. She could only manage single words.

"As a physician for some of the most powerful and influential in New Jersey, it wasn't difficult to call in a few favors and arrange your adoption. That way, we could bring you straight home from the hospital as soon as you were strong enough. We wanted to keep you out of the foster system."

"But my brothers?" It wasn't like her parents had been childless. Had they cheated the system and *bought* them too?

"Your five brothers are not adopted." Her mother huffed with a sad laugh. "I love my wild boys, and they've done your father and me proud—and as far as they know, you are their biological sister. With all of you so close in age, it was easy to *help* them remember what we wanted them to remember." She slowly shook her head while holding Emily's gaze. "But a year after your brother Henry was born, I had to have a hysterectomy to remove a large mass." Another heavy sigh left her. "Your father and I...well...mostly, me I guess, had always wanted a little girl to level out the playing field in our testosterone saturated home." She sniffed before pulling a tissue out of her purse and pressing it to the end of her nose. "I was so depressed after my surgery. Felt like I was not only less of a woman, but knew I had lost any hope of holding my very own little girl in my arms." She blew her nose, then rummaged for another tissue. "And then your father called me while doing his rounds at the hospital. About this sweet little girl that barely weighed a pound and needed someone to love her."

Emily risked taking a sip of her tea, thankful that it had cooled to a tepid level. With her hand pressed to the base of her throat, she shook her head. "Of all the things you could have said to me today, I never expected this."

"I am still your mama. Papa is still your papa, and Rob, Terrance, Jack, Miles, and Henry are still the greatest irritants and most loving brothers you could ever have. They would've come to Scotland with us, but we asked them not to this time." She pulled in another deep breath, blew it out, and sat taller in her chair. "And Mairwen told me everything. I now know why you and Jessa can never return to New Jersey, and how all of us can only meet and visit here in Seven Cairns."

"You're not supposed to know all of it," Emily whispered as a chill shot through her. They had made a vow, and Mairwen had broken it. "It's so...dangerous. None of what you know can ever be repeated—and you definitely can't tell the boys."

"I know. But Mairwen took pity on me because she understood my pain of losing my daughter."

Now, Emily understood. "Mairwen recently lost her son. He was murdered."

Her mother gave her a sad nod. "I know. She told me as we shared tea and tears." She reached for Emily's hand and gave it a squeeze. "Can you ever forgive me for lying all these years? Papa and I were so afraid to tell you. We were afraid we would lose you."

"Lose me? Are you insane?" Emily dove into her mother's arms, not caring that she nearly knocked her seat backwards. "I love you, Mama, and I love Papa too—and that's that." She pulled her chair closer and settled into it while still holding tightly to her mother's arm. "You and Papa need to retire and move here to Scotland. Buy a cottage from Mairwen. Right here in Seven Cairns."

Her mother wrinkled her nose. "We'll see. Your brothers may be scattered all over the East Coast, but they find their way back to Jersey on a regular basis."

"They've all got good, solid jobs. Maybe they would finally learn to cook if you and Papa moved over here."

Mama patted her hand and squeezed it. "Are you truly happy, Emily? *Truly* happy? Because that's all I have ever wanted for you."

"I am, Mama. I really am."

"Then that's all any mother can ask for." Mama shared another sad smile. "You'll understand when your babies reach their age of independence."

Emily just smiled and nodded. Mairwen might've told Mama all their secrets, or maybe just the few instrumental ones, but either way, Mama had no idea about her grandchildren's ancestry and what they might be capable of. Even Emily struggled to wrap her head around it. She pulled her mother into another hug. "I am so glad you're here." She locked eyes with Mama. "But I really want you to buy a house and stay. I think you'd love it here, and I know Papa would."

"We'll see," Mama said, but her tone implied that the *we'll see* was more of a *we will*.

CHAPTER 18

"I am bigger than your biggest Highland cow," Emily said through clenched teeth. She waddled around the solar, rubbing the sides of her enormous belly. "If I don't have these two soon, I am going to split open like an over-ripe watermelon."

All Gryffe could do was smile because, in his opinion, she was absolutely exquisite in every way. "Ye are the most glorious woman I have ever seen, my own. Yer beauty is beyond compare."

She stopped pacing long enough to throw a pillow at him. "Stop patronizing me! I am not a child!"

No. She was not a child, because children weren't nearly so dangerous when their tantrums overtook them. Most children didn't accidentally set fire to their surroundings because their anger caused their magic to spark and flare without being summoned.

He fell in step beside her. "What can I do to help ye, my own?"

"You can never have sex with me again!"

While he wasn't about to agree to that, instinct advised he best choose a reply with care. "What might I do to ease yer misery at this particular moment?"

She threw herself into his arms and crumpled into tears as she had done throughout the pregnancy after being uncontrollably surly. "I'm sorry to be such a bitch. I feel so much worse today. My belly keeps spasming into a rock hard pyramid, and my lower back is killing me."

"Spasming?" He was no expert on women giving birth, but he'd tended many a prized Highland cow, and their sides sometimes did as she described when they were trying to bring forth a calf. "Describe yer spasming, my love."

"Here." She grabbed his hand and pressed it atop her rounded middle. "It's doing it now. Feel it? One of the babies must be stretching—either that or building a brick wall."

Excitement building, he struggled to keep his tone even, in case he was wrong. "Have ye spoken to Tayda about this? Since old Grennove took to her bed and Breenoa is so damned flighty, she intends to help ye bring the babies into this world. She's been training with the Weavers for months now."

"I thought Mairwen was going to come." Emily groaned and doubled over. "On second thought, whoever is coming needs to get here. I don't care if this does turn out to be gas or false labor."

Holding her tightly, Gryffe aimed his roaring bellow at the door. "Mrs. Thistlebran!"

Emily sidled such a disbelieving look of disgust at him that he almost laughed, but knew he didn't dare. "The bell would work better, you know."

"I canna reach the bell at present because I am not letting go of ye. Shall we walk to the bedchamber now?"

"Probably so. But I don't want to make a mess of the bed when my waters break, so I'm not getting into it until after that happens."

"I feel certain Inalfi and Tayda will have that well in hand. The two have been preparing for this grand day for a while now."

"I was going to crochet another pair of blankets for the cradles." She halted and doubled over again, holding onto him so tightly that her fingernails dug into his hand. He didn't care. She could shred him to bits if need be.

"While they sleep, ye can crochet more." He carefully walked her down the hallway, shortening his steps to match hers. "Mrs. Thistlebran!"

"I am here, my chieftain!" The housekeeper huffed and puffed as she toddled around the corner at a remarkable speed. "Oh dear. Time to fetch the Weaver, aye? And alert Lady Tayda?"

"Aye. Now!"

"And send word to Nicnevin," Emily said through another groan. "She wanted to be here during labor rather than waiting till after."

"Feckin' hell," Gryffe muttered.

"If I have to be miserable," Emily said, "so do you." She halted and leaned against the doorpost. "Wait. I have to rest here a minute. I feel like the babies are hanging down to my knees."

"What?" Alarmed, Gryffe yanked up her skirts. Thankfully, his bairns weren't dangling downward like wee bats.

She smacked his hands away. "I said it *felt* like it. You really think I'd be this calm if the babies were coming out right here in the hall?"

"Probably not."

"Thank you."

"Why in the name of all the realms have ye got her standing here in the hallway?" Tayda demanded as she came around the same corner Mrs. Thistlebran had just vacated. "We must get her changed into her birthing shift and as comfortable as possible in the bed."

"I dinna rush my wife," Gryffe answered with a warning growl. "When she asks me to wait and let her catch her breath, I do so. And might I remind ye to whom ye're speaking?"

Tayda immediately bowed her head. "Forgive me, my prince. I was overcome with the excitement of the situation. Might I please take over now and help our lady bring the precious bairns into the world?"

"Absolutely." Gryffe started to step away but Emily clutched him tighter.

"Don't leave me!"

"But…"

The fear and pleading in her eyes undid him.

"I swear not to leave until ye send me away," he promised as he helped her through the door.

"I'm afraid," she whispered. "I keep remembering last time, even though this time is so much different."

That very reason had caused him to try to convince her to return to her time and have the babies there in the safety of one of her hospitals. But she had adamantly refused, since he could never set foot past the boundaries of Seven Cairns. While it honored him that she had made such a choice, it worried him as well. Her safety and the safety of the wee ones were so much more important than anything else in creation. But he couldn't tell her any of that. Not now. Now she needed reassurance.

"Yer blessed Cara is smiling down on ye," he said. "She'll keep our wee ones safe through this and yerself as well."

"I so want to believe that. It doesn't matter if I die, I just want them to live."

Her words struck terror into his heart, making him halt and lift her face to his. "Ye willna die and leave me. I refuse to allow it. Do ye ken what I am telling ye?"

"But the goddesses said—"

"I dinna give a feckin' damn what those three said. Ye know how they lie." He swept her unwieldy self into his arms and carried her the rest of the way to the bed. "Swear to me now. Ye believe ye shall live and be the mother our beloved wee ones need. Swear it, I say!"

"I swear," she said, but still sounded afraid. She caught hold of him with both hands. "Stay with me and keep me safe."

"I am here and here I shall stay." He sat on the bed and pulled her back against him as she curled into herself with another contraction.

"Lift her, my chieftain," Inalfi said as she and Tayda rushed forward with heavier linens. "We must spread the cloths to shield the bed for when her waters break."

"We'll start on this side and bring the coverings over to spread beneath her," Tayda said. "Lift her when we say."

"Where is Mairwen?" Emily asked. "I want her here to help with the babies."

"Mrs. Thistebran told Ferris to message her with the Defender's way. I am sure she'll be here quicker than quick." Tayda nodded at Grytte. "Lift our lady now, chieftain."

He cradled her in his arms once more, holding her as easily as a wee babe.

"How can you hoist me up with no effort at all when I'm this size? You're going to throw out your back." With her forehead peppered with sweat and her curls a mess, Emily had never looked more beautiful. He couldn't resist stealing a kiss.

"Ye are perfect as always, my love." He accepted a cool cloth from Inalfi and wiped Emily's face. "Absolute perfection, and I'm nay just talking out me arse like some fool intent on impressing ye. I am simply stating that which is true."

She sniffed and more tears overflowed. "I love you so much." She curled tighter and groaned again.

"And I love ye more than ye will ever know." He noticed Tayda and Inalfi standing close by with more linens and a simple chemise that would be a great deal more comfortable than the dress his dear one currently wore. "Are ye able to let them help get ye changed? It might bring ye a little comfort."

"I'll take all the comfort I can get." She patted his arm. "I guess I can let you go for a minute or two."

"I shall be right here," he promised.

"Good."

"Ye intend to stay in here for the birth?" his mother asked from behind him.

He turned and bared his teeth at her. "Stop entering my bedchamber unannounced, ye ken?"

"Mrs. Thistebran summoned me," Nicnevin said with a warning hiss. "I assumed that meant I was expected."

"Don't fight," Emily ordered. "Not today. Only good and positive *ju ju* in this room to welcome my babies."

"*Ju ju?*" Nicnevin mouthed at Gryffe.

He shrugged, not knowing what it was either. But if it mattered to Emily, it mattered to him. "We only fight *for* ye, my love, and for the wee bairns to hurry and join us."

"Absolutely," Nicnevin said. "I see the cradles are ready and waiting. My artisans are so proud to be the first for many an age to provide such special furniture for the royal family."

"Many an age?" Emily asked, back in bed now and propped among dozens of pillows. She fixed Gryffe with a curious look. "How old are you?"

"Why, he is in his prime, dear daughter," Nicnevin said before Gryffe could answer. "He's but a mere three hundred and forty mortal years."

The way Emily's eyelids fluttered sent a surge of panic through him. He dove to her side. "Emily!"

"Three hundred and forty years?" she repeated slowly while appearing to struggle to draw deep breaths.

"Aye."

"And you never thought to tell me that before now?"

"I nay thought it mattered."

"You *nay thought it mattered*? Are you insane? I am thirty-two years old, and if I'm lucky, I'll live until I'm well into my eighties or maybe even nineties. That doesn't concern you?"

"Nay, my love," he said. "Because as long as ye remain in this realm with me, ye will age the same as I."

She stared at him. "Are you serious?"

"Aye."

"What else have you not told me?"

"If we ever decide to reside in the Dark Kingdom, we will live even longer."

"Even longer than what?"

"Longer than is possible here—by several thousand years or so."

She drew up her legs, curled over onto her side, and hugged her belly, hissing with the pain. "We will discuss this more at a later date. But know that I am not happy with you. You don't keep me in the dark about important stuff. Understand?"

He offered a solemn nod. "I understand."

"I see the babes have decided today shall be the day," Mairwen said as she entered the room.

"They are taking their sweet time, though," Emily informed her.

"Patience, child. Bringing forth new life is an honor. Relish it. The pain will quickly pass as soon as ye behold yer babes." Mairwen moved to the other side of the bed, then frowned at Gryffe. "And why are ye still in here, grand chieftain?"

"Because I want him in here!" Emily snapped with a look that dared Mairwen to ask any other unwise questions.

"I believe my wife made that clear?" Gryffe said to the Weaver, unable to resist the temptation.

"Gryffe!" Emily squeezed his hand and groaned as her birth waters soaked the bed. "It goes faster now, right?"

He looked at Mairwen and Tayda, who both barely shook their heads.

"Deep breaths, our lady," Tayda instructed. "And tune yer mind to something other than the pain. Ye can control much of it, if ye but try."

"I am trying, dammit!"

"What names did ye decide upon, my own?" He had to get Emily to focus on something other than her increasing agony. "Did ye choose any of the ones I thought might do, or did ye settle on yer family names ye mentioned?"

"I settled on," she said, sharply huffing and blowing. "Quinn for our son, and Saersy for our daughter."

"Those were my favorites." He matched her puffing, trying to breathe the same to encourage her. "Are ye certain?"

Tucking her chin to her chest and groaning, she finally bobbed her head. "Yes. Quinn and Saersy. I like the way it feels to say their names. It's almost as if they chose them."

"Perhaps they did." He caught her as she sagged back against his chest, already exhausted from the pains.

"You know we could do this all night," she said, peering up at him with a hopelessness that broke his heart.

"I have nowhere else to be but here."

"Where is Grimalkin?" she asked, aimlessly looking around.

"Over there." Gryffe nodded at the other side of the room. "Pacing."

Hours passed, and the pains came fast and furious. If Gryffe had never admired and fully appreciated Emily before, or thought her strong and fearless, he did so now. She was braver and more resilient than any warrior wounded on the field of battle.

"The babies aren't coming," she said through a gasping moan as the most recent pain eased off. "I'm going to die, and so are they if you don't cut me open and save them."

"Dinna speak that way!" He cupped her chin in his hand and forced her to look him in the eyes. "Ye will not give up. Do ye hear me, Emily? Never will ye leave me or our babes."

"They always speak that way right before the wee ones come," Mairwen whispered from behind him. "Hold her and give her yer strength. She needs ye now more than ever."

He gathered her up by the shoulders, supporting her with his chest as she sagged back against him. "Our wee ones come within the hour. I shall not think otherwise. Hold fast, love, and stay strong."

"Another pain is coming," she said, sounding so weary he wanted to weep. "I am going to push. I don't know if it's time or not, but I'm going to push."

"Do ye not feel the need to push?" Mairwen asked.

"I feel the need to go to the chamberpot and unload a huge shit!" Emily snapped.

"That's it, child!" Mairwen told her, excitement resounding

through her tone. "Push yer bairns out, lass. We're all ready to meet them."

Gryffe helped Emily sit higher, straining as she groaned and pushed with every last bit of her energy.

"I see a head full of dark hair," Mairwen said excitedly. "Keep pushing."

And then the most magical thing Gryffe had ever seen in his life happened. His child, a tiny babe, slid into Mairwen's hands, as slippery and wiggling as a wee selkie. Red faced and angry, he squalled as Mairwen patted the soles of his feet to make him cry—for it was a him. Gryffe's firstborn son. Quinn.

"See him, my love," he told Emily. "What a fine, braw boy we have. Just look at him. Listen."

"He's crying so loudly. And breathing. I hear him breathing between cries. He's healthy, isn't he? He's fine?" Emily sobbed uncontrollably while reaching for the babe. "Give him to me. Let me hold him till his sister comes."

Gryffe stared down at his angry son, unable to speak as Emily cooed and calmed him, not caring that he had yet to be cleaned of the mess of his travels.

"Sorry, Quinn," she said as she handed him back to Mairwen. "Sister is coming."

Gryffe held her upright again and witnessed the second miracle of the day. A wee daughter. Red and angry. Smaller than her brother but a great deal louder. Little Saersy.

Then Tayda stepped forward and started massaging Emily's stomach, kneading her middle like pummeling bread between her fists.

"What the devil are ye doing?" he asked, ready to shove her away.

"All the afterbirth must come out, my chieftain. 'Twill make her ill, if it doesn't." Tayda kept kneading and pushing.

"It's all right, Gryffe," Emily told him. "It doesn't hurt, and she's right. Everything has to come out, so I don't get an infection." She lay cradled in his arms, exhausted but happier than he had seen her in a very long time. "Our babies are healthy," she whispered. "They're going to live."

"As are ye," he whispered back. "Say it."

She smiled. "As am I."

"I love ye, my own." He kissed her damp forehead, relishing her salty sweetness.

"I love you more."

EPILOGUE

Over a year later...
Seven Cairns
Highlands of Scotland
Christmastide (Neutral Reality Portal - Emily and Jessa's Modern Day)

THE MEETING HALL at the heart of the village, festooned in ivy, red ribbons, and a gorgeous tree with twinkling Christmas lights, rang with laughter and holiday music. All the villagers and Weavers, both light and dark, and Emily's parents and brothers feasted on every treat imaginable while enjoying the adorable antics of the MacAlester triplets and the MacStrath twins.

"Who would have thought we would be married and mamas to triplets and twins all because of a tarot app that refused to be deleted off your phone?" Emily separated Quinn from Jessa's son Lucian and aimed him at a different pile of toys. Just because all the babies were close in age didn't mean they always played well with each other.

"We don't hit our friends, Quinn. Stay here and play by yourself for a while."

Jessa laughed. "You know that's not going to work. Those two can't stand to be separated even though they pick on each other all the time—and yes, who would've thought a phone app would be the seed that grew into all of this."

"And we still have Mama and Papa and the fearsome five—all because of our stubbornness." Emily smiled at her mother, jostling Saersy on one hip and Jessa's daughter Meira on the other. The little girls, even though toddlers, already banded against the three boys and usually reigned victorious.

"We did good," Jessa said with a loving nod at her husband, Grant. "And we're happy."

"More than happy," Emily said with an adoring smile aimed at Gryffe. "We're content."

"To contentment." Jessa lifted her glass.

Emily did the same. "Yes. To contentment and finding the missing piece of our souls' puzzle."

GLOSSARY
PERTINENT STUFF TO KNOW

Auld Ways, The - Earth religions, Paganism, belief in the gods and goddesses

Bride - the goddess of healing symbolised by the element of water, goddess of the alchemical force of fire, and goddess of poetry

Caladbolg - the sword of Leite from the elf mounds

Cerridwen - a figure of significant importance in Welsh and Celtic mythology, often revered as a goddess of wisdom, inspiration, and rebirth

Crystal Athame - Ceremonial knife used for spell work, healing, and sometimes, binding ceremonies

Crystal Prison, aka Danu's Prison - where the mighty Goddess Danu imprisons immortals unwise enough to cross her

Danu - a central figure in Celtic mythology, specifically Irish lore, regarded as a primordial mother goddess associated with water, fertility, and wisdom

Domas - a spell to send one home

Dreaming, The - constantly fluid and ever changing plane of existence- all beings from every level can travel there because nothing is permanent, and there is constant chaos

Ether, The - The Weaver telepathic alarm system that does not include the goddesses or the Defenders.

Goddess's Ledger of Infinity - used to report the Council's meeting minutes to the goddesses

Highland Veil - a tapestry of time, energy, and mystical ether. Over the ages, it becomes worn and thins a bit here and there. Some beings, depending on their goddess given abilities, are sometimes able to slip through to other worlds or times and create havoc where they do not belong, giving birth to many of our myths and legends. There is but one thing powerful enough to keep the Veil's weave strong and intact enough to fully separate that which must be kept to itself for the good of all: Love.

Induciae - a spell or request for the suspension of hostilities

Kelpie - In Scottish folklore, a kelpie is a dangerous, shape-shifting water spirit that can appear as a horse.

Knowing, The - the way the goddesses speak to the Weavers as a whole. Their minds connect, and knowledge is shared.

Libero - a spell to release a subject from the effects of another spell

MacAlester Craig - village nearest to MacAlester Keep

Order of the Defenders of the Veil - mortals sworn to defend the Highland Veil and work with the Weavers. They also possess a few special powers and a longer than usual lifespan...but they are still mortal and eventually die.

Portal Bell - when an unsuspecting mortal rings it, they travel to another time; the time chosen for them by a Weaver.

Quies - a spell to freeze someone in place and time to prevent them from harming themselves or others

Recedo - a spell to put out fires

Septem Cairnēs - a spell to transport to Seven Cairns

Seven Cairns - a quaint Highland village that is so very much more ;)

Talam - the Weavers' word for the earth realm. Earth = Talam

Tarot Card Dating App - an irresistible phone application that helps the Weavers lure fated mate prospects to Seven Cairns

Tenete - a spell for strength to hold fast and stay together

Tranquillitis - a spell for tranquility

Unum Sumus - a healing spell that unites the powers of others

Weavers - the ten immortals charged with the protection and rejuvenation of the Highland Veil

SNEAK PEEK INTO: A FINE SCOTTISH DREAM

inemagic Horse Farms
Lexington, Kentucky
Early June 2025

Dr. Lexington "Lexi" Vine strolled down the center aisle of the main barn, breathing in the sweet perfume of healthy horses, clean stalls, and future derby champions in the making. Thumbs hooked in the pockets of her jeans, she tried to roll the day's tension from her shoulders and almost...almost succeeded.

She really had no excuse to feel stretched tighter than a fiddle string. It had been a good day. Three new foals. Excellent bloodlines, robust babies that their mamas had readily accepted. Yet the feeling of being wound too tight wouldn't go away, and she didn't know why. She had been this way ever since Mammaw died, and she had inherited the status of the sole family member left to run the extraordinarily successful Vinemagic Horse Farms.

Maybe that was what it was, but deep down, she felt like it was more than just grief or the weight of extra responsibilities. It was an odd restlessness that made little sense. Maybe it was because her grandmother, *Mammaw* in southern speak, had been a force to be reckoned with and left behind an impossible set of boots to fill. Old money and a high society southern belle, nobody crossed Mammaw. If they did, there wouldn't be enough of their reputation left to pray over by the time Mammaw finished with them. The Bluegrass Region respected Lexi well enough as a trainer, horse rehabilitator, and Doctor of Veterinary Medicine—but she was no Mammaw, and she knew it. She allowed herself a sad smile. Mammaw would tell her it was all right. If everyone were a *Mammaw*, where would the fun in that be? So how could this *itchy-twitchy* restlessness be from following in Mammaw's footsteps?

A familiar, mud-spattered pickup truck backfired as it pulled up in front of the wide-open doors at the front of the main barn. The building was the largest of four that housed, bred, and trained so many winning thoroughbreds they'd had to enlarge the trophy room. Lexi's friend, Maggie Siriton, also a vet, climbed out of the truck. She was covered in nearly as much mud as her vehicle. "Hey, Lexi! Come look. I brought you something I came across down in the bottoms."

Maggie had a habit of rescuing any varmint she came across. There was no telling what she had in the back of that pickup.

"No snapping turtles," Lexi warned as she joined her friend outside. "Remember?"

Maggie lifted both hands in surrender. "One time, I bring you a poor old snapping turtle, and you never let me forget it." She tipped a nod at the truck bed. "Seven puppies. And the mama dog. I figure somebody dumped them down there by the creek."

"I hate people." Lexi shook her head at the sweet, floppy-eared hound with the soulful eyes. The dog, along with seven puppies that hadn't even opened their eyes yet, filled the animal carrier to over-flowing. "Luckily for you, mama dog, we've got room in the kennels," she said. "You and your babies will need to be in isolation for a while until all the tests come back, but at least you'll be warm, dry, and fed. And there'll be plenty of cuddles too." She turned to Maggie. "You're going to help me with this bunch, right? You know they'll need worming, bathing, and, from the looks of them, a lot of attention while we make sure they're healthy."

"You know I'll help." Maggie reached into the carrier and rubbed the dog's ears. "And when it comes time to place them, I won't leave you high and dry either." She offered Lexi a broad smile. "I even brought lunch to bribe you. Mom sent over her famous fried chicken, hash brown casserole, and peach cobbler."

"Sold!" Lexi gave Maggie a high five. "Drive around to the kennels. Sam is back there. I'm sure he'll fall in love with them. He can get them settled, and we'll give them a good look over after we enjoy your mama's most thoughtful and scrumptious lunch. Meet me in my office. I've got a fresh pitcher of sweet tea in the fridge."

"Back in a few."

Lexi wasn't mad about today's rescue. Anger at whoever had done that to the poor dog, and the pups simmered low and steady deep in her gut, but she didn't mind taking the animals in and giving them the care and attention they deserved. She headed to her office in the main barn.

Settling down at her desk, she scooped up the tarot card spread she'd been studying during a break when word of the newest foal had called her to the barn. The cards had belonged to Mammaw, and whenever Lexi shuffled them and dealt the spreads, it was almost as if her grandmother was right there with her, a hand on her shoulder, pointing out the cards and either crowing with glee or groaning about what the symbols foretold. They had shared this love of tarot, and more often than not, the cards never lied. Sometimes the meanings were a little unclear, but once they happened, it was easy to see the symbols' advice and warnings had been accurate.

"What's Mammaw got to say today?" Maggie asked as she

lumbered into the room with a cooler so large she had to turn sideways to get through the door.

Lexi hurried over and grabbed one of the cooler's handles, and together, they toted it to the table in front of the large picture window overlooking the training paddock. "Holy crap. Did your mom pack enough for the entire crew?"

Maggie laughed as she opened the lid. "Well, you know she did. There's probably not a chicken left in Kentucky. She fried them all. And this isn't the only cooler. There's another in the truck. I told Sam to get it and pass the food around to everyone working today."

Lexi leaned over the chest and breathed in the mouthwatering aroma of spicy fried chicken, rich, cheesy hash brown casserole, and buttery sweet peach cobbler. "We'll need a nap after eating all this."

"You shouldn't need a nap. You left the Sanderson's party pretty early last night. You should be well-rested." Maggie set the food on the table without taking her gaze from Lexi. "I take it that it's over with Robert? You didn't look happy when you left."

"Well, it was never really *on* with Robert, now was it? It was just sort of hanging there. Kind of like a hair in a biscuit." Lexi went to the cabinet behind her desk and retrieved paper plates, napkins, and utensils. "He suggested, *again,* that another surgery might just do the trick."

"What—he considers you his art project or something just because he's a plastic surgeon?"

"Apparently." Lexi really felt no ill will toward Robert. That was the problem. She felt nothing toward him at all. "He wasn't too keen on the fact that I am done with surgeries." She touched the grid of scars that started at the outer corner of her right eye, spilled across her right cheek, and ended on her throat just below her chin. Past surgeries to replace shattered bone and repair muscle had helped some, but nothing would ever make her flawless, and with Mammaw's love and guidance, she had accepted that a long time ago. Makeup, if caked thick enough, filled in the hills and valleys, but it felt like a cloying mask that would crack if she smiled. She was what she was. Some folks couldn't get past her scars. She struggled to maintain the mindset that was their problem and not hers. "So, yes—Robert and I are officially over now with no bad feelings either way."

"Well, no bad feelings are good. I guess."

"You guess?"

"Well, the way you say it, there were no good feelings to begin with." Maggie fished out a drumstick and put it on Lexi's plate. "Here. Your favorite."

"I kind of want to dig into the cobbler first." Lexi couldn't resist a wicked grin. "Life is short. Eat dessert first—you know?"

"You don't happen to have any ice cream in that fridge of yours, do you?"

"Afraid not. But I did promise you some tea. Just made it this morning." Lexi filled two glasses with ice, then poured the already cold sweet tea into them. "Lemon or mint today?"

"Lemon, please. Save the mint for derby day."

"That's in May, remember? This is June."

"That's also because I don't like mint, remember?"

Lexi snorted a laugh. "Ah, yes. I forgot. Sorry."

"So—" Maggie settled into a chair, propped her elbows on the table, and tucked into a crispy chicken thigh. "What did Mammaw have to say today? In the cards?"

After fishing several of the choicest dumpling-like pieces of crust out of the peach cobbler, Lexi sat in the chair opposite Maggie. "She knows I'm restless and keeps telling me it's time for a change."

"That reminds me." Maggie pulled her phone from her pocket and tapped on its screen. "Have you seen this new dating app? It's with tarot cards. Watch." After tapping the deck on the screen, Maggie shook her head. "I keep getting a different spread of three cards and different guys, so I can't imagine it being very accurate. Some aren't so bad. But some..." She shuddered. "You try it, and see if it's just me or if the app really works and aligns with what Mammaw says."

Lexi shoved an overly large bite of pie into her mouth, then took the phone and tapped on the card deck on the screen. One card appeared: the death card. "Upright death card. End of cycle, beginnings, change, metamorphosis. That's what Mammaw's cards keep telling me, and I have to admit, I'm ready."

"See what guy you get." Maggie rummaged through the cooler, found a couple of chicken wings, placed one on her plate and one on Lexi's.

Lexi frowned. No guy appeared after she tapped on the link. Just a grayed-out silhouette with a big red question mark overlaid on top of it. She handed the phone back to Maggie. "What's that supposed to mean? Did they run out of men or something?"

The girl frowned. "That's weird. I've never seen that before." She shrugged. "Probably just a crappy app. I'll uninstall it and stick to your Mammaw cards and regular dating apps." She tore off a chunk of chicken and popped it into her mouth. "But that card you drew makes sense. You said you'd been all wound up lately...kind of like you need to be talked off a ledge. Are you feeling any better?"

Lexi shoved a peach around on her plate, trying to decide whether to lie or be honest.

"I want the truth, Lex," Maggie said, as if reading her mind.

"I need...something. Some kind of change. I feel like one shoe just dropped, and the other is still suspended in midair and about to fall at any minute." She slowly shook her head. "And I don't think it's got anything to do with Mammaw's passing. I was leaning toward anxiety-overload before she died."

"Any more dreams about her?" Maggie filled her plate with peach cobbler, frowning at the lack of crust left in the container. "You fished out the best bits."

"Of course I did," Lexi said with no shame. "I always do. You know that."

Maggie rolled her eyes and settled back into her chair. "Any more dreams?"

Lexi shrugged. "Just the same one over and over. Mammaw and me standing in a shadowy room, and her telling me, *"Stop stalling and just do it."*

"Just do what?"

"Good question."

"And you keep getting the death card in your tarot readings?"

Lexi went to her desk, cut the cards, shuffled them, then drew one and showed it to Maggie: the death card.

"That is freakin' eerie."

"What's freakin' eerie is I know I need a *change*. I just don't know how big or what to change." Lexi tucked the card back into the deck and placed them in a drawer.

With her fork in her mouth, Maggie took on a thoughtful yet frowning expression. Then she pointed the fork at Lexi. "You need a sabbatical."

"From what?"

Maggie rolled her eyes again. "From here. This place. Your practice. Kentucky. We both know if you take a break and stay here, you'll just get sucked right back into things. Lexington won't leave you alone, and the Horsey Set won't either. You have a way with animals that no one else around here has."

"And just how could I leave for any amount of time?"

"No one is indispensable, Lexi. You know that. Mammaw felt the same as you about taking time off, and yet this part of your world hasn't collapsed since she passed. I know a very large part of your personal world came crashing down around your heart when she left you, but the business side of things maintained the status quo until you worked through your grief enough to take the reins. She and your grandfather set this place up to run like a well-oiled piece of machinery." Maggie slowly nodded. "You could leave here for a while and get your head and heart together. I can cover the vet side of things, and everyone else, your board of directors included, can handle the business end of Vinemagic Horse Farms. It'll be fine."

"I don't know. I just wouldn't feel right about leaving." The idea was tempting and definitely tugged at her heart, but her stubborn sense of duty and accountability kept rearing its ugly head and bashing the temptation back down. There was so much to *handle* during this time of year. "It just wouldn't be right."

"What wouldn't be right about it? Everyone needs some downtime. Take a break before life breaks you."

Lexi continued fiddling with the slippery peach that was trying to slide off her paper plate. "Where would I go?"

"Wherever you want to go—just not here or close enough to *here* for anyone from this area to get in touch with you."

"But they might need to in case there was an emergency."

Maggie huffed with an exasperated groan as she rose to dump her leftovers into the covered trash can outside the open office door in the barn's primary thoroughfare. "I can be the point of contact and decide what is or is not an emergency. You know I won't let anyone bother you unless it's warranted—like one of the barns burning down or something."

"Don't even say that." Lexi shuddered. A barn fire with all the horses inside? That was the stuff of nightmares.

"Go to Scotland and search for unicorns. You always dreamed of doing that."

"When I was five." Lexi gathered up the rest of the trash and disposed of it in the garbage bin. "Unfortunately, that dream was dashed when reality told me unicorns weren't real."

"Scotland thinks they're real. Isn't the unicorn their national animal?" Maggie propped her feet on the corner of the chair beside her. "And weren't you having another recurring dream about unicorns and dark forests that was narrated by some deep, sexy voice?"

A shiver raced across Lexi. She was still having that dream, too.

She just hadn't told Maggie. "How do you remember all this stuff I tell you?"

"You're my friend. If it's important to you, it's important to me." Maggie made a show of yawning and rubbing her eyes. "Wow. You were right about the dangers of a big lunch. If we don't do something interesting, I'm going to be snoring soon." With a wicked gleam in her eye, she hopped out of her seat and hurried over to Lexi's desk and started typing on her keyboard. "I know. Let's check out some travel agencies. See if we can find you a good Airbnb overseas or something."

"Your acting hasn't gotten any better than it was in the third-grade talent show."

"Humor me."

Lexi joined her friend at the computer, more amused than excited about any traveling plans. When Maggie got on a roll about something, it was better to let her burn herself out than try to stop her. "What are you going to search for? Unicorns?"

Maggie laughed. "Why not?" She typed, *trying to find unicorns* in the search bar, and hit enter. "Well, will you look at that?" She nodded at the first item on the list that popped up on the screen, then clicked on it. "Seven Cairns, Scotland. Recommended by the Scottish tourism board as the place most likely to spot a unicorn. Cottages available for daily, weekly, and monthly rental."

Even though the scenic photographs of Seven Cairns pulled at Lexi, her dubious streak persisted. "Back up a page and see what else the search suggested."

"Hmm...looks like a place to make a stuffed unicorn, a place to buy unicorn costumes, and according to AI, unicorns do not exist. How rude, dashing somebody's dreams like that."

"Yeah, well, there is always someone ready to dash your dreams if you are willing to let them." Lexi chewed on the corner of her lip, ruminating about all that such a getaway would entail. She had always dreamed of visiting Scotland. According to Mammaw, her great-grandmother had been born there. "So, you'd be willing to handle my practice and make this your home base while I was gone?"

"Absolutely."

Lexi fully trusted Maggie. They'd been best friends since preschool. "You know everyone on the board will help if you need them. Mammaw trained them well."

Maggie nodded, already looking smug with victory. "I know."

"How long do you think I should take off? I don't want to be selfish."

Maggie waggled her head back and forth as though weighing all the options. "I've heard tell that unicorns can be very elusive creatures. I would think you would need at least a month. After all, you have to settle into their habitat and make them feel comfortable enough to trust you, especially since you're not a virgin anymore. If you were still a virgin, they wouldn't be able to resist you."

"Yeah, well, we can't exactly un-ring that bell now, can we?"

"Nope. That proverbial ship has definitely sailed." Maggie tapped on the keyboard again, then hit enter with a flourish. "I sent Seven Cairns your name and email address. The rest is up to you."

Another shiver rippled through Lexi, but this one was different. It was almost like the feeling she had always gotten whenever Mammaw praised her for a job well done. This must be the right thing to do. If Mammaw took the time to smile down from heaven, then it had to be the right decision.

"Here's to Scotland and unicorns," Lexi said.

"And finding the change the cards say you need."

"Amen."

June 1811

Sevenrest Manor

Highlands of Scotland - within the Fae world of the Seventh Realm

. . .

Queen Nyna, Prince Jeros's mother, exploded into the conservatory as if charging into battle. "Ye canna stay here at Sevenrest forever. No son of mine cowers. My son knows his duty to the Realm and accepts it."

A heavy sigh escaped Jeros as he turned from the window and faced the woman who had never cared about or understood him, nor ever been the least inclined to try. "Good day to ye as well, Mother, and how are ye this fine beautiful morning?"

"How do ye think I am? We arranged this marriage to appease the Fifth Kingdom, and ye failed to appear for the announcement. Failed to represent the Seventh Realm as it should be represented. How the devil do ye think I am? We are on the brink of revolution. Is that what ye wish?"

"Screeching is unnecessary. My hearing is impeccable, I assure ye." Jeros strolled alongside the wall of windows and concentrated on the peaceful view of the trees gently swaying and fluttering in the wind as if dancing to music. "Princess Faeniana can marry someone else of the Realm to appease her kingdom's agitators. I feel certain one of my lesser brothers would be more than happy to overlook her selfish wit and cruelty for the abundance of her physical attributes." He pushed one of the taller windows open a bit wider, concentrating on the shushing of the breeze through the leaves. The sound soothed him. Kept him from saying things to his mother that he might not yet wish to unleash. "And ye know as well as I that the Fifth Kingdom will still go to war. That is what they do. Warmongers. The lot of them. Not happy unless they are stirring chaos and leaving death in their wake. Too much Unseelie blood in them, if ye ask me."

"Ye speak of their Unseelie blood and yet it is yerself who choose to wear the mantle of darkness rather than the light." Queen Nyna charged forward, her teeth bared and lightning flashing in her pale eyes. "Ye are full blooded Seelie. Yet ye dress like one of *them*—"

"One of whom, Mother?" He knew who she meant. He simply wished to make her say it.

"One of those bloody Scots. Ye have always admired those mortals. For what reason, I canna fathom." She strode forward, shaking a finger. "And yer hair should be the shining white of yer father's and his father's before him. Not the blue black sootiness of a wicked raven's wing. Ye know that well enough. Ye look like an Unseelie yerself."

Jeros restrained himself, fighting to be respectful, although he had begun to wonder why bother. "I wear the mantle of darkness because it suits me, Mother, and the Scots are a rare breed of mortals whom I respect and admire. Let it go. And no matter how much ye rant and rage, I will not marry that woman. Match her with Warlen or Ganan. Or someone else from the Court. I feel certain that someone other than myself would welcome the challenge of taking her to wife."

"Ye are the prince. Heir to the throne. Only yer marriage to Princess Faeniana will appease the Fifth Kingdom."

"Then they will not be appeased, and if they are foolish enough to wage war against the Seventh Realm, they will die."

"War is no small thing. Have ye no care for those who would die?"

Jeros snorted, ready for this conversation to reach its end. "Ye speak of caring. Yet we all know yer worry is for the moonstone mines that lie within the borders of the Fifth Kingdom, not the subjects of the Realm. I am not a fool, Mother. I know how ye lust after their agates and fluorites as well."

She took a step back and glared at him.

Momentary regret washed across him. Perhaps he should not have said that, but he knew it was the truth, and if the Fae of light, the mighty Seelie, valued anything, it was the truth. "I have a fated mate. Ye know the prophecy. Would ye have me defy it and plunge the Seventh Realm into darkness for a thousand ages?"

His mother's scowl hardened even more. "How do ye know that Princess Faeniana is not yer fated mate?"

"Because all I feel for her is disgust and loathing. She is a cold, vain, heartless creature. Ye would shackle me to *that*?"

Queen Nyna yanked an orange off a nearby tree and tore it in half, slicing through it with her long, gleaming nails. "I would shackle ye to whatever it took to maintain peace within the Seventh Realm."

"And that is why yer word carries no weight with our son or within the Realm, my love," boomed the mighty voice of King Salfan as he shimmered into view. "Return to our chambers, wife. I would speak to our son. Alone."

Eyes flashing with fire, Queen Nyna sank into a low, respectful curtsy. "My king...would it not be better if both of us spoke to him?"

"No. From the ire in his eyes, I would say ye have already said enough. Be gone, Nyna. Do not test me."

Her head snapped up at the king's dropping of her title, but her lips pressed into a thin, tight line as she bit back her words. Jeros's mother knew better than to challenge his father. Theirs had been no love match. Their arranged marriage had taken place because she had once been deemed the most fertile Fae of the Seelie. Perhaps that explained her willingness to deny the prophecy of a fated mate for the king's firstborn.

After another curtsy, she disappeared from view, shimmering into the air like morning mist burning off in the sunshine. His father held up a finger and barely shook his head. "I can sense ye, Nyna. Enough games. Do as yer king bade ye."

Jeros arched a brow.

King Salfan nodded. "She has left us. Finally." His tensed stance relaxed, and he smiled. "Ye give me great pride, my son, but there is war to consider. What say ye?"

"I say the Fifth Kingdom will revolt no matter who anyone marries. If they canna blame it on a marriage gone wrong, they will blame it on the rain."

"I think ye have the right of it, lad." The king meandered deeper into the citrus trees, studying them with a critical eye. "Have ye sensed yer fated mate? Do ye know where she is?"

"I feel her unrest, but she is still verra far away."

"Have ye consulted with Mairwen? Seven Cairns brings fated mates together to strengthen the Highland Veil."

"She stalls. As does her assistant. They show me bits and pieces, then tell me the rest must wait."

"Must wait?"

"Aye," Jeros said, "puts me off, saying the timing is not right or some such other falsehood. I believe she fears the war and the Weavers becoming caught up in it."

"Aye," the king agreed. "The Weavers dislike war. At least, those of the light dislike it. Those of the dark side enjoy a good, mortal scuffle here and there." He palmed an orange as if weighing it for its ripeness. "Speak with her again. Mairwen has been known to wear down those she wishes to bend to her will. Let us use one of her tactics against her. Wear her down. When she grows sick of ye, she will tell ye what ye wish to know."

"I will speak with her today."

As Jeros crossed the boundary into Seven Cairns, the tingle of their magical wards swept across him like the burning sting of a sandstorm. The village of the mystical Weavers was hallowed ground, blessed and protected by the temperamental goddesses who would just as soon obliterate a Fae as look upon one.

The goddesses despised Seelie and Unseelie alike but tolerated the Seelie somewhat better, only looking upon them as lower-class creatures unworthy of their notice. Therefore, he could enter Seven Cairns. But the ancient gods and goddesses truly hated the Unseelie, fearing that the dark Fae might someday join with the forces determined to destroy the Highland Veil and throw all existence into even worse chaos. The Unseelie were forbidden access to the hallowed grounds of Seven Cairns.

"Prince Jeros." Mairwen waited for him in the doorway of the Weaver's ancient meeting hall. "I have been expecting ye."

"I am sure ye have." He offered her a polite nod, then followed her inside. Mairwen was as good as royalty among the Weavers. As the Divine Master Weaver and rumored daughter of the goddesses themselves, she deserved to be respected and handled with caution. "I shall not insult ye with useless niceties. Ye know why I have come."

"Aye."

"And?"

"She is coming."

Excitement thrummed through him. At last, he would finally meet his fated mate. "Show me."

Mairwen shook her head. "I fear that would be unwise, my prince. Ye should meet her when the Fates decide. But I swear she is coming, and that yer meeting will happen quite soon."

"Why would it be unwise for me to just look upon her, old one? I know ye have ways of viewing those whom ye wish to match."

Mairwen studied him, her expression unreadable. "Ye would not *feel* the connection with my ways, and it would be unwise, as I said."

"I will feel the connection when she arrives. Did ye not say she comes?"

"I did."

"Then allow me to see her so I know what to expect."

The old one pursed her lips, her somehow thoughtful silence grating on his nerves. "What if ye dislike what ye see?" she asked. "Will ye refuse her and spend the rest of this life denying that half of yer soul?"

Very few things possessed the power to frighten or make Jeros uneasy, but Mairwen was one of them. "Show me and allow me to decide."

"Very well." She moved to the table and picked up one of her strange flat slabs of mirror-like rock. "This is my assistant's tablet. She has connected it to Scotland's surveillance cameras. Do not ask me how. I leave all that to Keeva. But she has also somehow focused it on Lexington Elizabeth Vine with some sort of tracking device. It will allow you to see yer Lexi, as she likes to be called, as she approaches Seven Cairns." She tapped on the reflective surface of the rock, the tablet as she had called it, then handed it to him. "There. The lass with the long brown hair. There is yer fated mate, my prince."

The tall, young woman dressed in a shockingly tight pair of blue trews faced away from the camera, revealing a fine shapely arse and a thick mane of dark brown hair pulled back and knotted at her nape. It cascaded down her back in a river of tempting curls. His fingers itched to bury themselves in what looked to be their silky depths.

She was slight of build and had a delicateness about her, even though she walked with surety in her colorful red boots with the strange decorations and sharply pointed toes. He wished she would turn so he could see her face. But when she did, he gasped and drew back. The sight of her made his heart dip low, and all excitement left him. "She is…disfigured."

"Yes. She almost died in an automobile accident when she was naught but a small child. Yer Lexi has been through a great deal to become the lovely young woman she is today."

"Lovely?" He would not use that word to describe the hazel-eyed lady smiling and chatting with someone beside her. Pleasant enough, perhaps. But never lovely. The right side of her face was covered in scars, her cheekbone slightly misshapened and flatter, not full and high-boned like her left. Why did she not wear a mask? Or a scarf? Why did she not do something to try to hide that side of her face?

"So the rumors are true," Mairwen said. "Ye are the Prince of Perfection, unable to see past the surface of anything. It is one's soul, one's heart that is truly beautiful or ugly, my prince. What would I see if I looked within ye and viewed yers? Would I see beauty or ugliness in yer heart and soul?"

Indignance shot through him like a swallow of raw whisky. "That is not fair, old one. Ye knew I would be shocked by her appearance. Ye baited me."

"I did no such thing. I advised ye to wait. Ye refused."

"Why would the Fates match me with such a woman?"

"Yer souls were matched lifetimes ago. Would ye waste this lifetime and miss the joy the two of ye could share?"

"She is mortal. Her lifespan is but the blink of an eye."

Mairwen spat like an angry cat. "Ye know as well as I that as soon as the two of ye bind yerselves one to the other that her lifetime will match yers. 'Tis part of the Seelie alliance with the goddesses. Unlike the limits they place upon the Weavers who dare to love mortals. Consider yerself blessed."

The bitterness of her tone insulted him. He held out the tablet, ready to be rid of it. "Is there no way to heal her? Cover her disfigurement with a glamor?"

"Are ye truly that superficial? That vain?" Mairwen threw up her hands. "Perhaps ye would be better suited marrying that cruel princess of the Fifth Kingdom. Yer heart and soul are as black as hers. Now ye ken why I delayed this match. Mistress Lexi deserves much better than the likes of yerself."

"I am not that shallow!" Indignant rage charged through him. How dare Mairwen accuse him of such. He was merely shocked by the woman's appearance. He realized full well that it was what lay beneath the surface that mattered. "Ye trapped me," he accused again, trying to convince himself as much as trying to convince Mairwen. He was ashamed of his reaction, realizing he was no better than his mother. "If she is my fated mate, I will do right by her. I will not reject her."

"Well, my...my. Aren't ye generous?" Mairwen placed the tablet on the table and walked away. "I suppose we shall see if she accepts ye, yer high and mightiness. This meeting is finished."

"Ye dare dismiss me as if I were a young, thoughtless cub?"

Mairwen whirled about, the unsettling blue of her eyes brightening with an eerie light as thunder rumbled and lightning flashed outside. "Ye *are* a thoughtless cub, but I expected no less from the son of Queen Nyna. Leave, Prince Jeros, and do not return until ye have learned the lessons that Fate hopes to teach ye."

"What the devil does that mean?"

Deafening thunder split the air and shook the ground. "Ye will see," Mairwen promised with a calm just as unsettling as the thunder. "Ye will see."

TENTATIVE RELEASE DATE: **November 25, 2025**
Get your copy here: CLICK

If you enjoyed this story, please consider leaving a review on the site where you purchased your copy, or a reader site such as Goodreads, or BookBub.

Visit my website at maevegreyson.com to sign up for my newsletter and stay up to date on new releases, sales, and all sorts of whatnot. (There are some freebies too!)

I would be nothing without my readers. You make it possible for me to do what I love. Thank you SO much!

Sending you big hugs and hoping you always have a great story to enjoy!

Maeve

About the Author

maevegreyson.com

Maeve Greyson is a USA TODAY bestselling author, Amazon Top 100 bestseller, Amazon All Star, multiple RONE Award winner, and a multiple HOLT Medallion Finalist.

Maeve Greyson's mantra is this: No one has the power to shatter your dreams unless you give it to them.

She and her husband of over forty-five years traveled around the world while in the U.S. Air Force. Now they're settled in rural Kentucky where Maeve writes about her courageous heroes and the fearless women who tame them. Sometimes her stories are historical romances, time travel romances, or escapist romantasies, but the one thing they always have in common is a satisfying happily ever after. When she's not plotting the perfect snare, she can be found herding cats, grandchildren, and her husband—not necessarily in that order.

Also by Maeve Greyson

THE MAGICAL MATCHMAKERS OF SEVEN CAIRNS

A Fine Scottish Time

A Fine Scottish Spell

A Fine Scottish Dream

A Fine Scottish Love

A Fine Scottish Harmony

A Fine Scottish Curse

A Fine Scottish Keeper

SEVEN UNSUITABLE SISTERS SERIES

Blessing's Baron

Fortuity's Arrangement

Grace's Saving

Joy's Willful Wager

Felicity's Eloquent Earl

A less Than Merry Marquess

Serendipity's Suitor

The Making of a Duke

HIGHLAND HEROES SERIES

The Chieftain - Prequel

The Guardian

The Warrior

The Judge

The Dreamer

The Bard

The Ghost

A Yuletide Yearning

Love's Charity

TIME TO LOVE A HIGHLANDER SERIES

Loving Her Highland Thief

Taming Her Highland Legend

Winning Her Highland Warrior

Capturing Her Highland Keeper

Saving Her Highland Traitor

Loving Her Lonely Highlander

Delighting Her Highland Devil

ONCE UPON A SCOT SERIES

A Scot of Her Own

A Scot to Have and to Hold

A Scot to Love and Protect

HIGHLAND PROTECTOR SERIES

Sadie's Highlander

Joanna's Highlander

Katie's Highlander

HIGHLAND HEARTS SERIES

My Highland Lover

My Highland Bride

My Tempting Highlander

My Seductive Highlander

THE MACKAY CLAN

Blessed by a Highland Curse

A Heartsong Back to the Highlands

Beyond A Highland Whisper

The Highlander's Fury

A Highlander In Her Past

OTHER BOOKS BY MAEVE GREYSON

Stone Guardian

Eternity's Mark

Guardian of Midnight Manor

When the Midnight Bell Tolls

Once Upon a Haunted Highland Mist

Loving the Lady of Skye

THE SISTERHOOD OF INDEPENDENT LADIES

To Steal a Duke

To Steal a Marquess

To Steal an Earl

Printed in Dunstable, United Kingdom

66224371R00141